As Lady Kingsle y
bales and hurried throu f
helplessness and hop !
when James placed hi
back, she closed her to turn
around and bury her face in his chest.

"It will be all right," he said, softly. "For all her flirtation and playing around, Abigail is a good soul. She is desperately unhappy at court but makes the most of what is expected of her."

"She's unhappy?" Violet turned around, her senses filling with the musky masculine scent of him. "But she is always smiling and laughing. I thought—"

"A charade, a pretense that Abigail has perfected. One I fear she will be forced to carry on living once her parents choose her husband." His gaze dropped to her mouth. "I don't want you to suffer unhappiness any more than I do her, but there is little I can do to deter her family's martial expectations. But if I can find a way to set you free from your mother's dictatorship, I will."

Violet's heart hammered as the desire to kiss him grew stronger. "Why are you here, James? With me? Like this?"

He inched closer. "Because there's nowhere else I'd rather be."

She should step back, save herself, but it was too late. He cared about her, he was helping her, protecting her…

"James, I—"

His mouth touched hers, and any words were lost in his tentative, wonderful kiss.

Praise for Rachel Brimble

"Such a compelling read—one of Rachel Brimble's finest yet!"

~Clare & Lou's Mad About Books (5 Stars)

~*~

"I had to stay up to finish it. I just couldn't put it down!"

~Splashes Into Books (5 Stars)

~*~

"Rachel Brimble is one of my favorite authors. Her books are always engrossing, authentic, gripping and richly atmospheric."

~Dash Fan (5 Stars)

~*~

Rachel Brimble is the author of over 25 published contemporary romance, romantic suspense, and historical romance/fiction novels.

An Amazon bestselling author several times over, Rachel has thousands of followers from all over the world on Instagram, Twitter and Facebook.

Victoria & Violet

by

Rachel Brimble

The Royal Maids, Book 1

Victoria & Violet

Contact Information: info@thewildrosepress.com

Cover Art by *The Wild Rose Press, Inc.*

The Wild Rose Press, Inc.
PO Box 708
Adams Basin, NY 14410-0708
Visit us at www.thewildrosepress.com

Publishing History
First Edition, 2022
Trade Paperback ISBN 978-1-5092-4439-3
Digital ISBN 978-1-5092-4477-5

The Royal Maids, Book 1
Published in the United States of America

Dedication

For Mr. B—my husband, my rock, my boy…
Everything I do, you support.
Everything I dream, you dream for me, too.
I love you,
Rachel x

Chapter One

Windsor Castle, May 1839

"Violet, will you cease gawping at that painting and give me your full attention!"

Violet Parker inhaled a calming breath before reluctantly turning away from the magnificent portrait of Queen Victoria's paternal grandfather, Francis, Duke of Saxe-Coburg-Saalfeld.

She faced her mother—a woman possibly more hateful than the queen's mother, the Duchess of Kent, in whose bedchamber they now stood. "I'm sorry, Mama."

"So you should be. Now…" Her mother walked behind the gold brocade sofa from where the duchess sat staring at Violet, her eyes wide with unwavering expectation, her mouth pinched. "After all the hours I have sacrificed and all the frustration I have endured training you to the utmost level of perfection," her mother said, "I think you are finally ready."

Violet stilled, her thoughts of pigment and brush strokes dissolving. "Ready?"

"To serve the queen, girl! Why do you think I have invested so much time schooling you in conduct, decorum, and household skill?" Her mother's cheeks mottled, her icy-blue gaze growing impossibly colder. "I have secured you a place as the queen's personal housemaid. You will work under the authority of

Baroness Lehzen, of course, but there is little I can do about that."

"I am to leave the duchess's household?" Violet looked between her mother and the duchess. "I had no idea."

Her mother curled her fingers over the top of the sofa. "That's because everything you learn is on a need-to-know basis. But yes, you will leave us and work solely for the queen."

Excitement knotted Violet's stomach as the sunlit room suddenly grew a little brighter, the stuffiness lifting enough that her breath flowed easier. Was she about to find herself free of her mother's long-reaching fingers? Able to work in peace at the other end of the vast castle? Maybe paint without ridicule?

She inhaled, the combined smell of soot and beeswax that hung heavy in the room not nearly as irritating to her lungs as usual. "Then I am deeply honored."

Her mother's eyes narrowed. "Do not make the mistake of surmising this as an opportunity to escape my watchful eye. This new placement by no means allows you freedom from your duties to me *or* the duchess."

Violet tightened her laced fingers and held her mother's glare. "If I am to work for the queen, how can I possibly serve both her and the duch—"

"Oh, you are such an infuriating girl at times!" Her mother rounded the sofa, the blonde tendrils lining her forehead quivering with the force of her annoyance as she marched toward Violet. She stopped barely inches away and pointed her bony finger in her daughter's face. "The only reason you will be there is to orchestrate a reunion between the queen and the duchess. You will become Victoria's confidante, her friend, and do everything in your power to recall her love and need for her mother. Do you understand?"

Violet's tentative whispers of elation at possible liberty popped like soap bubbles as she snapped her gaze to the duchess and then her mother. "But how am I to cajole Victoria, the queen of England, to do my bidding? Mama, the queen does as she pleases, you know that. Why on earth would she listen to me?"

"The queen will listen to you because you will make it so. I did not raise your place at the palace for the good of my health, but for the happiness of the duchess. One way or another, you will ensure the queen's trust in you is secured."

As Violet opened her mouth to respond, the duchess waved a pink silk handkerchief in the air like a miniature flag. "Ladies, please, no more heated words. The last thing I want is for another mother and daughter to experience the wretchedness of an acrimonious separation."

Wretchedness? Violet could not think of anything more joyous than being away from her overbearing and often cruel mother.

The duchess rose from the sofa and came toward Violet, her dark hair gleaming under the sunlight that speared the carpet ahead of her. She gently took Violet's hand, her piercing eyes intense. "My dear, if you execute your duties to the queen with absolute diligence, this new appointment will give you more opportunities than you can possibly imagine."

The only opportunities Violet wanted were connected to painting, and it was highly unlikely she would find them at court where she was little more than a lackey, a shadow barely noticed by courtier or royalty. The fact the all-too-often aloof duchess had condescended to touch her meant this situation was grave and undoubtedly dangerous…especially for Violet.

"I beseech you to do all you can to help me and your wonderful mama." The duchess tightened her fingers on Violet's. "It grieves her equally as much as me that I am constantly separated from my dear Drina." She closed her eyes as though the pain were too much before snapping them open again, ruthlessness swirling in their hazel depths once more. "Your task is simple. You will ingratiate yourself into my daughter's good graces, and once she likes you—"

"But, ma'am, how can I ensure that Her Majesty will like me?" Violet swallowed, the underhandedness of this elevation tasting bitter in her mouth. "The queen has the baroness and at least half a dozen ladies devoted to her. She will hardly notice me among—"

"Oh, but she will." The duchess dropped Violet's hand and stepped back, annoyance shadowing her gaze. "Time and again, Drina complains of her lack of young company. Complains that her life is full of stuffy gentlemen and virtuous ladies who do not seem to care for fun, whereas she likes to dance and play. I have every confidence she will warm to you as soon as she sees you are a woman of her own age and understands her hankering for such nonsense."

Uncertain whether she should be flattered or insulted, Violet dipped her head. "Well, yes, I am young, but as for—"

"Then you are all you need to be to convince the queen of your value," Violet's mother interrupted as she joined them in the center of the room. "You will show

Her Majesty that without you, her life will be little more than duty as it had been before."

"And once you have gained her trust and companionship…" The duchess's smile was almost maniacal, her small white teeth reminding Violet of those she'd seen in the mouths of foxes. "Then you will tell her of your love for your dear mama and convince the queen she misses the company of hers."

Unease whispered through Violet as she looked from the wily gaze of the duchess to the conniving gaze of her mother. "I…need a moment to digest what you expect of me. What you ask seems impossible."

Violet walked to the window, away from two of the court's most detested women, her mind racing. The beauty of Windsor stretched as far as she could see, the greenery rolling and seemingly endless. Yet for Victoria—and Violet—the ancient and revered palace was little more than a theatre. A playhouse where their mothers leaned over them, pulling and yanking their strings, jerking her and Victoria this way and that, according to their wishes.

As far as Violet was concerned, the queen had endured so much at her mother's and Sir Conroy's hands during the first eighteen years of her life, Victoria had every right never to see or speak to either of them again. Even though she had managed to entirely banish Conroy from her presence, Victoria would not completely rid herself of her mother until such time as the queen married.

Violet understood that entrapment completely, her empathy and sympathy entirely with Victoria. Inhaling a strengthening breath, the first whispers of certainty swept through her. Whatever her mother and the duchess might ask of her, her loyalty would remain with the queen. A woman so different from her in a hundred ways but so alike in others. Their youth, entrapment, and frustration would surely be deep enough to act as the foundation to Violet becoming Victoria's ally rather than her backstabbing betrayer.

"Violet!" Her mother's voice cracked across the room. "Will you come away from that window? There is much to do."

Violet turned and smiled sweetly. "I have understood your instructions, Mama, Duchess. I will do all that I can to make the queen's life merry and turn her mind to familial peace and harmony."

The duchess clapped her hands and brought them together at her breast, her gaze glittering with happiness. "Oh, you dear child, I knew you would understand my anguish and work to vanquish it. Thank you."

Violet dipped her head. "My pleasure, Your Highness."

The duchess swept toward the door, leaving Violet's mother to follow.

But she didn't immediately shadow her mistress's footsteps.

Instead, her mother walked closer to Violet, her eyes blazing with undisguised warning. "I will be watching you. Do not, for one minute, make the mistake of considering this position your own. You are nothing without me and never will be. You would be a fool to ever think otherwise."

Violet locked gazes with her mother, her heart racing with suppressed fury. *God, how I hate her.*

With a dismissive tut, her mother turned on her heel and hurried from the room.

Violet slowly followed her mother into the grand, red-carpeted corridor. The lit chandeliers belied the darkness churning inside of her, and she looked heavenward, willing forth her previous elation. This change had to mean something. She would *make* it mean something.

She looked left and right and slowly smiled.

Once confident she was entirely alone, Violet lifted her skirts and danced a little jig, whispering over and over, "I'm the queen's housemaid. Bye, bye, mother dear. Bye, bye, forever," before she buried her euphoria and hurried after her mother, unable to entirely wipe away her smile.

Chapter Two

James Greene eased back from the voluptuous curves of lady-in-waiting, Abigail Kingsley and subtly tilted his face away from her searching lips.

From where they were hidden behind a marble pillar, he peered along the corridor as Abigail proceeded to slide her fingers over his chest and nip his earlobe. Narrowing his eyes, James watched Violet Parker almost break into a run in her haste to catch up with her mother and the Duchess of Kent.

How in the world the extraordinarily pretty housemaid hadn't seen him and Abigail, he had no idea. Violet had practically stood right beside the pillar as she squealed and danced and whispered. Even though he had absolutely no idea how on earth it could have happened, Violet's apparent elevation to the queen's household was all to James's good fortune. After all, as Lord Melbourne's assistant, James spent considerably more time in the queen's company than he did the duchess's.

And he was becoming mightily frustrated at failing to turn Mistress Parker's eye in his direction.

A fingertip to his chin turned his head, and he looked into Abigail's dark, smoldering eyes. "What is so interesting?" she asked.

He glanced toward the corridor. "Did you not hear that? Violet Parker could have been mistaken for a mouse being strangled."

"Oh, who cares about Violet Parker? She's a nobody." Abigail sighed and tugged him forward by his lapels. "Kiss me again, you scoundrel."

James gently grasped her wrists and lowered them, his mind still halfway along the corridor. Violet Parker was hardly a nobody in his eyes. How could anyone be when they had hair that shone ochre in the candlelight and gold beneath the sun? Not to mention eyes so blue a man could barely bring himself to look at them and not feel he was falling head-first into an ocean.

He peered into the corridor again as though he might conjure Violet's miraculous reappearance. A nobody, she was not. A conundrum? Most definitely. Despite managing to exchange a few words with her now and then, most of the time whenever they passed in the corridors and gardens of Windsor, Violet looked through him as though he were invisible.

"James, what is wrong with you?" Abigail twisted her arms from his grip, her lips pouting. "Is a lady in waiting not sufficient distraction from a servant girl?"

"Of course, you are," he said, before pressing a kiss to her cheek. "But I must go before my absence from the office is noticed. I will undoubtedly come by you again soon."

"But, James—"

He emerged into the corridor, adjusting his jacket and smoothing his necktie, just as Lord Melbourne strode closer, his dark head bowed to the papers in his hand.

James stood tall. "Good afternoon, sir."

Melbourne looked up, his blue eyes somewhat distracted. "Ah, Greene, just the person. The queen is agitated. Could you see to it that her horse is made ready for her to take a short ride in an hour or so?"

"Yes, sir."

Melbourne gave a curt nod of dismissal before turning his attention back to his papers and continuing along the corridor in the direction of his office. James waited until the minister rounded the corner and then glanced over his shoulder. Abigail lingered in the spot where he had left her, her flash of temper undoubtedly cooled by the sight of an approaching courtier James knew she had in mind to seduce.

James's shoes sank into the plush carpet as he walked from the palace, his path lit by the plethora of gold and gilt surrounding him. Being at court was never a stationary existence. Something was always simmering beneath the surface. Gossip and scandal as much an everyday occurrence as eating and drinking.

So, too, was relentless ambition.

It wasn't just Violet Parker with her eye on elevation, James had aspirations, too. Yet his motivation was not embedded in the hankering for monetary gain or power, but in his absolute resistance to returning home to his family estate in Oxfordshire.

Bitter resentment rose in his throat.

It had become his personal crusade to remain at court where many a man before him had found a pleasing and notable career. Surely, if he became important enough among the hierarchy of royal service, his father would have no alternative but to pass the estate to another relation. Hell, a distant cousin would suffice. Anyone but James or his younger brother. They deserved to be left in peace. After all, they had paid their dues, and both had grown to hate what their father represented and how easily his sons could follow suit if pushed…

Emerging from the palace into the bright May sunshine, James strode purposefully toward the mews, the smell of horses, manure, and straw hitting his nostrils. The stench once again brought thoughts of home and the pressures that awaited him there. James clenched his jaw against his rancor.

"All right there, Mr. Greene?"

James blinked and nodded at the jovial stable hand. "Afternoon, Pip. The queen wants to take a ride a little later. Can you ensure her pony is ready?"

" 'Course." The young lad frowned. "How come you've been sent down here with a message from the queen's household? I thought you were still working with Melbourne."

"I am, but I think everyone knows he deals with the queen's personal happiness as much as he does matters of state."

"Seems like, don't it?" Pip lowered a bale of hay to the floor and leaned back with his hands at the base of his spine, wincing as he twisted left and right. "You looked lost in thought when you came round the corner." Pip grinned and wiggled his eyebrows. "Thinking about some lady or another, I reckon."

Violet Parker immediately leapt into James's mind. "No, no lady, Pip," James lied. "I've got my mind on work and raising my position at court, nothing else."

"I'm sure you have."

Something in the way Pip spoke raised James's defenses. "What?"

"Nothing."

"Pip…"

The young lad's cheeks flushed, and he picked up the bale, clearly avoiding James's eyes. "I just think you're right to be looking to stay at the palace, sir. You belong here, not at that grand family house of yours. Let the whisperers say what they will and pay them no mind. That's what I think, anyway."

"Are the grooms talking about me?" James glanced toward the mews. "What are they saying?"

"Just that sooner or later you'll follow in your pa's footsteps and prove yourself to be just like him."

James frowned, knowing the insinuation was not in any way complimentary. "Are there people here who worked for my father?"

"Yes, sir."

"I had no idea." James stared at the stables. "Then I guess they too are happier at court."

"Soon enough you'll have your eye on marrying one of those grand ladies you like flirting with, and if you do, why should you be forced to leave? You got where you are by serving Her Majesty in her army and then earned a good place here. If you want to stay, that's what you should do."

As kind as Pip's sentiments were, it niggled that James was the topic of conversation. "What I do or don't do with the ladies, my position at the palace, or anything else is my business. Nothing wrong with some fun while you work."

Pip smirked, his kindly eyes amused. "I'll go and see about the queen's horse."

James walked back to the palace, tugging at his collar that now felt too tight. Even if he put aside the fact the grooms were discussing his inevitable departure, he could not ignore that marriage was often the prominent subject on people's lips. Who was likely to marry whom, where, and when. The entire palace was abuzz with such nonsense, day in, day out.

The truth was, if any woman scratched beneath the surface of his family history, they would soon learn James was not good marriage material. At least, he wasn't likely to be once children came into the equation. How could he when his father had beaten him and his younger brother more times than he could count? Made them sweat and toil in every part of the gardens and house until they were sick with fear or exhaustion.

James picked up his pace, hating the venom that built inside him. He would avoid marriage for as long as he could and thus not fall prey to the contemptable, dreaded future that awaited him once he matured into his father. A future potentially viler for his wife than it ever would be for him.

His mind wandered again to Violet Parker. Despite his reputation as a ladies' man, there was something about Violet that struck him as wholly unique compared to the hundreds of other women living and working at court. As beautiful as she was, she seemed entirely unaware of her appeal, and during their brief conversations, his superior position seemed neither to faze nor impress her. Clearly, she knew her own mind, relied on her own gumption, and someone like him did little to evoke her interest.

Her mystique and confidence drew him to her every time he came across her, more often than not, in her leisure time when she was sure to be found somewhere around the palace grounds with her ever-present sketchpad.

Yet now she would work for the queen as her personal housemaid. Such a position would lead to her learning of the queen's foibles, her likes and dislikes, what she felt was missing at court, and what she wished for in the future.

All vital intelligence of unquestionable help to Melbourne.

Tension eased from James's shoulders, and he smiled. Oh, yes, Violet Parker had now become so much more to him than a beautiful woman…

Chapter Three

As she entered the queen's private chambers behind Baroness Lehzen, Violet tried to breathe normally and ignore the threat that she might faint. Dressed in her tidiest but least flattering dress because her mother feared the queen might conclude Violet thought too much of herself, her nerves were stretched to breaking.

Yet she could not stop staring at the endless wonders around her.

The paintings and portraits on the walls were extraordinary, the artists of such extreme talent, they made her feel silly for even daring to dream that her own talents might one day take her far, far away from her circumstances. It would take her hours and hours of practice to come close to drawing even a leaf as exquisitely as these had been painted. Even longer to paint such mouths, strands of hair, hands…

"We are about to enter the queen's sitting room."

Violet jumped and looked at the baroness.

Lehzen pointedly widened her eyes as she halted outside a closed door. "Her Majesty is aware that you are joining her household this morning and seems particularly enthused by your youth. I do not know why, but the fact you are so young very much pleases her. Make sure all you do is to the queen's satisfaction, and I am sure you will do well enough."

"Yes, ma'am."

"Right then, in we go."

The baroness pushed open the intricately carved double doors and stood aside to allow Violet to enter first. She sucked in a breath, her mouth dry. Gold and silver glinted and glittered from every surface, the enormous chandelier in the center of the ceiling so big, Violet could not even begin to comprehend how it remained hung. A huge stone fireplace dominated one wall of the room, another lined with floor-to-ceiling bookshelves behind a beautiful, polished wood piano.

Quiet female conversation and the occasional tinkle of laughter punctuated the relaxed atmosphere. Something Violet had not expected at all. Through the stories her mother and the duchess had told her of Victoria and her ladies, Violet had pictured them continually indulging in either outright debauchery or their tempers flying with hair being pulled out by the roots from each other's scalps.

"Your Majesty?" The baroness stopped by a large wingback chair at the window. "I have Mistress Parker to meet you. She begins work today as your personal housemaid."

Violet swallowed. Only the queen's lap was visible, her hands busy at a swatch of embroidery.

"Well, don't just leave her standing there, Lehzen." The queen laughed. "The poor girl is likely to think me as rude as my mother."

Violet could barely hear above the pounding of her pulse, but on the baroness's nod, she stepped closer until she had full view of the queen. She dropped into a curtsey, her eyes lowered. "Your Majesty."

"Oh, how pretty you are!" Victoria exclaimed, putting her embroidery on a small table beside her. "And young. Rise, please. Tell me, are you my age? Twenty? Twenty-one?"

"Twenty, ma'am." Violet's cheeks warmed under the delighted, friendly gaze of the queen. "It is my birthday just next week. I will be twenty-one."

"Then I very much welcome the service of a lady so close to me in age." The queen grinned, her gaze traveling over Violet's hair and dress. "I hope you will be most content here, Parker. My household is generally a relaxed one, but if you need to know where anything is or how I like things done, my ladies will be happy to oblige."

"Thank you, ma'am."

Victoria appraised her from head to toe again before giving a satisfied nod and turning to speak with a dark-haired lady seated next to her. Just as Violet began to panic about how to retreat, Lehzen's firm grasp on her elbow relieved her of the dilemma.

The baroness led her across the room to the side of Victoria's enormous, beautifully carved bed and pointed at a basket of towels on the floor. "Those are the queen's. Fold them twice long ways and then place them in this drawer here." She led Violet to a bureau and opened the second drawer. "Place them neatly and in line as so."

"Yes, ma'am."

Lehzen gave a firm nod before narrowing her eyes and leaning close. "Your mother has warned me that you can have an obstinate way about you from time to time. Concentrate on proving her wrong."

She walked away, and Violet firmly closed her mouth, trapping any retort inside. Was Lehzen in cahoots with her mother? Violet always had the impression her mother envied the baroness's status at court. Quite likely loathed her for it. After all, no one could compete with Lehzen's importance to the queen, of the solidity of their long-standing relationship considering Lehzen had gone from being Victoria's governess to her most trusted confidante as the queen grew into adulthood.

Violet had never known her mother to choose any company at court other than the duchess's. Neither had she known anyone to seek her mother's friendship. Which meant she had most likely spoken to Lehzen in the hope her intimacy with the queen would provoke the baroness to watch Violet as closely as her mother.

Left alone to her work, Violet took the first towel from the basket and began to fold. All around her the queen's laughter and chattering mixed with her ladies, filling the room with warmth and deep, unexpected relaxation. Soon Violet was smiling as the women joked and jested, teased, and gossiped.

Could it be that she might find a semblance of happiness here?

"Oh, I am beside myself with impatience for my birthday ball," the queen suddenly exclaimed. "Lehzen? Tell me how the plans are coming along."

"Very well, ma'am." The baroness flashed the queen an indulgent smile. "The food and wine, music, and presents are all being taken care of and delivered as we speak."

"I am so thrilled by it all." Victoria laughed and pressed a hand to her breast. "Lord Melbourne is constantly boasting of the dignitaries who will attend, including a great number of suitors seeking my hand. What fun I shall have!"

Violet smiled at the sudden flush in the young queen's cheeks as she stood from her chair and swayed from side to side across the room as if dancing. She really was beautiful. Having only ever seen Victoria from a distance when Violet had been running errands for her mother or the duchess, she had never appreciated the queen's glowing skin, the shine of her hair, or the delicacy of her petite figure. She exuded youth and vitality, and Violet had no doubt that a hundred suitors would surround her at the ball.

Victoria came to an abrupt halt and turned in Violet's direction.

Embarrassed to be caught gawping, she dropped her gaze to the towels, her hands beginning to tremble.

"Parker, tell me, do you have a beau?"

Violet slowly lifted her gaze, holding a towel so tightly in front of her she worried just how badly her clammy palms would damage it. "I…well, no, ma'am."

"I don't believe it! A girl as pretty as you, who is free to come and go as she pleases, must have plenty of young men vying for her hand." The queen grinned, her blue eyes sparkling. "Do you not wish for a gentleman's attention? We are all maidens, are we not? But it's nice to contemplate such things. Well, at least, I imagine it is if you are not under constant pressure to wed as I am."

Was the queen really singling her out for such a conversation? Violet glanced from beneath lowered lashes at the other women. They stared back at her with interest or curiosity, soft smiles playing on their lips. What was the answer the queen wanted to hear? Why did her questions suddenly feel like a test? Or was she imagining the queen played the same games as her mother?

"Parker," Lehzen snapped, her face like thunder. "Her Majesty asked you a question."

"Oh, Lehzen," the queen admonished, her smile vanishing. "Do not scold her. Can you not see how afraid she looks?" She walked closer and put her hand on Violet's arm. "Do not wear such an expression of fear, my darling girl. You can talk freely here." She smiled and glanced around the room. "Isn't that so, ladies?"

A wave of murmured assent burst forth, and Violet lowered her tense shoulders. "All that matters to me is doing a good and worthwhile job at court, ma'am. I have neither the time nor inclination to think of such things as gentlemen or romance."

"But that is no life for a young woman. I keep telling Lehzen exactly that." Victoria frowned. "No, it will not do."

Violet's heart beat fast as the faces of her mother and the duchess appeared in her mind's eye. How she would be punished if she were dismissed from the queen's service on her very first day!

"All the young girls in the land deserve to have fun!" The queen snatched her hand from Violet's arm and clapped, her smile wide. "You included, Parker. For as long as you are in my service, I will see to it that you do."

She swept away into the laughing circle of her ladies, leaving Violet standing alone and gripping a towel that was now damp to the touch. She turned to Lehzen and was met with such a look of utter contempt that Violet abruptly returned to her task, her cheeks burning.

What in the world had the queen meant when she'd said she would ensure Violet had fun? She wasn't a lady or a maid of the court. She wasn't a friend of the queen or anyone else. Worse, what in the world would her mother say when she heard of Victoria's declaration?

Chapter Four

James lowered his pen as Melbourne strode purposefully into their assigned office at Windsor before sitting behind his desk with a grunt.

He leaned his head against the back of the chair and closed his eyes. "It seems the queen has entirely forgiven the Grand Duke of Russia's unexpected arrival yesterday. He will now be staying at Windsor for the next three nights at Victoria's invitation." He opened his eyes and heaved forward to plant his elbows on the desk. "The woman is as changeable as the bloody weather."

"I suspect then that, despite the queen's entourage doing all they could to soothe her, His Imperial Highness managed to pacify her temper by his own means."

"Indeed." Melbourne rubbed his hand over his dark whiskers, his brow furrowed. "So well in fact, that in her preparations for the ball, which the duke will now be attending, Victoria is behaving more like a little girl looking forward to a tea party than a queen entertaining foreign royalty."

"She is young, sir."

"That is something that becomes clearer to me every day. Now..." Melbourne pinned James with his piercing blue eyes. "The grand duke's valet has been taken ill. Therefore, I am assigning you the most important task of looking after His Grace whilst he is here. I know the position is not within your remit, but I want someone I can trust near him. I am not entirely sure what the man is up to arriving at a royal residence without warning."

James frowned. "Do you suspect an ulterior motive for him being here?"

"I'm not entirely sure what to think, but from what I've seen of the duke so far, he seems entirely without qualm with regard to protocol." Melbourne's jaw tightened. "I will be much happier having you adhere to his requests than a servant I do not know."

"Yes, sir."

Melbourne stood and walked to the window, his hands clasped behind his back. "The man is very self-assured, and it appears to me that the duke aims to court the queen. Why, I have no idea. There is little chance of a Russian heir to the throne marrying an English queen." Melbourne abruptly turned and strode back to his desk. "But let's not dwell on that now. Smarten yourself up, and we will go along to the duke's bedchamber where I will introduce you and then leave you to his demands." He picked up some papers. "Come along now."

James slid a comb from his drawer and faced the mirror behind his desk.

This new assignment not only illustrated Melbourne's growing trust in him but was also an elevation of sorts and would almost certainly be viewed as such by his peers. It was one thing to be at the minister's beck and call, quite another to have consistent access to a dignitary's bedchamber. Barely able to contain his smile, James pondered what he would write to his father about this new, unforeseen appointment. Not that James would reiterate it as unforeseen. Rather his telling of the position would present it as evidence of James's regard at court, the confidence in his discretion, and how this new role credited his services to Melbourne.

"Ready, Greene?"

"Yes, sir."

James returned his comb to the drawer and hurried from the office after Melbourne.

****

The queen's bedchamber bustled with activity as Violet ducked in between the ladies in waiting, picking up discarded fans and feathers. It was less than an hour before the queen's twentieth birthday ball, and tension enveloped the room.

Baroness Lehzen—self-appointed commander—issued orders as though she ruled the realm, rather than Victoria. "The lace, girl, the lace!" She flapped her hand at Violet. "By the blue ribbon. There, there."

Violet retrieved the swatch of lace, intricately folded and stitched into an exquisite flower, from atop the chest of drawers beside her. It was so light and delicate, Violet feared crushing it and gratefully passed it to the baroness. Standing back, she studied how the queen's dresser carefully attached the flower to the sash encasing Victoria's tiny waist.

"Will I do, Parker?" Victoria asked, her big blue eyes dancing with undisguised excitement. "Do you think the gentleman guests will be lost for words as I enter the ballroom?"

"Oh, yes, ma'am." Violet grinned, her hands together at her breast as she took in every detail of the queen's beautiful peach silk gown, adorned with lace at her waist and elbows. "You look like…like an angel."

"An angel?" The queen preened in front of the mirror, a slight blush darkening her cheeks. "Then I hope there is at least one suitor present this evening who is fond of all things heavenly, don't you?"

The queen's dresser removed the most breathtaking tiara Violet had ever seen from a black velvet box, the diamond and pearls shimmering beneath the candlelight. She hardly dared breathe as Victoria stood perfectly still, the magnificent headpiece slowly lowered and positioned upon her dark, plaited hair.

When Violet looked at the mirror, she met the queen's eyes in the reflection and quickly dropped her gaze to her feet.

"It would please me to see your pretty face at the ball tonight, Parker. Would you like that? To be in the ballroom where you might feast your eyes on all the dignitaries, the ladies' dresses and jewels?"

The queen's jesting brought a lump of longing to Violet's throat. "Oh, ma'am, I—"

"The queen does not speak in earnestness, Parker." Lehzen smirked as she slipped a diamond bracelet over the queen's outstretched hand. "You? At the ball? Oh, ma'am, you shouldn't tease her so."

"I am not teasing, Lehzen."

Violet stilled, her pulse thundering.

"But, ma'am, surely you do not think that your housemaid could possibly—"

"Tonight, Parker will not be my housemaid." The queen stood and walked closer, gently touching her finger to Violet's chin, so she had no choice but to look directly into the queen's eyes. "Do you have experience in serving drinks and the like?"

"Yes, ma'am."

"And it was your birthday this week, was it not?"

"Yes, ma'am."

"Good. Then tonight, you will go to the ball."

Lehzen stepped forward, fury burning in her eyes and her cheeks mottled. "But the idea is absurd. A servant girl cannot be in the ballroom. I will not allow it."

Despite the number of ladies present and the volume of excited chatter that had filled the space for the last two hours, heavy silence descended on the room like a dropped guillotine.

The queen's snatched her fingers from Violet's face and turned to Lehzen. "*You* will not allow it?"

Lehzen's color darkened further. "I merely mean to say—"

"I think you have said quite enough." Victoria's eyes flashed dangerously, her jaw tight. "Your tone implied that I cannot have Parker present wherever I see fit. Are you presuming to command your queen as though I am still a child and you my governess?"

"Of course not, ma'am. I just cannot understand—"

"Then I shall speak plainly." Victoria faced Violet, her gaze softening. "I want you to go to the servants' hall and tell them I am assigning you as one of the serving staff tonight. You can serve drinks and appetizers and spend the entire night listening to the music and watching the dancers. How will that be?"

Words flailed like a swarm of butterflies upon Violet's tongue as she glanced around the silent circle of ladies, their eyes wide with shock or sparkling with amusement. Some smiled their encouragement while others' lips were twisted in tight disapproval.

She quickly looked at the queen. "I don't know what to say."

"You say, thank you, Your Majesty." Victoria

laughed. “Now run along and do as I ask. The ball will start soon, and I do not want you to miss my entrance.”

“Yes, Your Majesty. Thank you. Thank you so much.”

With a quick curtsey, Violet glanced at Lehzen and met a glare so intense, Violet felt herself a gazelle under the gaze of a tiger about to rip her to shreds. Hurrying from the room, she burst into the darkened corridor, her heart hammering. For a servant to be favored so publicly was bound to provoke talk and judgment from every quartile of the court. Victoria had been nothing but kind and pleasant to Violet for the few days she had been serving her, and the last thing she wanted was anything to spoil her good fortune. Not when the complete and utter contrast to her mother and the duchess’s treatment continued to bolster her fragile happiness and confidence.

Violet lifted her trembling hands to her mouth to hide her smile.

Oh, how she loved the queen already! She would do all she could to repay Victoria’s benevolence toward her by anticipating her every want and wish. The happier the queen, the more likely Violet would not return to her mother’s and the duchess’s control, to the scathing remarks, backhanded slaps, and derision from her mother as the duchess looked on, doing absolutely nothing to stop the mistreatment.

The moment of distress Violet had felt about possible court gossip was slowly replaced with unadulterated triumph. She could not wait to see the duchess’s face when her eyes fell upon Violet in the ballroom, carrying a tray of champagne or the fancy delicacies she had seen chef preparing in the kitchens earlier that day.

Attendance at a grand ball! Even her mother had never managed such a feat.

Chapter Five

James battled his irritation as the grand duke swept the queen around the ballroom floor, his hand, which should have been at the small of her back, slipping dangerously low…

He looked across the room and met Melbourne's gaze, his face set in stone. He gave a curt nod indicating he was watching the duke with the same disgust as James. He turned back to the royal couple as the music came to an end, the tension that had stiffened James's shoulders for the last five minutes easing as the problem of the duke's roving hand was resolved.

The queen tipped back her head and laughed at something he whispered in her ear, her laughter far too loud and tittering. The crowds of gentlemen and ladies milling around the room constantly darted glances at Victoria, all undoubtedly wondering what the queen was thinking by so openly flirting with a man who could clearly not be trusted.

The Duchess of Kent, the queen's mother, approached her daughter, and Victoria immediately stepped back from the duke, her expression changing from one of unabashed happiness to one of complete gloom. James had never witnessed such open dislike from one person to another until he had come to court and witnessed the queen interact with her mother. Her bitterness toward the duchess was palpable, pungent enough to sear anyone who had the misfortune to come near them whenever they were together.

Wandering around the room, James admired the prettiness of the ladies, their pale pink, yellow, and blue dresses filling the already glittering ballroom with color. Feathers, pearls, and jewels adorned ears, necks, and wrists, glinting in beautifully arranged hair. James surveyed the room, catching the eye of one or two of the women who looked his way, mischievous intent clear in their gazes.

Then he spotted Violet Parker, and the other ladies vanished. What was she doing here? He had thought her the queen's personal housemaid, yet here she was dressed in the palace's black-and-white serving uniform, her natural beauty outshining those around her. Her eyes were wide with wonder as she looked at everything and everyone, a soft smile playing on her lips.

James slowly walked the circumference of the room. What was it about her that sent such irregular sensations coursing through his body? Time and again, he saw Violet around court and attempted to engage her in conversation, only for her to dip her head politely and hurry away. Was it her disregard of him that made him hanker her notice all the more? She was beautiful, yes, but she also held an aura—a presence—that made him yearn to be in her company. The notion was entirely mystifying.

He came to a stop at the edge of the dance floor, feigning interest in the dancers before glancing surreptitiously at Violet. She stared straight ahead, eyes he knew were the color of Bristol glass steadfastly directed away from him.

Yet pleasure swelled inside him to observe her

looking so happy despite standing on the sidelines, a tray of sweet treats in her hands, as all around her the aristocracy and gentry indulged in too much champagne, too much flirtation. He had no doubt Violet knew the ways of the court as much as he and was all too aware these people might smile and jest, but they also had a constant eye on elevation whether through appointed position or marriage.

He could not imagine Violet Parker indulging in such self-centered strategy. Then again, she was certainly rising. From helper to her mother to the queen's housemaid and now, here she was, serving at a grand ball alongside staff that would have been trained in such service for months.

Who was Violet Parker really? The fact he asked himself the question was concerning, but his desire for an answer had badgered him since he'd first laid eyes on her two months before. Well, this evening he was determined to exchange a few words with her. Taking a deep breath, James closed the few feet of polish parquet between them as he straightened his collar and smoothed his fingers over the hair at his temples.

Standing beside her, he made a show of glancing about the room as he lifted a small, peach tart from her tray. "Enjoying yourself, Mistress Parker?"

Her flinch was so slight, it might have gone unnoticed but not by him.

She continued to stare straight ahead, her poise more rigid than before. "I can't talk to you, Mr. Greene. You are far above me in station, and the queen pays me a huge honor by asking me to be here."

Surprised, it took all his restraint not to look at her as he lifted the tart to his mouth. "You are here by the queen's request?"

"Yes."

He quickly swallowed the minuscule delicacy. "Then, considering how long you have been in her service, she must have taken to you immensely and with speed."

"And the possibility clearly surprises you."

Her words were so clipped, so dripping with knowing, he turned to her. She stared at him with those ridiculously stunning eyes, her blonde hair shining and beautiful.

She lifted her brows, her gaze boring into his with undisguised challenge. "Am I right?"

So much for him being above her in station…

He bit back a smile and quickly looked ahead. "No, in fact you are very wrong. I imagine anyone in your company for any time becomes immensely fond of you." He glanced at her, pleased by her deepening blush. "Am I to gather your position as Victoria's housemaid is just the beginning of your ambitions?"

"How do you know I am her housemaid? I am hardly known at court." She frowned. "But I suppose my elevation could be deemed a snippet of gossip for devouring as much as any other."

"On the contrary, I have heard no one speak of it."

"Then how—"

"I overheard you, Mistress Parker." He smiled. "Better yet, I *saw* you."

"Saw me?" She continued to watch the dance floor but shifted slightly away from him. "Doing what exactly?"

"I suppose you could describe it as a…jig."

Her sharp intake of breath sent his stomach

quivering with suppressed laughter. She stared at him, her cheeks flushed but her eyes alight with mirth as though she often laughed at herself. "In the corridor? The day my mother told me I was to serve the queen?"

He nodded.

Her gaze slid over his face, lingered a moment on his lips before she returned her focus ahead. "Then you shouldn't be loitering in corners and behind pillars, or wherever you were, without announcing your presence," she said, clearly battling to diminish her smile. "It's unforgivably rude."

Duchess Sunderland stopped in front of them and gave James a passing nod before she lifted a treat from Violet's tray, her gaze warm. "Are you enjoying yourself, Parker?"

"I am, Your Grace. Very much."

"Good. The queen is delighted you are here, but I cannot say the same for the baroness. Which makes me enjoy your achievement twice as much." She glanced at James and straightened her shoulders before addressing Violet again. "A word of warning, Parker. Mr. Greene has quite the reputation. Don't be flattered by him. He is an incorrigible flirt."

Before he could even attempt to defend himself, the duchess swept away with her companion. Cursing the woman's appraisal and the impression it had likely left on Violet, James cleared his throat. "How is the queen?"

"She's wonderful."

"You genuinely like her, don't you?"

"I do. Very much." She faced him. "She has been so kind to me, and after working with my mother for so long, the queen makes me feel as though I can finally breathe." Her eyes shadowed with something indiscernible before she returned her gaze to Victoria as she was led onto the dance floor by her uncle Leopold. "I pray every night that I might remain in her service for a long time yet. I have absolutely no wish to return to my mother and the duchess."

The set of her jaw and the color that stained her cheeks provoked James's complete recognition, and he clasped his hands tightly behind his back. "Clearly, parental dislike and obligation is something we have in common."

"I am confident neither of your parents are anything like my mother. If they were, you would not be so happy and carefree."

"Happy and carefree? That is how you see me?" Although her summary was wholly inaccurate, pleasure whispered through him that she must have been watching him to come to such a conclusion, however mistaken. "I am neither of those things. In fact, I fight my inevitable depression every day."

"How can you say such a thing?" She glanced at him. "Your life must be interesting and privileged to work alongside Lord Melbourne."

"It is, but this life won't last forever." He drew in a breath, aware that he risked making a fool of himself or maybe provoking unwelcome gossip by confiding in her. Yet he sensed Violet was not prone to disparagement or tittle-tattle. "My father writes to me almost daily reminding me of my looming responsibilities, and I cannot avoid what awaits me forever. But until that time, I intend to work and play hard at court for as long as I am able, thus delaying returning home as my parents wish. Do you consider that very wrong?" Silence stretched, and James turned. "Mistress Parker?"

Her study of him was intense, her blue eyes narrowed as though trying to ascertain his sincerity.

At last, she spoke. "No, Mr. Greene, there is nothing wrong with that. Not at all." She faced the dance floor. "I should get back to the kitchens and replenish my tray. It was nice talking to you."

She moved to walk away, and James gently touched her arm. Suddenly, it was important that she hear him. That he shared with her what constantly harangued him. He instinctively knew she would not mock his confession—his fear—as so many of his other pointless conquests most assuredly would have, had he confided in them.

"What awaits me is marriage," he said. "But I am not a man any woman should want for a husband, so it's something I will avoid for as long as possible."

The curiosity in her eyes made his confidence falter, and James lifted his fingers from her arm. No doubt she thought him pathetic for fearing something that so many longed for. But Violet did not know him or what he might be capable of. Of the nasty, volatile temperament passed down through the men in his family for generations.

"Better marriage than imprisonment with a mother who has controlled and belittled you your entire life." She smiled wryly, her gaze sad. "Better a son who will one day marry than a daughter shackled to a mother who wishes her to scheme and spy upon the only person who has made her feel human, liked, and worthy of a modicum of respect for the first time in months."

He stilled. "Do you speak of the queen?"

Mistress Parker swallowed before looking at Victoria where she stood a few feet away. "What would you like to do if not marry?" she asked quietly.

James stared at her profile, unsure of her thoughts or disposition. "Stay at court where I am happy. Work hard. Rise within the hierarchy as a single man."

"I want to paint."

Had he heard her correctly? "Paint?"

She softly smiled as she faced him. "Yes. I dream of my landscapes hanging in every gallery and every grand house in the country. If you think yourself an oddity in this mercenary world, whatever must you think of me? Good evening, Mr. Greene."

James stared after her as Violet disappeared among the mass of finery, his heart heavy for the sadness that emanated from her, yet his inquisitiveness about her had only deepened. He looked at Victoria as she laughed with Melbourne and others in her circle. Could it be that the queen saw the same spark of something special in Violet Parker that he did?

Chapter Six

Violet smiled as she billowed a pristine white sheet over the queen's bed at Buckingham Palace. Three weeks had passed since the ball, and as the royal household had prepared to leave Windsor, Victoria announced—much to Lehzen's disbelief—that she wished to retain Violet as her personal housemaid at whatever residence she might occupy.

Ever since, Violet's elation had bubbled inside her even as she battled quiet dread that she lived on borrowed time. She had no idea how to stop the fear that her mother would find a way to quash her joy. The mere thought of returning to the duchess's rooms where tension and plotting filled the days from morning to night was more than Violet could bear.

"It's been almost a month since the grand duke's departure." Victoria sighed as she wandered in front of the fireplace and picked up a small porcelain ornament from the mantel. She turned it in her hands before replacing it. "Yet my thoughts are still filled with his eyes, hair, and exquisite build."

Violet smoothed Victoria's bedspread and stood back, satisfied with her work. "Well, he is very handsome, ma'am."

"The queen was not addressing you, Parker," Lehzen snapped from the corner of the room where she was inspecting one of the queen's gowns. "You only speak to Her Majesty when you are specifically spoken to."

Heat leapt into Violet's cheeks. "Sorry, Baroness. I did not mean to—"

"Lehzen..." Victoria's eyes flashed with annoyance. "I was addressing the whole room, Parker included." She lowered onto the carpet, her beautiful amethyst skirts splaying around her, to play with her beloved Dash, a charming Cavalier King Charles spaniel. "And you are right, Parker, the duke is very handsome. See, Lehzen? At least my maid doesn't find it necessary that I dismiss my emotions in favor of listening to my uncle's claims that my cousin Albert will fulfill all my heart's desires, and there is no other man on earth to match him."

"Your Majesty," Lehzen said slowly and quietly as though speaking to a child. "I urge you to accept that neither your uncle, nor your ministers, are likely to forget the importance of you marrying and marrying soon."

"As if I need reminding." Victoria scowled as she lifted Dash onto her breast, rubbing her nose against his. "Perchance I will marry my dog. How will that be?"

Violet plumped the pillows as she admired the exquisitely embroidered bedcover, her head filling with thoughts of whether she would one day have a wedding. Every now and then, her heart betrayed her by longing for a husband and children, even though her mother had made it clear Violet's sole duty was to elevate the family within the royal household. In her mother's grand plans, Violet's two older brothers would provide the next generation of Parkers. Violet and her younger sister, Elizabeth, would do as their mother commanded. Neither of them allowed to dream of a different life or contradict their mother's scheming.

"It felt as though every soul in England was in London for my coronation," Victoria continued. "I am queen yet still unable to make my own decisions. How can it be that thousands and thousands of my loyal subjects celebrate me as their sovereign, but I am still forced to propose marriage to a man found by someone other than me?"

"Because the matter is a state one, ma'am." Lehzen sighed, her gaze somewhat sympathetic. "You must listen to your ministers' and uncle's advice."

"The only advice I care for is Lord Melbourne's, and he is very subdued on the subject." The queen's eyes glittered with undisguised fondness. "Maybe he cannot bear to think of me marrying. His eyes were filled with tears when he knelt before me in the abbey." Victoria rose to her feet. "Parker, would you ever marry on the say-so of a relation who could not possibly know anything of your true feelings? Or would you follow your heart as I wish to do?"

Violet glanced at Lehzen before facing the queen. "Well, as common as it is from parent to daughter, I would still hate to be told who I could or could not marry."

"Hmm, but hate is such a strong word," Victoria mused. "I'm not sure that I hate the ministers' advice, but it *is* incredibly trying. Do you have any wish to marry, Parker? I would not blame you if you did not."

"Sometimes I do, but…" Violet hesitated, her abject feelings toward her mother simmering far too close to the surface. "My mother has other plans for me than marriage, ma'am."

"How unorthodox! What are these plans?"

"She is often keen to remind me how far I have come under her instruction and elevation. I belong here, ma'am, at court." She flashed Victoria a small smile. "Serving you, which has been an absolute joy since I first stepped into your chambers."

The queen's gaze softened. "And if we go along as famously as we have thus far, you will continue to serve me for a long time." Her smile faltered. "But I have absolutely no wish for your service to me to destroy any imaginings of love and happiness, if that is what you want."

Lehzen gave a theatrical sniff as she carried one of the queen's gowns to the bed. "Girls like Parker were born to serve, Your Majesty. Their only concern should be how they can work better and harder."

She pinned Violet with a stare so intense, she bent to the floor and retrieved a pile of discarded bed linen in an effort to calm her rising temper. It was so infuriating how Lehzen always felt the need to intervene whenever Violet and the queen were speaking. The baroness made it clear she was the only one who would ever be truly close to Victoria...although Violet suspected it was the Duchess of Sunderland whom the queen liked and trusted the most.

"Oh, Lehzen," Victoria admonished as she walked to her dressing table and sat before the mirror. "Leave dear Parker alone." She smoothed her hands over her jaw and neck. "Uncle Leopold is adamant Albert and his brother will visit before the autumn. I will have little choice but to be welcoming and courteous." Her eyes flashed impishly as she caught Violet's eye in the mirror's reflection. "But I have firmly stated that my uncle should not pin his hopes and dreams on a union or else risk being sorely disappointed."

Violet returned the queen's smile. "Is there anything else you need me to do, ma'am? Or shall I take these linens to the laundry?"

"You know." The queen sighed, clearly having not heard Violet's question or choosing to ignore it. "As queen I command that you never marry for any other reason than love, Parker." She turned on her velvet covered stool and grinned, her blue eyes shining. "Yes, I command that you work for me until a gentleman comes along who you find entirely irresistible. A man who makes you long to be nowhere other than in his arms. How will that be?"

Hope and possibility swelled inside Violet. The more often the queen spoke as though she wanted Violet by her side for the longest time possible, the more tightly Violet held on to the prospect of never returning to her mother's clutches. "There is nothing more I'd like than to continue serving you, ma'am. I am in no rush for romance."

"Good, then it is decided. From now on—"

"Your Majesty." Lehzen stepped toward the queen, her eyes like sharpened daggers on Violet. "You must not promise Parker such things. There is no saying when her mother might have need—"

"Her mother?" Victoria asked, sharply. "Do you have any wish to return to your mother or mine, Parker?"

"Not at all, ma'am," Violet said firmly, the vehemence in her words bouncing from the silk wall hangings. "That I can say unequivocally."

"There. You heard her, Lehzen," Victoria pronounced with triumph. "Parker wishes to remain with me as much as I wish her here. It's decided then. Your attendance to me is permanent until I say otherwise. Whether that be here at the palace, Windsor, or even if I must travel abroad. Now, Lehzen, would you please be so kind as to find my dresser? I have things I wish to discuss with her."

"Yes, ma'am."

Violet's throat dried as the baroness shot her a glare before marching from the room, her chin high and her shoulders rigid. As much as Violet enjoyed the queen's favoritism, she was building an enemy in Lehzen…a woman who had every chance of becoming as dangerous as Violet's mother.

Chapter Seven

"It's no use, Greene," Melbourne said, rising from his desk. "I must tell the queen it is imperative that she is seen behaving at least kindly toward her mother."

"People are still talking, sir?"

"Talking, speculating, and damn well gossiping. It's hardly news Victoria and the duchess are not the best of friends, but the queen must be regarded as the better woman. She must visit the duchess…preferably today."

James lowered his pen, the awkwardness between Victoria and her mother echoed throughout court, seemingly causing more and more possibility of fragmenting the courtiers from those loyal to the old ways and those keen to embrace the new ideas preferred by Victoria. "What can I do?" James stood from his desk, concerned for Melbourne and the queen. Should the backhanded chitchat continue in the same vein, it would only weaken Victoria's precarious popularity. "Why don't I speak to someone from Victoria's bedchamber? It might be more effective to have one of her ladies press the importance of maintaining an outward perception that she is trying her very best with the duchess—"

"As opposed to coming from me, you mean?" Melbourne's eyes flashed with anger. "Are you implying that the queen no longer trusts my judgement?"

Ever since Melbourne had almost lost his place as prime minister, he had been tense, to say the least. The gentleman who should have been his successor, Sir Robert Peel, a Tory no less, had insisted Victoria replace a number of her Whig supporting ladies with those more Tory orientated. The acrimony this request elicited between Peel and the queen reached such heights that he declared himself unable to form a ministry. Thus, Melbourne's somewhat shaky reinstatement to prime minister could never be considered a *fait accompli*.

"My confidence in your advice to the queen is stalwart, sir," James said, as he rounded the desk. "I merely think, as you and she are considered allies in a majority of issues, it might be wise if someone else addressed her about such a sensitive subject."

"Over and over, I have told Victoria she must try to find a way to bear her mother's company more often. Instead, she chooses to attend the opera and make merry with all and sundry in view of the whole of London. Did you see this morning's newspaper reports? It's as though the press intends to stir up a bloody revolt!" Melbourne's gaze bored into James's before the minister abruptly returned to his desk and snatched some papers. "I suppose you have someone in mind to speak to her?"

James stared at Melbourne's bowed head, indecision whispering through him before he said firmly, "Mistress Parker, sir."

"Parker?" Melbourne lifted his head. "I know of no lady by that name. Who is she?"

"Well, officially, she is the queen's personal housemaid, but people are speculating she is becoming much more than that to Her Majesty."

"More? In what way?" Melbourne lifted his pen from its onyx stand, his eyes narrowed. "Why don't I know about this girl? I assume she's a girl?"

"She's the same age as the queen, sir. It is that commonality which many are saying has made Parker such a sudden favorite. It seems she and the queen have many things in common they like to discuss."

Melbourne huffed a laugh, a wry smile curving his lips. "A housemaid and the queen? Don't be absurd, Greene. Fine." He waved dismissively. "Speak to this…"

"Parker, sir."

"Parker, yes. Speak to her and tell her that I advise the queen to visit the duchess as soon as possible. No, I advise the queen to visit her this afternoon."

"Yes, sir."

James left Melbourne's office and headed for the queen's apartments, infinitely pleased that the perfect excuse to seek out Violet had fallen into his lap. Their association—if he could call it that—could only be deemed tentative, but James intended to change that. It did not sit well with him that Violet remained so unresponsive to his charms. After all, he had little else on which to hang his hat. Possibly an untainted army record was to his credit, but still, his life at court did not count for much in the grand scheme of things.

God knew, his father would wholeheartedly agree with that sentiment.

Yet the one thing his father was keen for James to pursue at court was his search for a wife. Not that Violet would ever be deemed suitable by his parents, of course…which only made her all the more delectable.

As the days passed, James found himself less interested in his usual assignations with the grand ladies at court and more interested in Violet. Not just her beauty, but also her unusual desire to become an artist and the sadness that had lingered in her eyes at the ball. Although he had grasped the opportunity to speak to her if he happened upon her in the vast palace or gardens, their paths rarely crossed. Yet James was certain that a subtle connection and fondness slowly built between them.

He picked up his pace through the dark, gloomy corridors. Once he reached the queen's chambers, he was met by the Duchess of Sunderland as she emerged through a doorway into the anteroom.

She drew the door closed behind her and stared at him expectantly. "Mr. Greene. May I help you with something?"

"I'm looking for Mistress Parker, Duchess." He straightened his shoulders, determined to see out his mission to find Violet. "I have a small task for her from Lord Melbourne."

"Melbourne?" Surprise flashed in the duchess's eyes. "Are you sure he asked for Parker?"

"I am."

"Well, this is most extraordinary, but I trust you speak the truth. You are likely to find Parker on her way back from the laundry. She disappeared over an hour ago. If she dawdles much longer, the queen will notice her absence. I suggest when you find her that you relay your message and send her back here immediately."

James dipped his head. "Thank you."

Leaving the duchess staring after him, James quickly walked away, praying he didn't miss Violet in the maze of assorted avenues that ran throughout the palace. He finally reached a stretch of servants' stairs and asked after Violet. No one had seen her.

Cursing, he was about to retrace his steps when he

rounded a corner and there she was, standing in front of a landscape painting, her pretty brow furrowed and her arms laden with freshly pressed sheets.

He slowly approached, reluctant to interrupt her intense contemplation. “Mistress Parker?”

She jumped and turned, her cheeks flushing pink. “Mr. Greene, I was just…” She glanced at the painting. “Just…”

“Admiring a painting when you should be heading back to the queen?” He walked closer. “Your dallying will go no further, I promise.”

Her gaze flashed with a defiance that he suspected would get her wherever she wished to go in this unforgiving world. “I think you’ll find I am not answerable to you, so you can stop looking at me like a cat who’s caught a mouse.”

James smiled, unable to drag his gaze from her.

She glared at him before abruptly turning back to the painting. “It comes as no surprise that the paintings in this corridor do not warrant your admiration and, instead, you choose to stand there smirking at me.”

James raised his eyebrows in feigned nonchalance. “You think that I do not appreciate art?”

“Almost certainly if you can walk along these corridors and not be overwhelmed with the paintings on every wall.” She looked back to the landscape. “Art such as this should never be ignored, Mr. Greene. It deserves everyone’s full attention.”

He stared at her turned cheek, her whimsy stirring something awake in his chest. “I have a message for you.”

She met his gaze, a hint of panic in her wide eyes. “From whom?”

"Lord Melbourne. Or maybe from me considering I suggested your involvement."

"Involvement in what?"

A barrage of gentlemen's laughter burst forth from further along the corridor, and James gently gripped her elbow. "Not here. Come with me."

He quickly led her along the red carpet, past rows of glinting mirrors and paintings until he found a deserted doorway. Steering her into the small space, James's heart gave a jolt as he caught a fleeting scent of her hair. He had not been this close to her before, and suddenly every nerve in his body tensed, his entire being filled with awareness.

"Mistress Parker…" He cleared his throat. "Here, let me take those." He eased the heavy linens from her arms.

She looked at him expectantly, nothing in her manner indicating their nearness affected her as it did him. "Please hurry with your message, Mr. Greene. The queen is expecting me."

"Yes, the queen." He blinked from his pathetic stupor and turned his mind to the business in hand. "You must tell her to pay a visit to her mother this afternoon."

"What?" Her cheeks paled. "I couldn't possibly. The queen can barely hear the duchess's name without Lehzen sending for vapors. Why would you put this responsibility on me? She will not welcome me asking such a thing of her. I am certain the queen feels the same about her mother as I do mine."

"Which is exactly why the news is better coming from you."

"Why?"

"Because there is every possibility she likes and trusts you. Your empathy will shine through…certainly more than it ever could from Melbourne."

"But she trusts Lord Melbourne more than anyone else in the palace."

"But this is a matter, unfortunately, that Victoria refuses to speak to him about."

"But how am I to tell her? What words can I possibly use that will lessen the queen's inevitable annoyance?"

"Tell her if the court do not see her making a concerted effort to at least maintain amicability with her mother, they will begin to wonder of whom they should be more wary. The duchess or the queen. It will only be to the queen's benefit if she is deemed the nicer, kinder, more benevolent."

Her blue eyes were filled with doubt. "I really don't think she would ever pay attention to such speculation from anyone."

"Violet, please. If Victoria could just pay the duchess a quick visit this afternoon, it will satisfy Melbourne and lead to him halting his pestering of the queen. At least, for a while."

"This afternoon will be difficult. The queen has been in such a wonderful mood today." She sighed as she glanced along the corridor. "She has been talking about love and romance of all things."

James smiled. "And have you been contemplating such things along with her?"

She lifted her chin. "As if I would tell you anything of what is discussed in the queen's chambers, James Greene."

He grinned, pleased to hear her speak his first name.

She pinned him with a hard stare. "I will relay the message, but woe betide you if she maims the messenger. I am not comfortable with this. Not in the slightest."

"You know as well as I do how fond the queen is becoming of you. I would not have volunteered you if I thought it would in any way bring you strife. It's my intention to look out for you. Always."

"And why would you do that?"

"Because I am coming to care for you." He handed her the linens before walking backward out of the doorway. "And that care deepens each time I speak to you."

With a dip of his head, James turned and strode along the corridor, confident and immeasurably pleased that he sensed her studying him until he had rounded the corner, out of sight.

Chapter Eight

Her arms aching from the heavy bedclothes, Violet stood in the queen's apartments, her ears strained toward the private drawing room. She had not seen Victoria upon entering the rooms and could not hear her familiar laughter or piano playing. Although afraid of her determining Violet beyond insolent once she passed on the request from Lord Melbourne, Violet also longed to purge the words so that she might breathe normally again.

Entering the bedchamber, she stored the linens in the huge closet at the back of the room, her hands ever so slightly trembling. Just as she closed the double doors, Victoria's voice rang loud and clear above those of her ladies as they filed into the room.

"Oh, Parker, where were you? You missed the most unforgivable teasing from…" Victoria's smile faltered. "Whatever is the matter?"

Violet swallowed as the queen stared at her along with every one of her ladies, Lehzen standing to Victoria's side, suspicion in her eyes. "Her Majesty asked you a question, Parker."

Dragging her gaze from Lehzen's to the queen, Violet dipped a semi-curtsey, suddenly unsure if she should share her message so publicly. Maybe the queen would not want her ladies to know where she was going if she chose to visit her mother. "I must ask permission to speak to you alone, ma'am."

"Alone?" Lehzen's eyes widened, her cheeks mottling. "You have no standing upon which to speak to the queen alone! Leave this room immediately. I will speak to you—"

"It's quite all right, Lehzen." Victoria raised her hand, her gaze on Violet. "Everyone, please leave."

Violet's pulse pounded in her ears as one by one, the ladies and Lehzen left the room, each casting her a glare or a curious, lingering stare before they exited. The doors closed silently.

"Now, what is it that has you looking so terrified?" the queen asked as she walked to a small sofa by the window. "Come. Sit with me."

"Sit with you? Ma'am, I couldn't possibly—"

"Yes, Parker, you can."

Sickness coated Violet's throat as she walked to the sofa and sat a respectful distance from the queen, drawing her hands together so tightly in her lap, she felt the blood pump in her fingers.

Victoria raised her eyebrows. "Now, what is all this about?"

Violet drew in a long breath, then shakily released it. "It's about the duchess, Your Majesty."

"My mother?"

"Yes, ma'am. Lord Melbourne asked his assistant, Mr. Greene, to find me so that I might pass on a message to you."

"Melbourne instructed *you* with this message rather than come to me himself?" Irritation clouded Victoria's gaze, her mouth pinching tight. "I see. Well, I will most certainly be telling Lord Melbourne how I feel about such neglect in his duties. Come now. You must share this message the prime minister is clearly afraid to deliver himself or deems of such little importance it is beneath him."

"He feels it is imperative that you visit with your mother this afternoon, ma'am."

"What?"

"He…he fears that gossip and speculation is growing at court."

"What gossip?"

Violet's cheeks heated, her heart picking up speed. "Gossip about the status of your relationship with the duchess, ma'am. It's believed that popularity could become split between you. Not that I believe such a thing is ever likely, but if Lord Melbourne thinks it possible, then…"

Seconds ticked by as Victoria stared at her with such intensity, Violet battled to sit still and not fidget or flee.

Abruptly, the queen stood. "Fine. Then if I am demanded to endure such an ordeal, you will accompany me. I wish this trial over with as soon as possible, so we will go immediately. My mother will not be expecting me and no doubt my sudden appearance will cause a fracas, but I do not care for her feelings. Not one whit."

"But, ma'am, Lehzen will not like—"

"I am not asking you, Parker, I am commanding you. Now…" Victoria paced back and forth in front of the window, her gestures jumpy as she patted her hair and fiddled with the pearl and sapphire brooch at her throat. "You can escort me to my mother's side of the palace whereupon I will visit with her for the absolute minimum of time." She dropped her hands. "Why would Melbourne make me do such a thing on absurdly short notice? I will tell him my feelings in no uncertain terms when I next see him."

Violet trembled. The last thing she wanted was to return to the Duchess of Kent's apartments. Yet to refuse the queen was not an option. No matter how vile the prospect, it seemed inevitable Violet was about to see her mother again after a welcome two weeks of successfully avoiding her.

The queen marched toward the chamber doors. "Come now, Parker. I wish to get this dreadful task over with."

Violet hurried after the queen into the next room where her ladies and Lehzen stood stock-still, each poised as though awaiting a command or reprimand.

"As you were, ladies," the queen said, as she swept past them, her gaze resolutely focused ahead as her companions parted to give their sovereign an open pathway. "Parker and I will return shortly."

Lacking the courage to look at the Lehzen, Violet kept her eyes on the carpet ahead of her. As they made their way through the palace, Violet could barely contain her embarrassment as courtier after courtier, servant after servant, leapt into rushed bows and curtsies, their eyes lowered as they showed deference to the queen. Dressed in the basic gray-and-white uniform of her standing, Violet had never felt so self-conscious, and desperate explanations and excuses passed through her mind as she met one astounded gaze after another.

It soon became clear how rarely the queen came to her mother's household. Over and over again, Violet had to direct Victoria left and right through corridors which appeared barely known to her.

"Ah, here we are." Victoria drew to a stop outside the door to the duchess's receiving room and pulled back her shoulders, her petite frame rigid. "You will wait here, Parker. I shan't be long at all."

The queen entered the room, and the door fell closed behind her, the sudden silence enveloping Violet.

Blowing out a breath, she dropped her tense shoulders and looked back and forth along the deserted corridor, praying her mother was inside with the duchess and there was no chance of her appearing around the corner. Closing her eyes, Violet took a moment to steady her hammering heart, her mind once again on James Greene and what she would say to him when she next saw him. Lord only knew why she had come to his mind for such a task.

It did not matter how often his dark hair and eyes had infused her thoughts over the last few weeks. Or that his contagious smile and commanding height filled her mind's eye with ever increasing frequency. It would not be with subtle flirtation—or whatever it was that played out between them—that her words would be conveyed when she spoke to him. She was furious that he would put her in such an unconventional position. A maid escorting the queen? Who had ever heard of such a thing? Yes, she wanted to stay in the queen's service, but on footing unlikely to cause problems with Baroness Lehzen or any of the queen's ladies…not to mention her mother.

"Violet?" Her mother's voice echoed along the hallway. "What on earth are you doing?"

Violet startled and then stood tall, braced for the onslaught. "Mama, how are you?" she asked, forcefully holding her mother's gaze. "I am here with Her Majesty."

"What?" Her mother's eyes manically flitted from

Violet to the closed door beside them. "The queen is with the duchess?"

"Yes," Violet whispered, wanting her mother gone. "And she could come out at any second. So—"

"But this is madness." Her mother frowned. "Why would *you* be here with the queen?"

The derision and disbelief in her mother's voice stirred Violet's impatience, her annoyance matched only by the complete and utter triumph that unfurled inside her. She smiled softly. "Because she asked me to accompany her. We…the queen and I are becoming increasingly—"

"Don't you dare gloat in such an unbecoming way," her mother hissed, her blue eyes filled with venom as she gripped Violet's elbow. "If the queen has begun to seek your company, you have but a single task to complete. She might be here now, but how often have you even tried to urge Victoria to spend time with her mother? Asked her if she might consider regularly taking tea with the duchess? Go together to the opera?" Her mother shoved Violet's arm away. "No, all Violet Parker has been thinking about is Violet Parker."

Violet's body trembled with the effort it took not to laugh out loud or push her mother backward. "I will encourage a reconciliation when I think the time is right. Not before."

"You will do as I command."

The trust and kindness Victoria had shown her swept through Violet, and she lifted her chin. "No, Mama. I will not."

Color rushed into her mother's face, the tendons in her neck straining as she stepped forward, her hand raised…

The bedroom door opened, and Victoria emerged, her pallor frightening and her eyes icy-cold.

Violet abruptly stepped back, both she and her mother dropping into curtsies.

"Mrs. Parker." The queen addressed Violet's mother, her face set. "I am glad to see you. I believe I owe you my gratitude."

Violet raised from her curtsey and watched her mother redden further. "Your Majesty?"

"Yes, I thank you, madam," Victoria continued. "For the blessed and amusing company of your daughter. Parker is a welcome addition to my household indeed." She turned and smiled at Violet, her eyes warm and not without a hint of undisguised mischief before facing Violet's mother again. "Yes, I cannot see me wanting her very far away from me for a long time yet. Come along now, Parker. We have much to do."

Barely managing to bite back her smile, Violet held her mother's gaze as she brushed past her. "Mama."

Chapter Nine

James strode behind Melbourne as he marched toward the queen's apartments, his steps swift and his anger tangible.

James had returned to the office and told Melbourne the message had been delivered to Violet, but despite his assurances she would ensure the queen acted according to Melbourne's advice, no returning message had come from the queen's ladies or anyone else for the last two hours, leading to an increasing volatile Melbourne.

So much so, James felt he had no choice but to urge the minister to calm himself if he was to speak with Victoria. "Sir, I really think it best that you wait—"

"For what, Greene?" Spinning around, Melbourne's eyes bulged, his cheeks flushed with frustration. "Until I learn of what happened between the queen and the duchess in tomorrow's papers? Until I discover Victoria has smothered the damn woman?"

"Sir, you really must calm yourself. The queen is bound to be upset, whether or not she has yet visited the duchess. To confront her in this state of agitation will only lead to—"

"Repercussions?" Melbourne huffed a laugh, his eyes almost maniacal. "There is little the queen does without my say-so, Greene. There will not be repercussions, believe me. She will come to be grateful that I urged her to undertake this visit. Mark my words."

"Sir, I really think—"

"You are not in my employ to think. You are here to do my bidding," Melbourne said, leaning close. "I do not endure endless hours looking at picture albums, listening to her play and sing, or sit at a damn whist table until my legs are numb to have Victoria lose an opportunity to make some positive headway in a situation that is running out of the palace's control." Glaring, he stepped back. "Let that be an end to your objections."

They continued through the palace with James glaring at Melbourne's back. The man's conceit was renowned throughout court, and as much as James liked and admired Melbourne, it did not sit well with him that the minister could speak about the queen in such a throwaway fashion. It sometimes felt to James that the stars were one day bound to fall from Victoria's eyes and a new bright and shiny distraction would take her fancy in Melbourne's place.

They came to a stop at the main entrance to the queen's apartments where two uniformed guards stood sentry.

Melbourne adjusted his necktie. "You stay here, Greene. I will speak to her alone."

Once the minister had been granted access and the door closed behind him, James tipped his head back to stare at the ornate ceiling, unwelcome foreboding running up his spine. Had he unwittingly dragged Violet into a situation that was more involved, more turbulent, than he thought? In the months he had been working with Melbourne, he had never seen him so consumed with stress and anger. The man hid his feelings well—both professional and personal—but the continued chatter about the division between the queen and the duchess was clearly wearing on him. Or could it be that the increased contemplation of the queen marrying and her slow acceptance of its urgency had made Melbourne wonder, like James, whether his position at Victoria's side could be long-lasting?

Having returned to their stations, the two sentries suddenly stood to abrupt attention, their gazes directed behind James, chins lifted. James turned and then hastily lowered his head as the queen swept to a halt in front of him. Violet stood behind her, her expression inscrutable.

"You," Victoria snapped, her eyes narrowed. "Greene, isn't it?"

"Yes, Your Majesty."

"What are you doing here?" She looked sharply at the apartment doors. "Is Melbourne inside waiting for me?"

"He is, ma'am."

Color darkened Victoria's cheeks as she continued to stare at the door. "Then I will speak to him alone. Parker, you may return to your work elsewhere."

"Yes, ma'am."

James glanced at Violet, both of them standing stock-still until the doors closed behind the queen.

Violet's exhalation broke the tense silence. "Of all the things you might have asked of me," she said, brushing a fallen curl from her temple, her fingers trembling. "The queen emerged from her mother's rooms incandescent with rage. I have absolutely no idea what was said between them, but I fear the consequences." She faced him, her blue eyes anxious. "She is not happy with Melbourne. Not at all."

James glanced at the apartment doors before cupping her elbow. "Let's take a walk."

"Where are we going?"

Somewhat surprised she agreed to accompany him, James thought quickly. "We'll go to the gardens for a moment. I owe you an apology."

The clouds were heavy and gray as they emerged from the palace onto a gravel pathway, the stones crunching beneath their feet. Courtiers and guests milled through the flowerbeds and bushes, the fountains and trees, giving the required sense of him and Violet being among people in all propriety, yet perfectly able to snatch moments of intimate conversation without the risk of being overheard.

As they walked, James's mind raced with strategies of how to deepen Violet's attention toward him. He could no longer deny how much he liked her or that his fondness was taking a different form than his habitual flirtation. He liked talking to her. He liked spending time with her. He liked the way the difference in their stations did not seem to matter to her.

She confused and fascinated him in equal measure. One moment forthright, confident, and seemingly immovable. Another, quiet, vulnerable, and maybe even a little afraid. All of which made him want to take care of her.

A dangerous wish when he was not free to succumb to his emotions. His life's journey had been drawn out for him, no matter how long he might manage to delay his participation in it. Real, growing feelings for a housemaid were not part of that plan, and there was no way on God's earth he could allow his burgeoning friendship with Violet to escalate.

"What are you thinking about?" She smiled up at him, her gaze sparkling with amusement. "Your jaw is as tight as a piano string."

Forcing a smile, James dragged his gaze from hers. "Nothing. Come, there's a place we can sit."

He led her along a quiet path where a stone bench sat beneath an arbor that might afford them some privacy. Yet James could not relax his jaw any more than he could calm his beating heart. He hated what lay in wait for him, hated that a woman so lovely, gracious, and kind as Violet could never be his. She deserved a man of even temper, a man who would forever put her needs before his own. Deep in his soul, James knew he was his father's son, the proof evident in his meaningless flirtations, and his unpredictable temper when faced with a seemingly insolvable challenge that called into question his reputation as the consummate fixer. Add in his resentful frustrations and the endless need to work and play hard, and anyone would be pushed to convince him that he was any different than his father at all. Which meant once he had children, God only knew how he would treat them.

Shame struck deep in his heart. He did not want to be that man, but what the hell could he do about it?

"I really shouldn't be here with you like this."

Violet's voice scattered his thoughts, and James forced what he hoped was an encouraging smile. "I just want a few minutes with you." He gestured with a wave toward the stone bench. "Shall we?"

She sat and stared at the fountain in front of them as it spouted water into a small pond. "If you intend to apologize for asking me to speak to the queen, there is no need," she said quietly. "At first, I thought I would strip you into pieces when I saw you, but I'm coming to understand the perilous game you must have to play every day working for Lord Melbourne."

"Indeed, but he's amiable enough once you get used to him." James studied her, hating that her face was so much paler than usual. "What happened? The last thing I expected was for you to have to escort the queen to see the duchess. If I had thought you would have to go with her, I never would have—"

"You couldn't possibly have known. No one could." A little of the light he liked so much came into her eyes, and she smiled somewhat mischievously. "Most of all the baroness. I think Lehzen might well have popped a blood vessel."

He laughed.

"I gave the queen your message, and the next thing I knew, we were marching through the palace to the one place I have managed to avoid for days." Her smile dissolved. "The duchess's household."

"And with that your mother?"

"Yes."

"Did you see her?"

"Briefly." Her jaw tightened. "I might owe her all that I am and everything I have, but I like that the queen does not immediately assume everything I do well for her is due to my mother. Victoria sees me for who I am alone, I know she does." Her fervent gaze burned into his. "Does that sound fantastical?"

He wasn't sure how to respond. He had only seen her with the queen once, and Violet had looked far from happy. Yet he sensed she was unlikely to see any good in herself unless the queen's deepening regard for her proved true without doubt. Something he understood only too well…

"If you feel the queen's fondness, if you sense it,

then I have no doubt it's genuine." He looked into her eyes, and his heart ached to see such vulnerability, such need for approval. "But do you really want her attention? Trust me, it will not come without expectation and unforeseen pressures that could escalate on a whim. Victoria can be unpredictable. Service to her capricious. I have learned at least that much from working for Melbourne."

"Oh, I know." She inhaled a shaky breath. "But this position has given me the first liberty I have had since leaving home months ago. Yes, I am just a housemaid, but to be seen for who we truly are by anyone, let alone a queen, is something we all wish for. Don't you think?"

His father came into his mind, and James swallowed his shameful vulnerability. "Yes. Yes, I do."

They lapsed into silence, and James fought the urge to take her hand.

Chapter Ten

Although Violet suspected her mother would try to re-establish her control after their altercation, that awareness made the threat no easier to bear. So when Violet was summoned to the duchess's apartments two weeks later, she acquiesced. If she pushed her mother too far, the trouble she would create would be more profound and almost certainly more far-reaching.

Taking a strengthening breath, Violet entered the duchess's sitting room.

Purposefully averting her eyes from her mother where she stood in front of the fireplace, Violet turned to one of the two long, ivory damask-covered sofas beside her and curtsied to the duchess. "Your Grace."

The duchess silently regarded for her so long that Violet began to tremble.

Then the duchess flashed her a cold smile and stood. Violet instinctively stepped back and then cursed her cowardice.

Amusement flickered in the duchess's gaze as she held out her hands, the emeralds and diamonds, sapphires and gold on her fingers glinting. "My precious child. You have been away from us too long."

Sliding her hands into the duchess's icy grasp, Violet's foreboding deepened.

"Come. Sit with me by the window. Dear Geraldine," she said, addressing Violet's mother. "You, too. You must be as desperate to spend some time with your daughter as I am with mine."

Violet sat and clenched her hands in her lap, quick to notice her mother and the duchess exchange a loaded look before Violet's mother gave an almost indiscernible nod and turned to Violet.

Her smile was predatory, her blue eyes steely. "My dear. We have missed you."

Violet's pulse pounded in her ears, her dislike for her mother gathering strength. Why did her threat suddenly feel worse than ever?

"It has been weeks since you were assigned to the queen's service," her mother continued. "And it pains me to think that you might have come to mistakenly believe the position was given to you for your enjoyment…rather than to facilitate a certain reunion. One that has yet to transpire."

"The queen is busy, Mama. I am only her housemaid. You cannot expect me to—"

"But I do expect it, Violet. As does the duchess. I have eyes and I have ears, and I know you have grown closer to the queen, but I fear you fancy yourself important to her, too. Either that, or, as been reported to me, you are too overly occupied with meeting Mr. Greene in the gardens or corridors, rather than carrying out the task you have been given."

Violet fought to contain the anger twisting in her chest as she slid a glance at the tight-lipped duchess and then back to her mother. "You talk about Mr. Greene as though he is my beau, Mama. We are merely friends. He and I meet with one another through his work for Lord Melbourne and mine for the queen."

"Yet it seems you seek each other out when you are

not working, too."

"We—"

"Ladies, please." The duchess sighed. "Let us not waste this valuable time throwing accusations back and forth. What I wish to discuss with you is important, Parker. Not just to me, but to the entire country."

Tension tightened Violet's stomach. "Your Grace?"

"I am sure you are aware that discussions of finding a husband for the queen are becoming ever more frequent. These discussions often accelerating into heated debate. Now, I know Drina thinks she is enjoying running her life and Britain how she sees fit, but she needs a man beside her. A worthy consort. Lord knows, I miss dear Conroy so very much." She stared wistfully toward the window before focusing again on Violet. "My nephews, Albert and Ernest, are to pay us a visit. Possibly within the next few weeks. Therefore, it is imperative that we do all we can to improve relations between Drina and I before they arrive."

"I'm sorry, Your Grace, but Her Majesty cannot possibly be coerced. She is a grown woman. A queen, no less. She will soon grow tired of my interfering. I believe I have done all I can for the time being and—"

"Is that so?" The duchess glared, two spots of color darkening her cheeks. "Well, Mistress Parker, I'm afraid I do not agree. You have not done anywhere near enough for my cause."

Violet looked between the duchess and her mother, their glares searing her, as she scrambled for a response, her protectiveness of Victoria rising. Hadn't the queen implied that one of the royal brothers from the small duchy of Saxe-Coburg and Gotha was a possible candidate for her hand? Hadn't she also made it clear the notion was invariably unappealing? Marriage seemed to be the last thing on the queen's mind when she was so enjoying her liberty. A state which Violet coveted equally as much.

To add pressure to Victoria by asking that she further entertain the prospect of her mother's company would be too much. A scenario that would almost certainly result in Violet's dismissal from the queen's apartments…quite possibly from court.

She sat a little straighter. One way or another she would find a way to keep the duchess at bay for as long as possible. "I will do all I can to secure your wishes, Your Grace."

The duchess's smile was pinched. "Doing all you can is no longer enough if it means any more time goes by without me seeing my daughter regularly. Every day, if I had my way. Your dear mama and I have shown you nothing but patience thus far, but my tolerance of your delay has reached its end. I want you to ensure me a private visit with my daughter tomorrow."

"Tomorrow? But I cannot ask the queen to—"

"I know for a fact that Drina does not have anything of particular importance nor any pressing state business to attend to tomorrow. I am asking for a mere hour or two of her time."

Violet's resentment burned. The amiable relationship building between her and the queen was fragile and possibly fleeting. She would not allow her mother and the duchess to jeopardize the trust she saw in Victoria's eyes whenever she looked at her.

"I'm sorry, Your Grace, but if there is such urgency, I think it best that you speak to one of the queen's ladies. I am confident one of them will have more success in persuading Her Majesty to accede to your wishes than I ever would. The queen is fond of me, but she is hardly likely to listen to any request I might ask of her. I am her housemaid, nothing more."

Her mother sniffed. "Yet according to court chatter, you are so much more than that. It seems the queen speaks of you often and to anyone who cares to listen. She boasts of how she employs every level of society in her household. That she is sympathetic to all in her realm. I can only assume the person of low birth she refers to is you."

"She has been very kind to me, Mama. I hope she finds me invaluable to her comfort."

"But you are not invaluable. If you have the mistaken notion you are, then maybe it is time you returned to the duchess's service."

Violet glared at her mother, bitter words pinching and biting at her tongue.

"My dear." The duchess gently laid her hand on Violet's. "Your mother and I are happy to see you doing so well, but now is the time to carry out your given task and reunite me with Drina."

"You have been given more than enough time to manage your mission," Violet's mother snapped. "Yet we are no further forward. It will only take me asking Her Majesty for your return to this household, and you will be gone from her apartments forever. Do not push my patience."

The savagery in her mother's gaze and the threat in her words and tone provoked age-old intimidation that knotted Violet's stomach. But she would not falter. Not this time.

She stood from the sofa and made a show of

smoothing her skirts before finally meeting her mother's eye. "I am not convinced the queen would so easily release me, Mama."

A slow smile curved her mother's lips. "You think you know the queen better than I?"

"I do. Yes."

Her mother's eyes filled with anger. "Then maybe I will add your name to the list of women who are currently the subject of the most salacious gossip at the palace. Those risking ruin by their association with Mr. Greene, for example."

Defense of James burned inside her, and Violet glared at her mother. "James Greene is a good man. He has shown me nothing but politeness and friendly interest."

"Oh, you silly girl. He is a philanderer. A man who served in the army, who showed deference and bravery, yet now chooses to charm and bed weak, naïve ladies for a pastime. The queen is a romantic to be certain, but if any of her household is the least bit tainted because of loose morals, they will be dismissed regardless of whether that poor reputation is rumored or proven."

Violet trembled with the depth of her fury. "Mr. Greene does not deserve to have his name dragged through the mud because of what you want me to do."

"Mr. Greene's name? It's yours that should be the concern, Violet."

"I agree with your daughter, Geraldine. Mr. Green should not be a tool in our machinations." The duchess rose to her feet, Violet's mother also rising. "Which is why I know, Mistress Parker, your fondness for him will aid in your decision making once you return to the queen's apartments. You care for him as you do for the queen. Therefore, let us leave all men out of our agenda. It is your duty to make Drina understand the need for her to be guided and advised by a softer hand than Lord Melbourne's. Men stick together as women should. They care only for their own successes rather than ours. Isn't that so, Mistress Parker?"

Violet swallowed. "Well, yes, but—"

"There is no but, sweet girl. Women at this court, indeed around the entire country, are pawns in men's games and visions. It is up to us to use our wits and guile to outmaneuver their every strategy so that we might gain a modicum of say and pleasure in our existence." She arched an eyebrow, her gaze calculating. "Surely you would want nothing less for your beloved sovereign?"

Annoyance rippled through Violet, spreading in ever-extending circles through her veins. None of what the duchess wanted would be for Victoria's contentment, only for the continuation of her mother's power. There was no difference in her motivation than there was in Violet's mother with her.

But how was she to maintain her appointment to the queen unless she arranged a reunion as she had been commanded? Even if she managed to orchestrate a second afternoon meeting between Victoria and the duchess, the underhanded, sickening betrayal of Violet's manipulation would hover over her like an axe waiting to fall.

She had to find a way to halt it. But how?

"Violet?"

She jumped at the mother's curtness. "Yes?"

"There is no need for you to stay any longer. Return to the queen. I expect to receive good news from you very soon."

Violet curtsied to the duchess and then walked to the door. She had thought herself free, but she was still trapped, still caged in her mother's invisible dungeon. She needed to ensure her liberty and Victoria's.

And the only friend she had at court, the only person she trusted to help her was James Greene.

Chapter Eleven

As James ducked behind a suit of armor to avoid Abigail Kingsley, the steel antiquity wobbled precariously, the whole thing threatening to fall apart.

"There is no use attempting to hide, you naughty man." Abigail laughed, her green eyes showing her delight. "I will catch you wherever you are."

Hissing a curse, James stepped out from behind the armor and feigned interest in an old portrait which was most likely worth more than his family's entire estate. "Good evening, Abigail."

"Do not good evening me, James Greene. And look at me when I'm talking to you."

Pulling on his flirtatious persona like a well-worn cape, James turned and eyed her up and down. "You look beautiful."

Her smile widened as she pressed the tip of her fan to his chest. "I'm glad you think so. Once dinner is over, I will come and find you. It's been far too long since we've spent some time together." She leaned close to his ear. "Kisses and caresses are no longer enough to satisfy my hunger, Mr. Greene…even though I fear our association is coming to an end."

James looked along the corridor as gentlemen and ladies gathered, making their way to dinner with the queen. Her entourage seemed to grow more and more expansive with each week that passed. "What do you mean coming to an end? Our association has always been…imprecise to say the least."

"You've been avoiding me."

"I've been busy. Besides, I have no wish to be the reason behind any gossip that might affect you. It's for the best we ease things off, don't you think?"

She stepped back. "You do not care for anyone's reputation but your own…well, almost anyone's."

"Meaning?"

"Meaning I thought our little trysts were a fun and welcome release for us both, but I fear there might be a certain housemaid who has caught you in her trap. I believe my darling James is beginning to tip a little off-kilter."

His protectiveness toward Violet rose hot and fast. "Leave Violet out of this."

"Violet? Well, well."

"Abigail…"

Her smile widened. "Oh, James. Mistress Parker might be a passing favorite of the queen, but you would be a fool to develop feelings for the girl. One, she is far beneath you, and two, her mother will never allow her to lead her own life. The poor girl is a puppet. Her mother the master. Everyone knows that. Even the queen, I suspect."

"Violet Parker is far from being anyone's puppet, believe me. She is intelligent, hardworking, and regards the queen above all others. She has integrity, honesty, and a will to get on in this world without the need for plotting and scheming." He looked along the corridor again, nodded at an associate of Melbourne's. "That is something to be held in high regard."

"I couldn't agree more."

James turned, her tone had sounded incredibly sincere. “What?”

Abigail’s gaze softened. “If you like Mistress Parker, that is no concern to me. I will officially call a halt to our flirtations. Leave you be if that is what you want. All I ask is that you be careful.”

James huffed a laugh. “Are you suggesting that she might endanger me somehow?”

“That’s exactly what I’m suggesting.”

“But how could she possibly—”

“Love, James. It hurts.” Abigail’s eyes shadowed with genuine concern. “Be careful. But if you ever need my help, all you need to do is ask.”

She walked away along the corridor and slid her hand into the elbow of an aristocrat who stared down at her as though all life’s fortunes had unexpectedly dropped into his lap. Love! What in God’s name did Abigail know about love?

Shaking off his annoyance, James strode in the opposite direction toward Melbourne’s office. He would spend a couple of hours working before retiring for the night. Then maybe he would have some hope of sleep. Melbourne had left him a list a mile long to tackle before the week’s end, their tasks having fallen behind because the minister had been at Victoria’s incessant beck and call, day and night, over the past few days.

The entire court felt the tension rising with parliament’s insistence she marry. Something the young queen passionately resisted. And James sensed Melbourne was doing little to alter her mind. Which only reinforced James’s suspicions his master was fearful of losing his unique position by Victoria’s side.

He turned the corner to find Violet pacing back and

forth in front of Melbourne's office door, her movements jerky and nervous.

"Violet?"

She abruptly turned, her shoulders lowering as she hurried toward him. "James. I'm so glad I caught you."

"What are you doing here? If Melbourne had seen you—"

"I knew he was attending the dinner. Victoria has spoken of little else in her excitement to see him."

"Come into the office. We'll have more privacy." Gently cupping her elbow, he urged her ahead of him before closing and locking the door. "What has happened? You look dreadfully pale."

She stood in front of the fireplace, her brow furrowed and her arms tightly crossed. "I was summoned by my mother to the duchess's apartments this afternoon. Their patience for me to further encourage the queen's reconciliation with her mother is thinning. I can see no other option but to find a way to press Victoria even more firmly in that horrid direction."

Hating the agitation in her eyes, James took her hand, pleased when her fingers curled around his. "If you see no alternative, then that is what you must do. I don't like seeing you like this."

Her huge blue eyes pleaded with him as though begging him for a solution. "But if I do, it will anger the queen. Then I will be sent away, back to my mother, whose rage at my failure will match Victoria's. I am doomed either way."

"Come. Sit down." He led her to the sofa, reluctantly releasing her hand as she sat. He walked to the drinks cabinet and poured them each a glass of claret. "I'm amazed you've managed to delay things this long. It will soon be August, and it is rumored the queen's cousins will likely be here by September."

"Yes, the duchess mentioned them."

She took the glass he offered and sipped before giving a slight grimace. James smiled as he sat beside her, amused by her obvious naivety to wine when many at court were in a state of intoxication morning, noon, or night.

"Is their visit as significant as the queen has implied?" she asked. "That her uncle and the ministers wish her to propose marriage to Albert?"

"They do, yes."

"Which is exactly why the duchess is pressing me to move quickly. I am more aware of why the urgency has increased than she thinks."

"Oh?"

She sipped her wine, some color coming into her cheeks. "Don't you see? Once Victoria marries, she will be personally answerable to her husband rather than her mother. And that will be more than the duchess can stand."

"Not to mention that once married, Victoria will no longer be under obligation to have her mother living with her."

"Precisely. The duchess wants to literally court the queen in the hope of some fondness growing between them before the duke arrives." Violet's brow creased. "Isn't the queen's prospective husband a concern to Melbourne, considering how much Victoria relies on him?"

"He is, but the minister is unlikely to try to dissuade her against a proposal when the entire country will rejoice with news of a royal wedding. The biggest aspect bothering Melbourne is whether or not the British public, or even parliament, will accept a German as a consort."

"I see." Her eyes glazed as she thought. "But the queen has not mentioned any desire for either of the brothers. At least not in my presence." Hope flashed in her eyes. "Do you think if I told the duchess as much, it might delay her wish for me to speak to the queen about their reunion?"

James placed his glass on a small table beside him. She looked so worried, so tense, but he suspected if Violet did not conform, at least in some way, to the duchess's request, she would ensure that Violet's service to the queen was severed forever.

Desperate to comfort her, James tentatively covered her hand with his where it lay in her lap. She stiffened for a moment, before entwining her fingers with his.

He looked into her wonderful eyes. "Do you think you could share with the queen how you, too, are being controlled by your mother? Garner her sympathy with a circumstance she knows and resents to her core?"

She shook her head, her eyes wide. "No, I could never. It is not my place to burden her. I am there to help her."

"Yet I'm convinced if she knew, she would react in your defense. She might even confront your mother. She might work for the duchess, but your mother is still under the queen's command. Moreover, so is the duchess."

Her worried gaze swept over his face, lingered a moment on his mouth before she looked at their joined hands. "I don't think I could speak to the queen so intimately. She is fond of me, but I am by no means one of her ladies or Lehzen. Most of whom are kind to me but do not include me in much conversation. I am merely in the background."

"I think you underestimate your importance to Victoria." He suddenly thought of Abigail and her offer to help. He slipped his hand from hers and stood, their skin-to-skin contact making it hard for him to concentrate. "What you need is an ally. Someone who is friendly with the queen's ladies. Someone who could ask perhaps the Duchess of Sunderland to speak to Victoria and tell her about the threat hanging over you."

"But who would do such a thing? I have no friends at court."

"You have me, and soon you will have Abigail Kingsley."

"*Lady* Kingsley?"

James smiled. "Yes."

Chapter Twelve

Violet hurried into the palace courtyard and headed for the royal mews.

Her every instinct was on high alert, her body tense as she sent up a silent prayer that James's prediction that Lady Kingsley would come to her rescue was not entirely unfounded.

She had seen her only occasionally throughout the palace corridors and Victoria's apartments. As one of the court's young beauties, Lady Kingsley was inevitably surrounded by men eager to have her notice them. Her midnight-black hair and brilliant green eyes could not fail to attract any man…sometimes even women it was rumored. Of course, one of the predominant admirers who was often linked with her name happened to be James.

Something that had not bothered Violet until she had gotten to know him better. Any notice of him—and certainly any thoughts of him—had passed her by until he'd purposefully placed himself in her path over and over again. His eagerness to speak with her so flattering that eventually she was coerced by his attention.

What that said about her, she had no idea. Why her feelings for him had shifted when so much uncertainty continued to badger her seemed misplaced somehow. Beginning to care for a man so above her in station, wealth and prospects was hardly the recipe to follow to solve her problems, and miraculously aid her dreams of becoming an artist.

Although her fingers sometimes itched to touch his thick, chocolate-brown hair and his dark, dark eyes made her feel as though she were the most important woman in the world whenever he looked at her, Violet had managed to keep her wits about her as far as her attraction to James was concerned. Or she had thus far.

Always mindful of his reputation as a seducer, a player of women's affections, she had believed herself completely capable of controlling whatever might pass between them. Yes, she had allowed him to take her hand of late, sit close to her and lean into her, his breath enticingly soft on her ear, but James could not know how her defiance to resist him had started to wobble more and more.

And not because of flirtation, but because of something far worse. Genuine care…care in his eyes that she had not seen in any man's gaze when they looked at her, apart from her father's. It was frightening because it evoked a deeply buried need Violet had no idea she harbored. The need for a man other than her father to love her…

The smells from the mews drifted on the warm July air as Violet neared, and she slowed her pace, burying her thoughts and growing regard for James deep inside where it could not distract her. This meeting between herself, James, and Lady Kingsley was of utmost importance.

"Psst, Violet…over here."

She spun around. "James?"

"I'm by the hay bales."

Violet hurried to a huge stack of hay at the entrance

of a makeshift barn, and James poked his head out from behind the pile. Whether it was her stretched nerves, or the relief that he had not retracted his promise to help her, she could not stem her giggle.

"What are you doing?" she whispered as he gripped her wrist and pulled her behind the bales. "Lady Kingsley will hardly meet us—"

But then she appeared alongside him. "You'd be surprised what I will do, Mistress Parker."

Violet jumped and snatched her wrist from James's grasp. "Lady Kingsley!"

She smiled, her green eyes twinkling with amusement. "Did you think meeting in such a place beneath me, Parker?" She arched an eyebrow at James. "Clearly, you have a lot to share with our new friend, James."

A jolt of jealousy shot through Violet at the teasing flirtation in Lady Kingsley's voice. Swallowing hard, Violet glanced at James.

His cheeks flushed, his irritated gaze locked on Lady Kingsley. "Behave yourself. We are here to help Violet."

"I know, I know." Lady Kingsley took Violet's hand, gently squeezed her fingers. "I am merely teasing Mr. Greene. Do not pay any heed to our banter. I want to help you. More than that, I want to help the queen."

Instead of the teasing brightness Lady Kingsley had in her eyes when speaking to James, sad somberness lingered there now, which Violet found as disconcerting as she did surprising. Lady Kingsley epitomized confidence and female strength, yet in that moment, Violet recognized a small chink in her demeanor. She cared about people. A lot.

As much as she would love to have had Lady

Kingsley as a new ally at court, Violet eased her hand free and stepped back, uncertain whether she could be trusted. “Thank you.”

“Thank me if I am successful. James told me about how your mother orchestrated your appointment with the queen and the terms on which your attendance to her is based.”

Humiliation whispered through Violet, and she turned to James. “Did you really have to share everything?”

He nodded, his gaze intense on hers. “Yes. If we want Abigail’s help, she deserves to be forewarned about who and what she is dealing with.”

Lady Kingsley’s eyes softened with sympathy. “What James told me has left no doubt as to why Victoria has taken to you so quickly and so deeply. She must recognize something of herself in you. You certainly carry the same look of mistrust in your eyes.”

Knowing she had little other option than to accept whatever help Lady Kingsley could provide, Violet slumped her shoulders. “I have been under my mother’s instruction and control for so long, to trust anyone as sincere is daunting. I want to trust you…” She glanced at James. “Both of you, but this court hardly provokes a sense of trust in anyone.”

James crossed his arms. “Maybe not, but we are here and willing to help you. Everyone at court has secrets, wishes, and wants. None of us are without fears and failures. It is those things that make us human, Violet. Abigail is willing to speak to the queen on your behalf. Your mother is expecting a message from you today, is she not?”

“Yes.” She looked at Lady Kingsley. “Do you know

my mother?"

"No, but I am on marginally friendly terms with the duchess, and where she is, so often too is your mother. I understand the risk I am taking in helping you, Parker. After all, the queen will not welcome any mention of the duchess, but I believe if Victoria is made aware that sharing an additional hour or two with her helps you, she will agree to it."

Tentative hope swelled in Violet's chest. "Do you really think so?"

"Her ladies know you matter to her. I think Lehzen does, too. The queen enjoys frivolity, but she was raised under an iron hand, and the resentment she harbors for the duchess and Conroy will linger in her bosom for the rest of her life, I'm sure."

"Which means..." James came closer, his gentle gaze gliding over Violet's face making her blush. "Victoria is likely to fight in your corner when she learns you are suffering now as she has in the past. Maybe still is and will continue to do so until she marries."

Desperation to keep the queen's love set nerves fluttering in Violet's stomach as she faced Lady Kingsley. "It's important the queen knows my loyalty is to her. That if I am forced to leave her service and return to my mother, I don't think I could bear it. Not now that I have known true happiness with the queen."

Lady Kingsley touched her hand. "It won't come to that."

Violet covered Lady Kingsley's hand with hers. "But the last thing I want is for the queen's anger to be directed at you when it should be me who she reprimands."

"Her anger should be directed at your mother and

hers. This entire situation has been provoked by *their* scheming. No one is to blame but them, Parker. Trust that the queen is intelligent enough, experienced enough, to know that." She squeezed Violet's fingers. "All will be well. Now, I must go." She turned to James. "I will send a message of what happened between me and the queen to Melbourne's office, and then you can tell Violet."

He nodded. "Thank you."

As Lady Kingsley crept out from behind the hay bales and hurried through the courtyard, a strange mix of helplessness and hope simmered inside Violet. And when James placed his hand gently on the small on her back, she closed her eyes, fighting the need to turn around and bury her face in his chest.

"It will be all right," he said, softly. "For all her flirtation and playing around, Abigail is a good soul. She is desperately unhappy at court but makes the most of what is expected of her."

"She's unhappy?" Violet turned around, her senses filling with the musky masculine scent of him. "But she is always smiling and laughing. I thought—"

"A charade, a pretense that Abigail has perfected. One I fear she will be forced to carry on living once her parents choose her husband." His gaze dropped to her mouth. "I don't want you to suffer unhappiness any more than I do her, but there is little I can do to deter her family's martial expectations. But if I can find a way to set you free from your mother's dictatorship, I will."

Violet's heart hammered as the desire to kiss him grew stronger. "Why are you here, James? With me? Like this?"

He inched closer. "Because there's nowhere else I'd

rather be."

She should step back, save herself, but it was too late. He cared about her, he was helping her, protecting her…

"James, I—"

His mouth touched hers, and any words were lost in his tentative, wonderful kiss.

Chapter Thirteen

Violet hauled fresh towels from one of the huge cupboards in the palace laundry, nodded goodbye to three of the other maids before starting the long trek back to the queen's apartments. Her usually positive attitude had been lacking all afternoon, her mind turning over with imagined scenarios of how Lady Kingsley raised the subject of Violet's mother and the duchess with the queen.

That…and James's kiss.

Every time she thought of herself in his arms, pulled so close her breasts were pressed firmly against his broad chest, her cheeks grew hot, and her lips tingled. She had exchanged maybe three or four stolen kisses with young men in her twenty-one years, snatched moments that had felt illicit and exciting, but once the seconds were spent, Violet rarely thought of them again.

Her kiss with James had been entirely different. Entirely magical. Entirely—her core pulled shamefully—enticing.

She had wanted more. Wanted his lips to travel along her jaw, her neck, her collarbone…

"Parker! Quickly, come with me."

Violet jumped, almost dropping her bundle as she looked along the corridor.

Lady Kingsley flicked her hand back and forth, gesturing Violet closer. Dread dropped like a stone into her stomach. Lady Kingsley's expression was not one of elation but anxiety. Clearly, her talk with Victoria had not gone well.

She followed Lady Kingsley into an empty room with chandeliers running across its ornate ceiling and upholstered chairs lining the walls. This was where drinks were often served before dinner, and Violet knew she should not be in here…whatever the circumstances. Ever. Gold glinted from every direction, her feet sinking into the rich, ruby-red carpet, the numerous mirrors shining. A space full of wonder and possibility.

"I shouldn't be in this room," she whispered. "If anyone should see me in here—"

"Don't worry, if anyone sees us, I'll say you were assisting me with something." Lady Kingsley glanced toward the door and then took Violet's elbow, leading her further along the wall out of sight of the open doorway. "I managed to persuade the queen to see her mother earlier this afternoon, but I have no idea how things went between them."

"You haven't seen her since?"

"No, and she was not at all happy about the prospect, but once I told her the pressure your mother was putting you under to arrange a meeting, her anger was clear, and she immediately agreed. I have no doubt she would have said a few choice words to her mother and possibly yours, too."

Violet clutched the towels tighter, her throat dry. "Oh, what have I done?"

"You've done nothing," Lady Kingsley said firmly. "Victoria said she would speak to you upon her return from the duchess's apartments, but it is not you she is upset with. Not at all."

Sickness unfurled inside Violet. "But this will no doubt lead to my dismissal from her service. My mother could easily demand my return once the duchess is reunited with Victoria."

"Demand? Your mother or the duchess cannot demand anything of the queen. Anyway, I very much doubt your dismissal or a union between Victoria and her mother is likely." Abigail smiled, her green eyes glinting with satisfaction. "Once I informed Her Majesty that the duchess is apt to use Victoria's refusal to see her as reason enough to call you back to her service, the queen's expression spoke volumes. She is on your side, Parker."

A glimmer of hope brightened inside of Violet. "I don't know what to say."

"There's something about you that the queen clearly likes…James, too."

"We are just fri—"

"There is no need to deny what is between you and James to me." Lady Kingsley laughed. "He is a wonderful man. What he and I shared was mutual flirtation. Nothing more. Yet I see something very different in his eyes whenever he looks at you."

Violet swallowed, trying to fathom if Lady Kingsley's observations held any grain of truth. "I'm sure you are mistaken."

"And I am sure I am not, but just be glad of the outcome with the queen and breathe easy that you will not be returning to your mother anytime soon. Now…" She glanced at the door. "You should get back. Victoria will have questions for you, and it won't help if she finds you missing."

"Thank you, Lady Kingsley. Thank you so much."

"You're welcome. Now go."

Violet rushed from the room and along the back stairs, walking as quickly as she could to the queen's private apartments. Once there, she drew to a stop and inhaled a steadying breath. She needed to remain calm and act as though she knew nothing of Lady Kingsley's intervention. Victoria might be fond of her, but Violet had also overheard enough conversations to know that the queen did not fully trust anyone except Melbourne and Lehzen. If she had misconstrued Lady Kingsley's words as an attempt of manipulating her into seeing the duchess for Violet's advantage, then…

"Parker! There you are."

Lehzen's voice cracked through Violet's reverie, and she stood tall. "Baroness."

"Come along, girl. Her Majesty is asking for you." Lehzen grasped Violet's elbow and steered her through a row of two or three rooms to a storage alcove between Victoria's drawing room and her bedchamber. "The queen is in the most agitated state after meeting with the duchess this afternoon. Why Her Majesty sought to see her is beyond me, but I'm sure she will explain everything once she and I have a private moment."

Violet's heart raced, her hands turning clammy around the towels. "Is the queen upset?"

Lehzen tossed her a scornful look. "Yes, Parker, she is. Now, quickly. Put those towels away."

Violet stored the towels and closed the huge bureau.

"Right, now straighten your clothes and hair. The queen was adamant you be brought to her the minute you were found." Lehzen's eyes flashed with customary annoyance. "It seems there is something she wishes to discuss with you that cannot wait until your evening duties."

The late afternoon sun spilled through the bedchamber's tall sash windows beyond Victoria's dressing table where she sat, her hair being pinned by her dresser.

As soon as Violet entered the room, Victoria spoke, her tone far from happy. "Parker, there you are. Come closer, please."

Violet rose from her curtsey and approached the queen, her hands tightly folded. "Your Majesty."

The queen stared at Violet in the mirror's reflection, her head erect on her rigid neck, her color pale. "I have just returned from taking tea with my mother at the request of Lady Kingsley. Apparently, my doing so means it is less likely your mother will harangue you into returning to the duchess's service. Is that right?"

Violet's heart pounded, her cheeks hot as she glanced at Lehzen, the Duchess of Sunderland, and two other ladies who stared at her expectantly from their places in the room. Now everyone was aware of Violet's mother's influence over her, which could provoke her yearning to remain in the queen's service to be used as ammunition against her by one or all of the ladies present.

"Yes, ma'am." Violet met the queen's unwavering gaze in the mirror. "I told Lady Kingsley how much I enjoy serving you and how I feared returning to the duchess if you did not agree to—"

"See my mother."

"Yes."

"If that is case, can I assume you were purposely and carefully placed in my household by my mother and yours? That you are here as their interloper?"

Violet's legs trembled so hard she feared they might give out completely, her head suddenly light. "Ma'am, I—"

"Yes or no?"

"Your Majesty, I beg of you. My mother—"

"Do not say another word, Parker. I understand all that has been going on here perfectly well." The queen stood so abruptly her dresser stumbled back. Victoria's dark-blue gaze burned with fury. "I have chosen to give you the benefit of the doubt that you were forced into this position for my mother's reasons rather than your own…for now. It is my deepest wish that you have played no part in their scheming, but believe me, this has most certainly altered things between us. I am no longer confident that I can trust you."

Violet's heart hitched, to lose Victoria's trust was so painful it physically hurt. "Ma'am, my mother never tires of reminding me that anything I have achieved, personally and in service, is due to her say-so and arrangement. She believes I am nothing without her, incapable of making any wise decisions or taking any worthwhile action. She makes me feel as if I am—"

"Nothing without her. That you were born to do her bidding and act on her will." Victoria's shoulders lowered. "I understand only too well." She inhaled. "You'll be relieved to learn I have agreed to have tea with my mother on a regular basis. Possibly once a week if I can tolerate her company. So with that agreement, I hope you will enjoy a reduction in the harassment you have endured thus far."

Tears leapt into Violet's eyes, relief washing through her as she quickly blinked them back. "Thank you, ma'am."

"But you should know that neither your mother nor mine are in any position to command anything from me or my household. They are playing a game they will most certainly lose. However, from now on, I will keep a closer eye on you. Now that I have uncovered the real reason you were sent to me, it will take time and commitment for you to regain the trust I have given you so freely."

"Thank you, ma'am. I understand."

Silence stretched as Violet stood before the queen, her disgrace and shame complete, but at least she had told Victoria the truth, and whatever happened next, she could be proud she had admitted her sad existence in apology and supplication.

"Good, then I will see you later this evening."

The queen swept past her, her ladies following. Violet kept her head bowed until Lehzen stopped beside her, her taunting shadow enveloping her.

Violet raised her head, and Lehzen smirked before quietly leaving the room.

Chapter Fourteen

Although mid-August, rain ran in rivulets down the windows in Melbourne's study. There could be no doubt that the summer of 1839 would be recorded as one of England's wettest. The gloominess only served to deepen the tension that had emanated from Melbourne for the past few days, thus hindering James's concentration as he worked his way through the post that had arrived for the minister that morning.

"Anything needing my urgent attention, Greene?" Melbourne asked from where he sat hunched over his desk.

James lowered a letter from yet another member of the public wanting to make reverence to Victoria. "Not yet, sir. There were letters from Peel and Palmerston, which I put on your desk yesterday evening, but so far today, there has been nothing pressing."

"Good, then I shall leave you in peace." Melbourne pushed his pen into its marble holder and abruptly stood before walking to the coatrack by the door. "I am due at a parliamentary meeting. The chances of me being waylaid as I make my way through the palace are high, but the least I can do is show willingness by leaving earlier than strictly necessary."

James reached for the next letter on his pile. The familiar inscription scrawled across the envelope evoked a muttered curse. Why was his father writing to him again so soon? His last correspondence—just over a week before—had been teeming with the comings and goings at the family estate. The detail so repetitive, so obviously deliberate and pressing toward James's future responsibilities, that it had left him with no doubt of his father's frustration that his son was still at court. However, James's returning letter should have made it clear he would remain at the palace for the foreseeable future.

As Melbourne walked about the office collecting his papers, James slipped his silver letter opener beneath the seal and scanned the usual salutation and reports of his family's health. Melbourne's mutterings faded into the background…

It is my request that you return home for a few days so that you might share with your mother and me what your new position entails and how you are faring. It has been over three months since you visited, and your mother is saddened by the increasing length of your absences. Therefore, I urgently press you to ask Lord Melbourne for a week's leave so you might regale your family with your presence.

"Did you hear a word of what I just said, Greene?"

James lifted his head, his father's voice echoing in his ears. "Sorry, sir. I was—"

"Entirely enthralled by what you were reading." Frowning, Melbourne slipped his hand from the doorknob and approached James's desk. "What or who has put such a strange look on your face?"

"My father. He wishes me to return home for a week or so."

"I see. When?"

"As soon as possible. I have not been home for

several months, and it seems my parents are growing tired of my absence."

"Yet it is clear you are not tired of being away." Melbourne threw him a pointed look. "Well, I'm afraid all of us must bear the burden of duty, Greene. Whether that be from family, parliament, or royalty." He strolled back to the door and waved his hand dismissively. "Take some time with your family. I will be perfectly all right without you for a short time. I need you here first thing in the morning, but after our work is done, you are free to leave."

"Sir, I really do not have to—"

"Yes, you do." Sadness shadowed the minister's eyes, his expression grave. "Believe me, family is a precious thing. For once it is gone, you will forever be haunted by its void. No, you must go. That's an order."

Shame engulfed James as the door quietly closed behind Melbourne. A man who had not only borne the public humiliation of his wife's affair and obsession with Lord Bryon, but the loss of his daughter within a year of her birth and then the death of his only son just a few years ago.

Dropping his head into his hands, James slumped under the weight of his guilt and disgust. God only knew what Melbourne must think of him for avoiding a family who merely wished to see him…merely wished him to think of a future that he wanted no part of. His defiance suddenly felt abhorrent, and in that moment, James concluded he would leave for Oxfordshire in the morning.

Violet immediately filled his mind along with the unexpected insistence he must tell her of his imminent absence. James swiped his hand over his face and sat back in his chair, staring blindly ahead. Since when had he felt the need to tell any woman of his movements? His feelings for Violet were growing, bordering on selfish lunacy. There could be no future with her, yet despite the futility of their relationship, the bond between them grew ever stronger. And as their fondness for one another deepened, so did the frequency of their stolen kisses. Didn't he owe it to her to tell her of his temporary disappearance before she heard about it from someone else?

Standing from his desk, James shrugged on his jacket.

Each time he returned home, the problems and demands his father presented him with escalated. He suspected this visit would be no different. But this time, his days away from court would bother him more than ever when had no wish to see Violet less than he already did. He'd not pursued any other woman for weeks, and it had not gone unnoticed or without comment.

Especially from Abigail, who seemed to find his friendship with Violet either incredibly amusing or intolerably foolish, depending on her mood.

James left the office and walked along the carpeted corridor. The path his life had taken over the last couple of months had begun to fulfill him as he had always wanted. As much as he revered his time in the army, the company of his comrades and the hardships they endured, nothing had ever felt so right as working with Melbourne, learning about the politics and bills of Britain.

It felt as though he served the Crown on a more intimate basis than he ever did in the army. As prime minister and private secretary to the queen, Melbourne's work was integral to the success of the country, and James now played a part in that. How could running an estate ever be as rewarding? It was clear to him—as it must be to his father—that he did not have the passion for the land that his forefathers had. Maybe his younger brother would have better suited the role, but considering how quickly and fervently George had chosen the clergy, he too had fears and reservations of becoming as tyrannical a man as their father, grandfather, and great-grandfather.

Landed gentlemen who had done terrible, terrible things to their respective wives and offspring.

Well, whatever his father might say or want, James would not leave court or his life here until absolutely necessary.

Upon reaching the queen's private apartments, he was granted access without preamble, the guards outside her rooms no doubt assuming him to have a message from Melbourne. He prayed the queen absent and Violet present, otherwise, his plan to see her would be in vain. As their time together was scarce and often fleeting, James decided he would propose a short outing together tomorrow afternoon during her half-day's leisure so that he might say farewell to her properly.

He entered the queen's drawing room and stopped, clearing his throat.

Baroness Lehzen turned from some flowers she was arranging in an enormous porcelain vase. "Mr. Greene, how might I help you? Her Majesty is currently walking the gardens with the Duchess of Sunderland."

"I would like a word with Mistress Parker, if I may."

Her expression hardened, and she glanced toward a door on her right. "She is busy in the queen's bedchamber. You would be best advised to time your courting *after* Parker's morning duties."

"I am not here courting, madam. I merely wish to give her a short message."

Lehzen pursed her lips, her gaze beady and emotionless. "You must think me blind *and* stupid if you think I cannot see what is in your eyes whenever you look at Mistress Parker. The girl is here to work, not—"

The door opened, and Violet entered, carrying two boxes stacked on top of one another. "Oh, James…I mean, Mr. Greene."

Pleasure swept through him at the sight of her, and James dipped his head to hide his smile. "Mistress Parker."

When he raised his eyes, he noted the flush in Violet's cheeks as she faced Lehzen. "I have finished in the queen's bedchamber, Baroness. I will take these things to her dresser if you don't need me for—"

"Mr. Greene is here to see you, Parker. I will leave you alone to speak with him and then expect you to be quick with your errand and straight back." Lehzen looked from Violet to James, her gaze steely. "You do not have time to waste on nonsense."

As soon as they were alone, James took the boxes from Violet's arms and placed them on a table beside him.

He took her hand, smoothed his thumb over the soft skin on her wrist. "I have to leave."

"Leave?" Her eyes widened. "Forever?"

He smiled. "Just for a few days. My father is insistent that I return home for a visit, and Lord Melbourne has urged it. So, unfortunately, I have little choice but to concede."

"I see, and you came to find me before you left…" She softly smiled, her blue eyes showing her pleasure. "That is very nice of you."

He gazed at her mouth, longing to kiss her. How fast he had taken her into his heart. After years of noncommitment and flirtatious contentment, now it seemed James Greene was well and truly caught.

Embarrassed by the depth of his passion and how words so often failed him in her company, James released Violet's hand and took a step back. "I thought before I leave we could take a walk in Hyde Park. Hopefully, there will be a break in this constant rain, and we could spend a couple of hours tomorrow afternoon watching the riders and coaches."

"That sounds wonderful. I finish at two o'clock and will meet you then, but for now, I must press on before Lehzen reports me to the queen." Her smile dissolved, her gaze worried as she glanced at the door. "The atmosphere between Victoria and I is marginally improving, but I dare not do anything that might make things worsen again."

"You have no reason to doubt the queen's regard for you. You would not still be her housemaid if she blamed you for any of your mother's or the duchess's actions."

"I know, but I must be careful."

He picked up the boxes, handed them to her with a wink. "Until tomorrow then."

Chapter Fifteen

Violet could not remember a time when she had been happier.

The sun had finally emerged after days of heavy clouds, and the whole of Hyde Park was bathed in the most wonderful summer warmth, the clouds wispy and few. It was as though everyone in London had leapt at the chance to enjoy this unexpected break in what had been a terribly wet summer. Men, women, and children, dogs, horses, and coaches swarmed the park in an explosion of color and sound. How she longed to paint just a tiny aspect of it!

"Do you think your smile wide enough, Violet?"

She laughed and tightened her fingers on James's arm. "It's all so wonderful. Thank you for suggesting we come here. It's impossible to take everything in."

"Have you not been to the park before?"

"Once or twice with my mother, but only as a walk through to the palace. She considers the flamboyance and endless show of parading wealth, as she calls it, vulgar."

"Whereas you find it…"

"Absolutely exhilarating!" Violet's cheeks ached from the breadth of her smile, but she could not contain it. "After the decorum and formality of the palace, this is so freeing. So exciting. I wish I could paint it all. There is something so satisfying about capturing a moment, an object, or person in time. I fear all the talk that the new photography phenomenon will destroy people's love of art, but I will continue to paint regardless. I must believe there will always be a desire for painters."

"I would love to see an example of your work. Do you think you might show me one day?"

Violet's heart picked up speed. "Except for my family, I haven't shown anyone my paintings."

"If you truly want to be an artist, you must gain the courage to share your work outside of family and friends. I bet the queen, an art lover, would be impressed by your industry."

"Are you suggesting I show her my paintings?"

He shrugged, his dark eyes glinting with challenge. "Why not?"

Violet stared at him before lifting her chin, his confidence in her fueling her determination to take pride in her passion, rather than hide it away as her mother so often ordered her to do. Her painting was the only thing her mother could not take an iota of credit for. "Maybe I will." She smiled. "One day."

They joined the crush of people lining the pathway known as Rotten Row, and James firmly held her hand. He led them to a space on the periphery, which gave Violet a clear view of the spectacle ahead of them. The long and wide thoroughfare, lined on either side with spectators, gave the aristocracy, gentry, and even the burgeoning middle classes the space and opportunity to show off their finery and wealth.

Violet breathed in the atmosphere.

Laughter and gaiety rang all around them as she and James sneaked glances and smiles at one another. She stared in awe at the grand gold, black, and white carriages, the horses preening as much as the passengers. This special time would be printed on her memory forever. Couples walked along, arm in arm, the silk and satin of the women's dresses, the plumage in their hair and the jewels glinting from their ears, necks, and wrists eliciting untold stories that sparked Violet's artistic imagination.

She looked at James, his handsome profile rousing a flutter in her stomach. As much as she cared for him, she held herself back from the folly of fully trusting him. His reputation was one of a fancy-free joy-seeker who loved women as much as he did his work.

Yet when he looked at her, Violet longed to believe the softness in his eyes was authentic and entirely for her and her alone.

"Shall we see what the food sellers have to offer?" He raised his voice above the din. "We could watch the crowds while we eat."

They found a stall selling spice cakes and lemonade and took their treats to a nearby bench. Although they ate in comfortable silence, the fact he was leaving, even only for a few days, took a little of the joy from what should have been a perfect day.

"Will you miss me while I'm gone?"

She smiled and turned. Did he sense her thinking about him? His eyes glinted with mischief.

"I won't even notice," she said, teasing. "We have barely seen one another for the last two weeks. Your absence will be no hiccup for me, James Greene."

"Is that right? Well..." He sipped his lemonade. "That is noted and will be remembered. Let's hope my return is not delayed by my father lest you come to regret your disregard."

Despite the laughter in his voice, Violet also detected a hint of concern, and she regretted tormenting him. She had no idea of James's homelife. The only aspect he'd ever shared with her was his resistance to marry. Not that she had designs of them marrying, but his reluctance showed something of his attitude to commitment.

As he stared ahead, his expression hardened, and Violet suspected that it was not the pressure of romance that made him so grave. He had also compared her dislike of her mother to the distance between him and his parents.

She grappled with how to raise the subject of his mother and father, questioning whether she should mention them at all when her relationship with her mother had already led to Violet adding aggravation to his life. No, it was better that they not speak of their familial problems when their separation was imminent. But she wished she had not ribbed him.

"I fear my disregard for you might be a little harder to come by the longer I know you," she said softly, her heart quickening at her admission and the vulnerability it evoked. "You have somehow come to matter to me…a little."

His smile was roguishly slow as he turned, his eyes sparkling with unforgivable satisfaction. "Have I, indeed?"

She nudged him with her shoulder, trying not to laugh. "There is no need to look so pleased with yourself. I still have your reputation to contend with."

"My reputation? Please tell me you are not concerned by court gossip. Surely, after all this time working for the queen, you have learned her ladies are more prone to talk nonsense than many of the servants."

"I don't need to listen to gossip." Violet popped the last of her cake into her mouth and swallowed. "I've seen all I need to see with my own eyes. You are an incorrigible flirt. Just as the Duchess of Sunderland warned me at Victoria's birthday ball."

"But that's hardly fair," he protested, color darkening his cheeks. "I have not felt the need to dally as I used to for a long time now."

"And why is that?"

Violet shamelessly searched his feelings for her, but she could not help it when her heart softened toward him. To what end, she had no idea, but the thought that James might consider her little more than an interesting conquest rankled.

His gaze settled on a young father and mother tossing a ball back and forth to their little boy. "Because of you, Violet. You are different than the others. You are…I don't know. Just different."

There was no happiness in his explanation, only quiet melancholy which left Violet no more knowledgeable than before. "I'm sorry. I didn't mean to upset you with my teasing."

"You've not said anything I don't deserve. Come, let's walk." He stood and held out his arm, his gaze unreadable and his jaw just a little too tight. "We will have to return to the palace soon enough."

She stood and slipped her hand into the crook of his elbow, regret coiling inside her. James had shown her more tenderness, laughter, and respect than she had ever had the pleasure of experiencing, and now she felt she had ruined their day, the atmosphere, possibly even their friendship. Shameful tears pricked her eyes, and Violet hastily blinked them back.

She was stronger than this. She knew deep in her heart she should not afford to rely on James's loyalty to her any more than anyone else's at court. Everyone was out for their own elevation, their own success, and if Violet were truly honest with herself, she was no different.

Her main ambition was to stay in Victoria's service, the second to paint. Not once had her aspirations stretched to love, and they would not now.

"Do you leave this afternoon?" she asked, looking around at the hundreds of people surrounding them, the bright afternoon sun glinting on parasols, hats, and canes. "Will it take you long to return home?"

"Not too long. I will take the coach, and if the skies remain as clear as they are now, I should be halfway to Oxfordshire by nightfall. I'll find a place to stay for the night and resume travelling tomorrow." He drew her to a stop, his gaze hesitant. "Please don't think the attention I pay you, the time I spend with you, is anything less than open and honest. I hate to think you might distrust my words or regard for you. But…"

That one word obliterated all that he had said before it, and Violet's heart sank despite the talk with herself just moments before. "But?"

"But my feelings, whatever they might be or come to be, are not mine to act upon. I have…"

"Responsibilities, I know. A responsibility to marry well and so much more I suspect."

He stared into her eyes, his own dark with regret. "Yes and marrying well is a pressing priority for my family. It is my duty to marry someone who understands the burdens as well as the privilege of inheriting an estate. I cannot allow myself to act recklessly on feelings alone, Violet. I just can't."

Her heart suddenly felt inexplicably heavy, and she swallowed hard, forced a small smile. "You do not have to tell me any more about your life, James. There are things I do not wish to tell you either. We are friends. Friends who have shared a few kisses and much laughter. Let us hold on to that for as long as possible, shall we?"

He opened his mouth as if to protest and then closed it. He nodded. "Yes, that would be best for us both, I think."

They continued to walk in the direction of the park's grand entrance, and Violet held her head high…despite feeling unhappier than she had since James first spoke to her months before.

Chapter Sixteen

At dusk, James approached the gates of his family estate.

The house loomed large at the end of the long gravel pathway, huge beech trees lining either side, casting the avenue in shadow much like the feeling that had settled over his entire being.

Lifting his cane, he rapped on the roof of the hired carriage and leaned back, taking a moment to gather himself—strengthen himself—to face his father. Already James's hackles had begun to rise, his self-protection slamming into place like plates of armor as he metamorphized into the man his father made him become whenever James was home.

Hardened. Somber. Defensive.

The carriage drew to a halt, and he disembarked, staring at the double doors at the front of the house as the driver retrieved the luggage. One of the bags contained the minimum of clothes and personal effects needed for a short stay, the other work papers, and some small gifts he had purchased on Violet's urging.

Despite her acrimony toward her mother, it only bolstered James's fondness for Violet that she would encourage kindness in him toward his parents…even if she had no idea the presents would remain in his case. His mother and father would think he had lost his mind or was someone in disguise if he showed any sort of emotional care for them.

Such sentiment had been beaten out of him a long time ago.

Having paid the driver, James picked up his bags and started along the pathway to the house. The lengthy walk would give him time to prepare himself for what lay ahead.

Time and again, he waylaid the inevitable. Yet as his father neared his sixtieth year, James could no longer ignore that sooner or later he would be forced to step into his role as heir of the estate. A place that had been in his family for generations.

Once the site of a modest farmhouse, each successor had added something to the house. James's grandfather had greatly extended the main part of the house a couple of decades before, and then James's father added the pillared portico and wings. Throughout the generations, more and more acres of land around the residence had been purchased, tenants' cottages installed, and employment given to many from the surrounding village.

The estate was a living, breathing entity. A source of income and prosperity—James tightened his fingers around the handles of his luggage—and, for all his dread and misgiving, his pride prevented him from truly turning his back on his inevitable duty. He could not fail his ancestors or the people who relied on him to provide work, now and in the future.

But as for marrying and siring children, that was a different matter altogether. Yet if he did not produce heirs, the link between the estate and his family would be broken forever. On his doing.

He reached the end of the avenue as hatred of his

inheritance pressed down on him, conflicting with the gratification that swelled inside him as he took in the magnificence of the house's façade. He might fear what sort of man he would become once all this was his, but he could not deny the love he held for the bricks and mortar of his family home, the dirt and bracken of the grounds.

The day's rain had given way to a beautiful evening, and the lowering sun cast the house's yellow stone in hues of rose-gold, its chimneys reaching toward a pinkening sky and its many windows reflecting wisps of cloud and shadow.

Cassington Park was indeed wonderful.

James walked up the stone steps, pushed open one of the double doors, and stepped into the entrance hall. From the drawing room to his right came the soft melody of his mother's piano playing, the odd murmur from his father, and James guessed he perused the evening's paper. After all, tradition rarely changed at Cassington.

He carried his bags to the bottom of the stairs and strained his ears for sounds of the staff and was greeted by the muted conversation of Cook and the family's loyal butler, Branson, from the kitchens on the lower level. No doubt the three maids who also worked for his parents were busy with tasks elsewhere, and James was glad that no one had heard him arrive.

The element of surprise would serve him well in gaining the upper hand rather than his father.

He left his bags by the stairs, took a deep breath, and entered the drawing room. "Good evening, Mother. Father."

The piano playing came to an abrupt halt.

"James!" his mother exclaimed. "You're home."

"I am." He kissed her cheek, her dark eyes wide with surprise and delight. "Are you well?"

"Of course. It's wonderful to see you." She stood and took his arm, her gaze turning anxious as she looked toward the wingback chair where her husband sat. "Henry? Are you not going to say anything to your son?"

James fought to hide his shock as he fully looked at his father for the first time since entering the room. He had lost weight, his once salt-and-pepper hair now silver, his robust face drawn and gray.

Forcing a smile, James walked forward, his hand outstretched. "Good evening, sir."

His father's face remained stalwart, just a flicker of what might be relief flashing in his eyes before it was replaced with habitual coldness. "So my latest letter was not written in vain." He lowered the paper to his lap and held James's hand in a surprisingly firm grasp. "I am glad this one was not ignored."

"On the contrary, I sensed its urgency." James cautiously withdrew his hand, foreboding twisting his stomach. His father did not look at all well. "Lord Melbourne has generously granted me a week's absence."

"A week?" His father grunted and nodded toward the sofa opposite him. "Take a seat." With his gaze on James, he reached for the bell pull beside him and tugged. "Time for a spot of brandy, I think. Tea, my dear?"

"Lovely." His mother sat by James on the brocade sofa and clasped his hand. "It's so wonderful to see you, my darling. Tell me, how is the palace? Do you often speak to Her Majesty?" Her usually dull eyes were almost feverish with excitement. "No, I don't suppose you do. What of the minister? Any gossip you can share?"

"Millicent, that is quite enough," his father barked. "James is not here to impart gossip, for crying out loud. He's here to learn all that needs to be done on the estate."

James patted his mother's hand and stared at his father. "I understand it is because of the estate that you called me home, but I'd prefer our discussions wait until morning. I would very much like to hear how you both are faring. And George, of course. Is he well?"

"Why wouldn't he be when he believes God himself walks beside him?" His father faced the door just as the butler entered. "Ah, there you are, Branson. Tea for my wife and a snifter of brandy for myself and my son, please."

"Yes, sir." Branson bowed to James. "Welcome home, sir. Shall I arrange for your bags to be taken to your room?"

"Yes. Thank you." James nodded, pleased to see the butler who had been with the family since before he was born looking so well. With silver hair and moustaches, half-rimmed spectacles balancing on his nose, Branson, now in his sixties, often acted as tactful mediator between James and his father. "It's good to see you."

"And you, sir."

Branson left the room, and James addressed his mother. "To answer your questions, I do not see the queen too often but often enough. As for Melbourne, I am immensely enjoying working for him and hope to continue to do so for a long while yet." The statement was said with intent, and James turned to his father. "And what about you, Father? Are you well?"

"Far from it, as you can see." He leaned back in his

chair, his gaze steely and his cheeks mottled. "It does not matter how much you *enjoy* working for Melbourne, your responsibilities lay with this house. First thing in the morning, we talk. It is time to start planning for your permanent return."

"Which won't be straight forward, I'm afraid. I have obligations at the palace. I am ultimately in service to the Crown, am I not?"

"That may be, but it is impossible that your service last forever."

"And I will return when it is absolutely necessary. Not before."

His father glared at him. "And what if it is absolutely necessary now?"

As his temper rose, James turned to his mother so that he might have some time to curb the bitter retaliations that burned on his tongue. To hotly argue with his father as soon as he returned home would not do either of them any good.

James cleared his throat. "So tell me, Mother. How is your project coming along in the east garden? The last time I was here, you were adamant that only a fountain would do along the far side of the main walk."

Their conversation continued for a few minutes before Branson returned with their drinks. The atmosphere grew ever more tense as the butler gave his father and James a glass from his silver tray before turning to their young maid, Ava, who stood waiting with a tea tray for James's mother.

Glancing from the staff to his father, James drew back his shoulders. His days of being bullied and intimidated by Henry Greene were over. Both James and George had each found a way to escape the past and live better and happier presents. The future would come soon enough.

Just not yet.

As Branson and Ava left the room, the ornate, ivory-painted doors closing behind them, James's father cleared his throat. "If it is too much to ask for your permanent return home right now, the least you can do in the interim is use your position at the palace to search for a suitable wife."

James's mother gave a nervous titter. "Henry, please."

"Please what?" He glared at his wife. "Be quiet? Leave him be? Not try to make your fool of a son understand how bloody privileged he is to have the pick of some of most eligible young women in the country?"

Anger burned in James's chest as he gently laid a hand on his mother's arm and stared at his father. "There's no need to defend me, Mama, and I know how privileged my upbringing was, sir. You never tired of reminding me or George…often with more than words."

"And still it doesn't sink in! Your languorous attitude to taking over the running of Cassington ends now. Before long, you will be a baron. You need a wife and heir."

James shook his head, smiled wryly. "Are you suggesting I just walk into the queen's chambers, choose a lady in waiting, and get down on one knee?"

Color leapt into his father's cheeks. "This situation amuses you? By God, you are waste of space. Shirking your responsibilities has reached its climax. I am drawing a line in the sand. You will marry and marry well. I do not want to die without knowing there is an heir ready and waiting after you."

Memories of how his father had treated him, demanded and demeaned him for years before James's calculated escape to the army, rose bitter in his throat. "I am well aware of my legacy and my duty to take the helm one day. But for now, I am needed at the palace. I will return home when I must and not before."

"And in the meantime, you *will* choose a wife." His father's cheeks mottled, his gaze icy-cold. "There is no more time for your dallying. I am ill, goddamn you. Very ill, indeed."

Chapter Seventeen

Violet finished rereading the last letter she had received from James over two weeks ago and returned it to the box she kept hidden beneath her bed. She placed her hand on the closed lid and stared toward the window of the bedroom she shared with three other maids at Buckingham Palace. Despite their company when some or all of them were not working, Violet had never felt so lonely. And that loneliness was due to missing James. A sad state of affairs that occurred because she had not paid enough attention to guarding her heart.

She was a fool. A fool in love? There was every possibility. Worse, he had unashamedly admitted there would never be a chance of them having a future together. Why in heaven's name had her understanding that he would eventually marry a highborn woman begun to waver…begun to hurt? She should be glad he was gone for a while; their time apart gave her a chance to build a barrier around her heart. To keep it safe from harm whenever he chose to return.

He had said he would only be away for a week, but it had been much longer already. She hoped everything was well with his loved ones, and his long absence was not due to a family member falling ill.

Violet returned the box to its hiding place and walked to the small dressing table the women shared and set about pinning and tidying her hair. She was shortly due at the queen's apartments, but first she had no choice but to answer her mother's summons.

Life at court was as busy as ever, and Violet's relationship with Victoria was gradually returning to where it had been before the queen reluctantly agreed to regularly take tea with the duchess—something Victoria had honored once a week ever since.

Violet forcefully pushed a pin into her blonde curls, her fingers trembling. But despite the teas being a huge step closer to what her mother had assigned Violet to do, she continued to pressure Violet to work harder to reconcile the queen with the duchess, heart, body, and soul. A frankly stupid imagining. Every time Violet saw her mother, she fumed that it was not enough for Victoria to merely make polite conversation with the duchess. She must make her feel loved and needed. Surely her mother had Victoria confused with another woman entirely!

The queen grew in confidence and authority day after day. Her role as head of the country and head of her palaces could no longer be disputed among her ministers or, indeed, by her subjects. Victoria led the charge with only her beloved Melbourne and Lehzen holding any semblance of influence over her.

Also, with the arrival of the dukes of Saxe-Coburg and Gotha looming, there was every possibility a marriage proposal would soon be announced. What that would mean for courtiers and staff, or the entire country, no one could say.

Turning from the dresser, Violet retrieved a clean apron from a chest of drawers and tied it at her waist, her thoughts drifting to James and what he might be doing. After he first returned home, his correspondence to her had arrived regularly, but for the past two weeks, he had been painfully silent, her last letter to him remaining unanswered.

Not that he could really say anything in response to her meandering reports of life at court and the difficulties she continued to endure with her mother. Tears pricked Violet's eyes. How could she tell him how much she missed him? That he had somehow burrowed a place in her heart so quietly, so discreetly, that she had not even noticed until he left.

Glancing at the clock on the mantel, Violet quickly smoothed the front of her dress before leaving the room and heading across the palace to the Duchess of Kent's apartments. The last thing she needed was to be late for her appointment with her mother and the duchess and add further displeasure to what was guaranteed to be a ghastly and vile visit.

She rounded a corner to find her mother pacing outside the duchess's drawing room, her movements agitated and her face set.

"Where on earth have you been, girl?" she demanded. "You deserve a slap for your tardy insolence. Come quickly, the duchess is waiting."

Pure loathing burned inside Violet as she followed her mother into the room, glaring at her back. *God, how I hate her…*

"Ah, there you are, child." The duchess flashed Violet a pinched smile. "Come, sit with me awhile. We have much to discuss, and I'm sure you are due with the queen very soon."

"I am, Your Grace. In the next half an hour, in fact." Violet fought to remain steadfast and composed and not surrender to intimidation. "My mother told me you wished to speak to me urgently?"

"I do. My nephews, Albert and Ernest of Saxe-Coburg and Gotha, will be arriving a mere ten days from now. It is imperative Drina continually seek my counsel and company both before and during their visit. I understand she wishes to entertain them at Windsor?"

"I believe so, ma'am. There has been little talk of the preparations in front of me, of course," she said carefully. "After all, I am neither a person of influence nor any particular importance to the queen."

"That is not the case, and you well know it," Violet's mother snapped.

The duchess raised her hand, silencing her. "My dear, I have been most patient with you, and as much as I fully appreciate your participation in facilitating my weekly meetings with Drina, her impending marriage is a different matter altogether."

"I understand, ma'am."

"Do you?" The duchess glowered, her feigned amiability slipping like water through a sieve. "Because it seems to me, your cavalier attitude regarding my guidance and advice to Her Majesty is insufferably nonchalant."

The duchess's face turned puce with anger, and Violet's mother looked fit to burst with fury.

To hide her sudden need to laugh, instigated more by hysteria than hilarity, Violet lowered her gaze. "I am sorry, ma'am."

"An empty apology means nothing," her mother admonished. "Do something to help the duchess today, Violet. Her Grace needs to be with Victoria when she greets the dukes, when she spends time with Albert. Not to mention being entirely involved in the arrangements beforehand. You will see that all comes to fruition."

Are they blind or just stupid? Victoria hates her mother, and I hate mine. Knowing she had little option but to placate her mother if she were to escape this meeting unscathed, Violet raised her eyes. "I will do what I can."

"Not good enough!"

Once again, the duchess raised her hand, and Violet's mother pressed her lips into a firm line.

"I am taking tea with Drina the day after tomorrow," the duchess said quietly, her eyes flashing with spite. "Maybe it will come into conversation that you have been talking ill of the queen, questioning her authority and actions…her relationship with Melbourne."

Violet froze. "I would never—"

"Oh, yes, my dear." The duchess grinned wolfishly. "As powerful as Drina might be, she is woefully paranoid about her household and their loyalty to her. It would only take me saying a few things in her ear, and she would begin to look at you in an entirely different way. She might even agree to my suggestion that you permanently return to my household. Something she has refused to sanction thus far."

Violet looked from the duchess to her mother who smiled at her, her eyes equally as gleeful as the duchess's.

Knowing she was beaten, Violet's next words threatened to clog her throat. "I will turn every minute I am with the queen to your purpose, Your Grace. Please, just give me a little more time, and I will do all I can to encourage Her Majesty to your counsel and company."

The silence stretched.

At last, the duchess spoke, her tone once again

sickeningly sweet. "Good, then you may go, my dear. I will eagerly await a summons from my daughter saying that she would very much like to speak to me privately about the dukes' arrival."

Violet stood, her legs trembling as she sank into a curtsey, entirely ignored her mother, and walked from the room. The farther she strode from the duchess's side of the palace to the queen's, the more profound Violet's anger and determination became.

She would try her best to capture a moment alone with the queen and tell her all that the duchess had requested. Then Violet would advise Victoria not to become caught in their mothers' treacherous web of trickery and scheming as she had, that neither of them could be trusted regardless how lovely—or not so lovely—the duchess might be at their teas together.

But what if Victoria thought Violet insolent for suggesting her incapable of seeing through her mother as easily as Violet saw through hers? She could easily dismiss her from her service for daring to talk to her about such an official matter as the visiting dukes. State business that had nothing whatsoever to do with a servant.

Yet what choice did she have but to try?

Chapter Eighteen

Later that evening, Violet was turning down the queen's bed with only Lehzen for company in the royal chamber. The more Violet considered how to broach the subject of the dukes' arrival and the queen consulting the duchess about her intentions, the more convinced Violet became that the best path was to speak to Lehzen first. That way, Victoria would hopefully accept that if Violet had confided in the queen's most trusted companion, she could not possibly be working in cahoots with her mother and the duchess.

Inhaling a steadying breath, Violet stepped back from the bed. "Baroness? I wonder if I might speak with you?"

"Hmm?" Lehzen continued to examine one of the queen's nightgowns, her eyes narrowed as though assessing the quality of the lace. "About what exactly?"

"The dukes' arrival."

Lehzen spun around, her brows lifted. "Why on earth would such a thing be of any concern to you?"

Nerves leapt in Violet's stomach. How she hated her mother for jeopardizing everything she now enjoyed. "My mother and the duchess have spoken to me about the dukes' visit."

"And?"

"And the duchess would very much like the queen to speak to her about her plans so that she might help and advise her."

Lehzen's gaze was unreadable as the seconds ticked by before she crossed her arms, her eyes dark with annoyance. "So you have resumed your place as their puppet."

"That is what they think, but my loyalty lies first and foremost with the queen, and…"

"And?"

Violet swallowed. "And I need your help to prove I speak the truth."

"Well, well, this is quite the turnaround. Considering how you have risen in Her Majesty's regard, I assumed you considered yourself without need for anyone." Lehzen walked closer, her eyebrows raised. "Are you asking me to speak to the queen on your behalf about this matter?"

"No, this interference by my mother is hers alone, and it should be me who speaks to the queen. I have no doubt she will be angered by what I have to say, and therefore, I must put myself in the firing line, no one else."

"Then why come to me?"

"Because I would like you to be there. That way, I hope Her Majesty will see that I am not keeping to myself what my mother and the duchess ask of me. And that my willingness to share their request with you is proof that I want no part in their scheming."

Lehzen studied her before returning to her task at the other side of the room. "You do the queen a discredit, Parker. She would never think such a thing. She knows her mother better than anyone at court." She glanced at Violet, her jaw tight. "She knows, as well as I, how easily the duchess would take advantage of someone as young and impressionable as yourself."

"So you will be there when I speak to Her Majesty?"

"I will." Lehzen walked with the queen's nightdress to the bed and laid it out, her brow furrowed. "It appears your mother placed you here to spy and cares very little for the queen's happiness. Am I right?"

"Yes."

"Then I have no choice but to support you. Victoria's happiness has been my priority since she was a child, and considering her regard for you and my appreciation of your coming to me first, your reaction to the duchess's commands is commendable." She gave Violet a pointed stare. "I hope we can continue to work alongside one another with honesty and respect."

Hope bloomed, and Violet smiled. "As do I."

"But…" Lehzen did not return Violet's smile, instead her gray eyes remained suspicious. "I am perturbed by the hold your mother must have over you that you would allow this ridiculousness to continue. You are very much liked by the queen. Why risk her wrath? Why not have it out with your mother once and for all?"

Gathering her strength, Violet pulled back her shoulders, determined to show Lehzen—show herself—how her mother's control over her diminished every day. That she grew stronger, more committed to Victoria the longer she served her and could only see that allegiance deepening.

"My mother has always been immensely cruel and manipulative to me and my siblings, but as my brothers have managed to escape her, I will, too. Being in the queen's service is all I want. I love and wish to serve her for as long as possible. I want to be honest with Her

Majesty. Show her that my first loyalty will always be to her. I promise you my mother's supposed control over me has reached its end."

Laughter and excited chatter suddenly erupted in the next room as the queen and her ladies returned from an after-dinner play, breaking through the tense silence that had enveloped Violet and Lehzen.

Lehzen stepped closer. "I will arrange for you to speak with the queen once she is abed. I will be here, but that does not guarantee she will not be angered, regardless of my involvement. If that anger is turned on me, trust me when I say your mother will be the least of your concerns."

The baroness swept from the room, and Violet blew out a breath as Lehzen's overly loud, overly enthusiastic salutation to the queen drifted through the open doorway.

For the next hour, Violet did all she could to stay busy and out the way of the queen and her ladies. The company remained buoyant as Victoria was prepared for bed, regaling them with anecdotes of past dinners. Uncertain what to do when she was not usually in the queen's bedchamber at this hour, Violet kept her distance, almost trying to disappear into the walls so that she might not be noticed.

At last, Victoria climbed into bed and settled back against the pillows as Lehzen dismissed her ladies. Sickness churned in her stomach as Violet stepped closer, feeling like an unsavory stalker appearing from the shadows.

Lehzen glanced at her and discreetly nodded. "Your Majesty, Parker would like to speak to you about the duchess."

The queen's soft smile vanished. "You of all people

should know my mother is the last person I wish to discuss before I close my eyes at night, Parker."

"I'm so sorry, Your Majesty, but I did not want to wait until morning and risk my mother or yours telling you of my conversations with them before I did. I would hate for you to assume I have been talking with them behind your back."

Victoria's gaze shadowed with anger. "They summoned you again even though I have kept every infernal tea with my mother as agreed?"

"Yes, ma'am. I fear they will keep summoning me until you are *fully* reconciled with the duchess."

The queen folded her hands on the bedcovers, her knuckles showing white beneath her pale skin. "I see. And what is it my darling mama would like from me now?"

Violet glanced at Lehzen who ushered her forward with a wave of her hand. "Go on, girl. Speak honestly with Her Majesty as you did with me."

"You knew about this, Lehzen?" the queen snapped. "Have you spoken to my mother, too?"

"No, Your Majesty." Lehzen approached the bed, her expression twisted with distaste. "But when Parker spoke to me, I soon understood the depth of the duchess's nefarious employment of her, and it is deplorable. Hence why I agreed to stand in support of Parker when she spoke with you. In truth, I applaud her honesty…and heartily condemn the subterfuge Mrs. Parker and the duchess seem determined to continue throughout Parker's service to you. It must be stopped."

"I agree." Victoria faced Violet. "What does my mother want?"

"She wishes to be brought into your confidence

before and during the dukes' visit, ma'am. She wants to advise you and have you share with her your concerns and plans."

"Does she now?" The queen slapped and smoothed at the bedcovers, her brow furrowed. "Then it is obvious she has concluded that I will propose marriage to Albert, just as my uncle has. Well, there will be mammoth disappointment throughout the palace because if she and Leopold continue to harass me this way, I have the mind not to see Albert at all!"

Violet lowered her gaze, her knees trembling. The queen looked incandescent with rage. "Yes, ma'am."

"Do not, *ma'am*, me, Parker," Victoria cried. "What I want to do and what I will *have* to do are not nearly the same. You have worked in my household long enough to know that I often feel as much pulled and used, manipulated, and held to ransom as you clearly do. To have you pity me or, God forbid, have you even think I will do my mother's bidding, makes me utterly furious."

Violet trembled harder, bile rising in her throat. This was it, she would be dismissed.

Lehzen cleared her throat. "I do have an idea if it is your wish for Parker to stay in your household, Your Majesty."

"Of course, I wish her to stay." Victoria shot Lehzen a glare before turning to Violet. "You will not leave my service for as long as your mother and mine continue to use you as a pawn in their pathetic games. You have my word."

Relief swept through Violet so strongly, she swayed back on her heels, her hand pressed to her chest. "Thank you, ma'am."

"There is no need for your ideas, Lehzen," the queen

said firmly. "The fact of the matter is I have little choice but to convey my plans and thoughts to my mother about Albert. The same as I am obligated to keep Uncle Leopold informed." She looked at Violet. "My mother pressing you to urge my love for her once again has only increased my malevolence toward her. Her mission to bring her and I closer has failed again. Just as it always will." Victoria's eyes flashed with malice. "As Lord Melbourne reminded me just a few days ago, my marrying will be the most delicious retribution of all toward the duchess. If I choose to marry Albert, the moment I return along the aisle of the Chapel Royal as his wife, I have absolutely no onus to continue living with her." She softly smiled. "Which means you, Parker, will be equally as free from your mother as I will be from mine. After all, they come as a pair, do they not?"

Violet grinned. "Indeed, they do, Your Majesty."

Chapter Nineteen

Plastered with mud and dirt, James returned from his inspection of the estate and entered the main house through the servants' entrance. As he started to remove his boots, Branson immediately leapt up from the scrubbed pine table where he'd been polishing silver.

"My lord, let me help."

"I am more than capable of removing my coat and boots, Branson." James tugged off his second boot and placed it beside the other. "The ground is abominable considering it's only the first week in October. Then again, if you consider the summer we've had, it comes as no surprise the fields are like a damn quagmire."

"Indeed, sir."

Slipping off his scarf, James stood in stockinged feet and glanced at the backroom door. "Where is my father?"

"In his study, sir, and my lady is upstairs with Ava, sorting through items for charity. May I bring you some coffee in the drawing room?"

"I'll take some here, if it's not too much bother." James sat at the table and stretched out his legs, tilting his stiff neck from side to side. "I'd rather stay out of the way of my parents for a while longer, if possible."

Branson gave a small smile before moving to the stove and lifting the kettle. "How are you getting on reacquainting yourself with the estate, sir? I understand you have visited most of the tenants, and they have been very pleased to receive you."

James swiped his hand over his face and settled back on the wooden chair. "They have been welcoming. Most behaving as though I have never been away with their kind words." He sighed. "Having said that, each was as keen to know when I intend to wed as they were to share any difficulties or successes they might have with their work."

"Unfortunately, your fate of inheriting Cassington will be no less on the tenants' minds as it is your father's, sir." The butler raised his eyebrows, his gaze concerned. "Are you no easier about what awaits you? It would make his lordship incredibly relieved if you can find it in you to accept—"

"What? That I need to stay at home from this day forward? Not return to the palace?" James clenched his jaw and held Branson's stare. "That is not going to happen. Not yet. I have seen the lay of the land, spoken to tenants, and been into town to see Father's banker. I am as abreast of things as I need to be at this juncture and intend to tell my father as much this afternoon."

"I see." Unease whispered through the room as Branson filled the kettle and returned it to the stove, reaching for a box of matches. "A letter came from the palace for you. I will set this to boil, and then I'll get it from the hallway tray."

James stood. "I'll go. Actually, on second thought, coffee in the drawing room would be welcome."

"As you wish, sir."

James left the room and hurried upstairs to the hallway. Once there, he snatched a thick cream envelope from the silver tray by the front door before heading upstairs. Entering his bedroom, he walked to the window and ripped open the royal seal.

Dear Greene,

It has been confirmed that the royal dukes are likely to arrive from Germany in the next day or so. I need you to return to Windsor immediately. I have decided you are best placed to look after His Serene Highness, Albert, while he is here. You excelled in your attention to the Grand Duke of Russia, and I know you will serve this duke just as well.

If your return is not possible due to the commitments that have already kept you from the palace for this unexpected length of time, please let me know by return message. Alternatively, please do all that you can to enable your departure so that we might discuss the dukes' needs before their arrival.

Yours sincerely,

Melbourne

James smiled and looked out the window along the tree-lined avenue toward the estate's iron gates. "God bless you, Minister."

James quickly undressed and approached his dresser. Making hurried use of the bowl and jug of water there, he swilled his face and patted it dry, grimacing at the day-old growth on his chin. He would shave and make himself more presentable at whichever inn he stayed at overnight tonight before leaving for the final run to London in the morning.

Quickly dressing in the travelling attire he wore to Cassington Park over four weeks ago, James straightened his jacket knowing his apparel and countenance would leave his father in no doubt of his son's determination to leave that very afternoon.

Heading downstairs, he walked straight to his father's study and knocked on the door.

"Enter."

Adrenaline pulsed through him as James strode into the room and closed the door. "Afternoon, Father."

"How were things this morning?" His father did not lift his head from the papers in front of him, but continued to frown as he read, a pen between his fingers. "I understand there are several horses you would like sent to the farrier."

"Yes, three. Father, I have received—"

"A letter from the palace. I know. I saw it in the hallway earlier." Henry Greene finally lifted his head, his beady eyes boring into James before he ran his gaze over his clothes and boots. "And I see you are wasting no time escaping."

"The letter was a summons from Melbourne. One I cannot refuse."

"Cannot or will not?"

"Once you have heard why he wishes me to return, I think you will be more than happy for me to leave. The assignment is rather honorable."

His father put down his pen and slowly removed his spectacles. "Oh?"

"Melbourne has requested that I attend to his Serene Highness, Duke Albert of Saxe-Coburg and Gotha, who will be arriving in the next couple of days. A man who, according to popular opinion at court, is likely to become king consort." James paused for his father's reaction, but his face barely twitched. "Hence there is no time for delay. I will be leaving immediately."

The ensuing silence was only broken by the sound of the birds in the eaves outside the window and the odd shift of gravel crunching beneath the boots of the stable hands and the horses' hooves as they walked back and forth to the stables.

His father rose and came around his enormous desk before purposefully placing his hand on James's shoulder. "This is a significant appointment."

"It is."

"But you will return to estate forthwith thereafter."

"Whenever that might be, yes."

Their gazes locked before his father slipped his hand from James's shoulder and stepped back. "I am neither surprised nor dissatisfied by your elevation, but your true place is here at the helm of our estate, not at court."

"I have given you and the house an entire month when I expected to be here no longer than a week," James said, battling to keep the impatience from his voice. "I have done all I am willing to do, learned all I need to for the time being. Leave me to return to my duties at court, and I will come back when the need next arises."

His father shot him a final glare before he strolled to the door and opened it. "Then go, but you have a continuing duty to find a wife, James. A wife suited to becoming the next mistress of this house. Someone compliant, yet intelligent. Kind, yet capable of sternness when necessary."

"I will find a wife of my own choosing in my own time," James said as he walked to the door. "And when I do, I will make her fully aware of all that awaits her should she agree to be my wife. I will not marry anyone who stands in ignorance of what this family is and what it runs the risk of always being."

His father nodded with satisfaction; his gaze filled

with pride. "Good, because we are indeed a grand and honorable family. Any woman should be proud to stand beside you."

"You are missing my point. We are a grand family, yes, but honorable?"

His father's cheeks mottled. "What is that supposed to mean?"

"We are also a family of tempers and miscalculations. A family prone to reprimand and abuse." James's stomach tightened with suppressed resentment. "And any potential wife of mine will be aware of that. Now…" He walked into the corridor and curtly dipped his head. "I will say goodbye to Mother and be away. I will write to you in due course."

James had barely taken more than a few steps along the corridor when he heard his father's study door click shut behind him. He stopped and turned. He had expected an argument, raised voices, and rage from his father when he had so blatantly pointed out the family failings, but his father had met James's outburst with uncharacteristic silence.

Disquiet shrouded him as James approached the drawing room where he hoped to find his mother. His father had shared little about his illness, saying there would be time to deal with it as long as James returned home more often. It seemed the most pressing issue his father harbored at this time was want of an heir.

An heir whose mother must hold breeding and prestige. That much had been made crystal clear by both his parents during this visit. Yet as James thought of the women at Buckingham Palace, of Windsor and beyond, the only face that filled his mind's eye was Violet's.

Chapter Twenty

"Make haste, Greene. The dukes have arrived." Melbourne strode to the office door. "The queen will want us in attendance when she greets them."

James quickly shrugged on his jacket. "What is Her Majesty's current feeling, sir?"

"About marrying Albert, you mean?"

"Yes."

Melbourne stopped, his hand on the doorknob. "It appears her earlier reluctance to wed is no more. In fact, she has spoken of nothing but Albert for the last few days. Apparently, she is happy with the reports she has received regaling his increased handsomeness since she last saw him, but somewhat perturbed by his purported hesitancy to come here." He opened the door. "But I'm confident all will be well. Come."

"They have met before?"

"Several years ago. I cannot be certain when, but it was far enough in the past for both to have noticeably changed." Melbourne raised his eyebrows. "Only time will tell if that is a positive or negative circumstance. Now, come along, enough chitchat."

The dukes of Saxe-Coburg and Gotha's arrival had been as per the minister's prediction, giving James and Melbourne only two brief days to prepare. Long discussions and agreement on James's role and that of Melbourne's while the royal guests were at Windsor meant James had been entirely entrenched in duty. Thus, he had not found the opportunity to seek out Violet to let her know of his return.

Now, with the dukes' entrance, James had even less of an idea when he would have a chance to speak to her.

As he and Melbourne turned into the corridor leading to the queen's apartments, Victoria strode ahead of her ladies toward them. The minister and James dipped their heads.

When James looked up, Victoria's blue eyes held Melbourne's, her gaze revealing just an iota of nervousness. Yet it was clear something indiscernible passed between them before she abruptly continued walking. James glanced at Melbourne. Yes, the minister looked decidedly more cheered than he had before seeing Victoria.

Whatever the message, it had been an encouraging one. Maybe Melbourne had been silently reassured that Victoria marrying would not mean his redundance.

James followed the royal procession beside Melbourne until they reached the top of the grand staircase. Victoria came to a stop, her head held high. It was here that she would greet her exalted guests alone.

The rest of her household, James, and Melbourne continued down the stairs, each taking their places at the bottom of the staircase. Melbourne positioned himself next to a gentleman named Henry Barrow and nodded. James knew Henry to be a reputable steward and assumed he would be serving Duke Ernest as James would Albert. The three of them stood to attention side by side. The formality of the situation and the possibility Albert could be the future king consort was lost on nobody.

At exactly seven thirty, horses' hooves and the jingle of harnesses sounded outside as the dukes' carriage pulled up at the open double doors. A few moments later, the royal brothers entered the candlelit entrance hall, side by side, straight-backed, and somber faced. Dusk settled behind them, enveloping them in amber light, the grandeur of the castle entrance glinting all around in an array of gold, silver, and crystal.

Both men were dark haired with almost identical moustaches and whiskers, tall, and well-built, inarguably striking in looks.

James bowed as they passed and continued to the colossal set of stairs where Victoria stood stock-still at the top, a small smile about her lips and her blue eyes wide with unabashed curiosity…maybe even delight, her gaze barely straying from Albert.

The dukes each bowed before taking Victoria's hand in turn, pressing a kiss to her glove before she swept ahead of them, leaving them to follow.

As soon as they were out of sight, it was as though a collective sigh of relief echoed from the walls before the household and guards dispersed to their various duties.

Melbourne approached two gentlemen who had surreptitiously entered behind the dukes and stood waiting near the door. "You are the dukes' valets?"

They nodded. "We are, sir."

"Very good. Well, I am the queen's prime minister and private secretary, Lord Melbourne. This…" He held out his hand toward James. "Is Mr. James Greene who will be assisting you in looking after His Serene Highness, Duke Albert, and this is Mr. Henry Barrow who will assist you with His Serene Highness, Duke

Ernest."

James learned Albert's valet was named Charles Carr, and he seemed, on first impression, amiable and suitably deferential to the minister.

Melbourne glanced at the open double doors. "Do you need to collect the dukes' luggage?"

"It will follow shortly, sir," Mr. Carr said. "There has been a slight delay with its arrival. Therefore, it would be appreciated if you could inform the queen that my master finds it impossible to attend dinner tonight without his formal dress."

Melbourne glanced uncomfortably at the stairs. "I am not sure how Her Majesty will receive that news, but I will speak to her. Now, if you would follow me?"

James joined them as the party followed Melbourne to the grand staircase. "We have arranged rooms for the dukes overlooking the great Windsor Park," the minister said over his shoulder. "I am sure they will be more than comfortable."

Once in Albert's designated room, James was left alone with Charles who visibly relaxed as he held out his hand. "Glad to make your acquaintance, Greene. I am sure we will work well together."

Clearly, Charles was a man mild in both manner and temperament, and James took an instant liking to him. Around James's age, Charles was smartly dressed, his dark-blond hair and whiskers neatly combed despite what was bound to have been an arduous journey.

James nodded. "Let me show you around the rooms. The duke will be pleased with them, I'm sure."

Half an hour later, James stood at attention as Albert entered the room and released a heavy sigh, pulling on his necktie. "I am exhausted," he said, in clipped

English, looking at the bed rather than Charles or James. "I fear Victoria is not happy about Ernest and I missing dinner, but I refuse to sit at a dining table in my travelling clothes."

"Sir." Charles stepped forward, his hand held out toward James. "This is Mr. James Greene who has been assigned by Lord Melbourne to work alongside me whilst we are here."

Albert's brilliant blue eyes bored into James's before he offered his hand. "Delighted, Greene. I am confident Charles will tell you all you need to know and how I like to be attended." He gave an almost imperceptible smile. "I consider myself of much lower maintenance than my brother."

The jibe was laced with fondness, and James smiled. "That is good to know, sir."

"So." Albert strolled to the window and planted his hands at his waist, staring out at the vast parkland now shadowed with oncoming nightfall. "How closely are you associated with the queen? I assume you have regular contact with her considering you work for her private secretary?"

James stared at the duke's turned back, caution whispering through him. "I know her very little, I'm afraid, sir. Lord Melbourne spends much of his time alone with Her Majesty and returns to his office where he duly assigns me any tasks he'd like done."

Albert turned, his eyes narrowed. "So you know nothing of the queen's interests outside of state business? What sort of woman she is away from the constant glare of courtiers and officials?"

"Well, no, sir. Her leisure time is spent with her ladies in or out of her private apartments."

"But it is my wish to get to know her. Understand her." Albert's tone was brusque as he paced the room, his hands clenched behind his back, his expression somber. "I have no intention of doing what is asked of me without knowing the queen a little better. We have exchanged many letters, but still, it is important to me that we get along well and with mutual regard." He glanced up from the carpet and pinned James with a stare. "I need to know that Victoria is a woman of intellect and purpose."

Defense of the queen simmered in James's stomach. Victoria was proving herself a good and fair monarch. A woman of integrity and purpose in a male-dominated world. A sovereign James was privileged to serve. The thought that the duke might judge her in any way did not sit well at all. Somehow, he had expected more of him despite the manner of the last suitor who came calling.

"The queen is both of those things," James said, holding Albert's gaze. "As well as enjoyable company from what I have witnessed when she is relaxing."

"Meaning?"

"Meaning when we have held balls, she is full of laughter and can dance until the early hours. She likes to joke and gossip with her ladies and tease her ministers. But when it comes to state business—"

"Joke and gossip?"

"Yes, sir."

Albert's frown deepened. "And you think it acceptable that she teases her ministers?"

"That only occurs amid informal circumstances, sir. The queen never veers from complete solemnity when dealing with official business."

"I see. You might presume me harsh, Mr. Greene,

but you are wrong. I am not harsh. I am prudent. It is important that Victoria and I are relaxed and could grow fond of one another."

The sincerity in Albert's voice went some way to lessening James's growing tension. "Yes, sir."

"So to that mind, I would like you to speak to the ladies she enjoys spending time with and trusts. Try to find out what she likes to do when alone, the things she speaks of." Albert began pacing again, his gaze on the carpet as though deep in thought. "Her desires and dreams. That sort of thing."

James glanced at Charles who gave a subtle shrug, his green eyes amused.

Clearly, Albert's stern, inquisitive attitude came as no surprise to his valet.

James cleared his throat. "I will find out what I can, sir."

"Please do." Albert stopped and flashed his first proper smile. "I am sure you find it no hardship to talk to the beautiful women at court."

Chapter Twenty-One

Wandering along one of the pathways that wound between the countless flower beds in Windsor's gardens, Violet stopped beside a particularly colorful arrangement. She lowered to her knees and set down her basket, her imagination filled with romantic notions of His Serene Highness, Duke Albert and Queen Victoria.

It was the afternoon after the duke's arrival, and Violet could not help but smile as she thought how the queen had behaved while preparing for bed the night before. The entire chamber had been in a state of girlish euphoria as she rejoiced in Albert's handsomeness, remarking on his wonderfully blue eyes and exquisite nose, his beautiful figure and fine waist. There was every possibility of a love match between Her Majesty and the duke, considering Victoria seemed to have fallen head over heels for Albert almost immediately upon seeing him again.

Violet carefully snipped at the stem of a flawless ruby-red rose and lifted it to her nose, her mind filled with romance but also Victoria's current fragility. Despite her admiration of Albert, at any unprovoked moment, the queen spiraled into a state of agitation as her confidence plummeted, and her worry Albert might not admire her in the same way she did him escalated.

Maybe that was how true love felt? Constant leaping from one emotional state to another. Doubting your lover and yourself. How fervently she hoped that Victoria and Albert came to love one another and were happy.

Violet wiped the back of her hand across her cheek before pushing the brim of her straw hat higher on her head, the sporadic summer heat pressing down on her. She could not afford to trust that the fondness, which slowly deepened between her and the queen, would not vanish once Albert entirely filled Victoria's heart. There was as much chance of Violet being dismissed as anyone else once Victoria married.

After all, there could be no doubt how quickly the queen would instruct her mother to find her own place of residence. Who was to say the queen would as much as blink if her mother suggested Violet leave court with them, too?

Sickness churned ominously in Violet's stomach, and she forced her mind to her task. Carefully selecting and cutting a few more blooms, she added them to the foliage already collected in her basket. She would live in the moment and not worry about the future. Only Victoria could decide Violet's fate. And no matter how deep Violet's fear that she would never be capable of anything without her mother's orchestration, for now at least, she soared in the queen's affections.

The crunch of gravel turned Violet's head, and her heart jolted. James approached, a roguish, toe-curling smile on his lips.

Warmth rushed into her cheeks, and she quickly looked at the flowerbed, humming to herself as she feigned intense interest in a rosebud. She had overheard several of the queen's ladies commenting on James's return the night before, and now that he had finally sought her out, Violet's heart pounded like a hammer against an anvil. She had also heard talk that Melbourne had put James in service to Duke Albert.

Something she was certain pleased him.

"Good afternoon, Mistress Parker."

Slowly, Violet lifted her gaze, her heart racing with pleasure as James smiled down at her. "Mr. Greene. What a surprise. I had no idea you'd returned to court."

"Did you not? I'm astounded."

"Why? Did you send me a message?" She turned back to the flowers, her fingers tight around her scissors. "Only I have not received any correspondence from you for over two weeks."

The jab was assured and sharp, but one she could not resist, even if her treacherous lips tugged with a smile.

His shadow enveloped her as he leaned down and gently removed the scissors from her grip. He took her hand, easing her to her feet. The moment Violet looked into the dark depths of his eyes, her heart swelled with deep affection and an immeasurable awareness of how much she had missed him. His gaze wandered over her face, her lips, before he brought his thumb to her face and wiped it softly over her cheek.

He held up his gloved thumb, his eyes shining with amusement. "You have been playing in the dirt it seems."

Embarrassed, she wiped both cheeks and dragged her gaze from his to pick up her basket. "I'm collecting flowers for an arrangement in the queen's bedroom." She glanced at him as she straightened. "I should get back."

They slowly started along the pathway, neither of them in any hurry to return to their duties. Looking up at him from beneath the brim of her hat, Violet admired his handsomeness. The hard line of his jaw, his perfect nose, and tempting lips that she had not remembered in nearly as much detail as she thought.

"When did you get back?" she asked, looking ahead.

He nodded hello to a pair of male courtiers as they passed them. "Three days ago. I'm sorry I did not find you sooner. Melbourne had been in a state of nervousness over the dukes' arrival and kept me in attendance from early morning to late at night. Once dismissed, I readily fell into bed."

"Well, there can be no one more important at court than Duke Albert at the moment. The queen is quite besotted with him. You must be in good favor with Lord Melbourne for him to assign you to the duke's chambers."

"It's an honor. Although not nearly as much of an honor as you enjoy with the queen." He leaned closer, his breath brushing her ear. "Which pleases me immensely since the bond between Albert and Victoria appears to be growing stronger and inevitably means we will spend more time together if their relationship is a success."

His proximity sent a flash of heat through her entire body, and Violet quickly looked around them. "Must you walk so close to me?" She bristled. "I am not one of your many ladies, you know."

"Will you never stop referring to my reputation?" He laughed, leaning away from her as they continued to walk. "Surely, you know by now that I am not the rogue they make me out to be."

"Hmm, only time will tell."

Violet smiled, enjoying their playful companionship and wanting to pull the feeling close. It made her happy that James seemed as delighted to see her as she was him.

"Would it please you for us to spend more time together?" he asked. "Whether that be purposely or by accident?"

"Possibly." She looked at him, his gaze lit with flirtation, but there was something else there, too. Hope? But what could he possibly hope for when their relationship had no future? "Maybe."

He gently cupped her elbow, drawing her to the side of the pathway and into the shadow of an elaborately manicured bush. "Violet, I need to ask you something. Something about the queen."

The change in his tone, his sudden seriousness raised her caution. "Yes?"

"As much as it might suit us for Victoria and Albert to marry, I am not yet convinced they will."

Violet's hope for the queen's happiness faltered. "Why not?"

"The duke is asking a lot of questions."

"What sort of questions? The queen is fond of him. I presumed the feeling mutual."

"Albert is serious, reserved. A proud man who, as far as I can tell, is not prone to relaxation easily and most certainly has no desire to waste time on frivolity." He pushed some fallen hair from his brow, his expression exasperated. "You and I both know how much the queen enjoys dancing, playing the piano, laughing, eating. The duke has noticed or been told of those things, and I'm not sure he likes it."

Annoyed that Albert would judge the queen so harshly when she was only guilty of enjoying herself when not dealing with state business, Violet took a step back. "Well, maybe if the duke finds it felonious that Victoria manages to find snatches of enjoyment amid her service to the realm, he is not the man to be her consort."

"You could be right, but there is something in his countenance that I think will complement the queen's sense of fun rather than hinder it. I suspect they could come to balance one another and be a formidable partnership given time." He frowned. "Are there other things Victoria enjoys privately that might change Albert's presumptions about her?"

"Are you asking me to divulge private happenings that occur in the queen's apartments so you can convince Albert she is worthy of him?"

"Well, I wouldn't have put it exactly like that, but yes. If he understands that she—"

"Then you are no different than my mother and the duchess."

"What?"

She hitched her basket higher on her arm, her cheeks warm. "You have the audacity to ask me to reveal the queen's privacy as though, if I should do so, it would not be treacherous."

"Violet—"

"Why must everyone use me for their own underhanded wants and wishes? First my mother, now you."

"I merely—"

"You merely nothing." She stepped away from him, anger speeding her heart. "If you want the queen to be happy, then it is your duty to persuade Albert to do everything in his power to woo and love her. To use his time uncovering her likes and dislikes, making her smile and laugh. If he cannot do that, then he doesn't deserve her."

"Sometimes men haven't the time."

Violet stilled. "Sorry?"

"All I'm saying is, Albert does not strike me as the sort of man capable of wooing. He is very serious, straitlaced. Almost eternally business like."

"I see. Well, maybe you and he assume too much about the opposite sex. Think your positions give you a free hand to push and pull women to your own advantage."

"That is hardly fair. I am asking you to do this for me as a courtesy from one friend to another."

"A friend?" She huffed a laugh, indignant and hurt that James would seek to use her in such a similar way as her mother. "I never thought it possible that you would regard our friendship as a tool for your own dealings. Well, now I see the real you, James Greene, and I'm not sure I like what I see. Bullish brutes have no place in my life."

Gripping her skirt with one hand and her basket in the other, Violet hurried in the direction of the house, praying he had not seen the tears that so painfully pricked her eyes.

Chapter Twenty-Two

As the royal party returned from their afternoon ride and gathered in the courtyard, James sat astride his horse and looked around at the courtiers and ladies, all dressed in their finest riding clothes. It was a regal sight indeed and left no doubt that the dukes were here for a reason far past a usual dignitary visit.

The brothers' third day at Windsor had broken overcast and gray, but the weather did not deter Victoria's request that they go riding. She had been adamant in her wish to show Albert Windsor's Great Park. She had never shown any enthusiasm for the vast space until she learned of his interest in botany.

James softly smiled and turned from the ladies and gentlemen surrounding him to the spectacle of Baroness Lehzen's sour mouth as she fussed and fawned over Victoria as she was helped down from her horse by her groom. But it seemed that even Lehzen's gloominess would not ruin the queen's day, judging by the breadth of Victoria's smile, her eyes shining with undisguised happiness. She had never looked more beautiful or so young.

James's satisfaction dissolved as he shifted his gaze to Albert, dismounting just a short distance away. The man had barely broken a smile in Victoria's company since he'd been here. They had played the piano together, sat side by side like intimates, danced with hands clasped and looking into one another's eyes, which only made the duke's aloofness all the more confusing. Frowning, James vowed to mention Albert's conduct to Melbourne the next time they were alone in his office.

Swinging his feet to the ground, James handed his reins to Pip. "How are you, young man?" he asked. "Keeping busy?"

"As always, sir. You looked mighty pleased with yourself when you came into the courtyard. I'm glad to see you happy in your work with the minister."

"And the duke, Pip, and the duke."

The young stable hand stared at Albert. "Is he likely to become a more permanent presence around here, do you think?"

James winked. "I'm not one for gossip. You know that."

Laughing, Pip shook his head and clicked his tongue, urging James's horse in the direction of the stables. "You take care, sir."

James joined the back of the royal entourage as they made their way to the castle entranceway. When they entered, his heart stumbled. Violet looked as beautiful as ever where she stood inside, lined up with other staff to greet the royal party, her gaze respectfully lowered.

As James drew even with her, she lifted her eyes and pointedly stared at him, her mouth drawn into a thin line, her eyes flashing with contempt.

James's heart beat fast.

Her accusation of his bullish behavior yesterday had cut deep. It was as though she had seen the future and the conceited man he was destined to become. There was little he could do to rectify his mistake now, and regret twisted inside him—her new dislike and distrust of him clearly written on her face. James gave her a curt nod and looked ahead, pulling back his shoulders. In a different life, one of simpler means and pressures, every instinct told him Violet would be the sort of woman with whom he could have lived a happy life. But his life was not his own and far from simple. He should push her to the back of his mind and from his heart, abandon the foolishness of pursuing her. She would not understand anything less than people being true to who they were.

After all, he very much doubted masquerade and falsity existed in her world as it did in his.

However, he would do whatever he must to rid the disdain from her eyes. Moreover, he would tell her how entirely wrong he felt her admonishment after his perfectly innocent request for her help. God only knew what sort of man he might be a few years from now, but the man who had stood in front of her yesterday was open and honest.

How could he have known his words would provoke such hostility in her?

Pride welled inside him, diluting his regret and fanning the flames of James's annoyance. Yes, he could have a temper when goaded, but he had hardly hounded her. And yes, her relationship with her mother was strained, but had he really deserved to be compared to her? He did not scheme and plan; his temper and intentions were plain for all to see. Whether they be good or bad.

Maybe it was to his detriment that when it came to the opposite sex, he only knew flirtation, cajoling, and banal mind games, innocent male-female interaction that he was confident would lead nowhere and no one would be hurt. Unfortunately, that was no longer the case with Violet, and James suspected she knew it as much as he.

Charles Carr stepped in front of him. "We are to return to the duke's chambers, Greene. He has decided on something particular to wear this evening, and I thought it might be worthwhile to show you how he likes things laid out should I be elsewhere on occasion."

"Of course." James glanced along the corridor, catching a glimpse of Melbourne as he spoke briefly to the queen before turning and heading in the direction of his office. "I just need a quick word with Lord Melbourne, and I'll be right with you."

Carr followed the party up the stairs, and James hurried after Melbourne, managing to catch up with him just as they reached his office.

"Greene, good to see you." Melbourne walked to his desk and put down some papers before sitting. He laced his hands on the desk, his gaze somber. "How was the ride this afternoon? The queen has just stipulated that she not be bothered with state issues for the rest of the day."

"I can't say I'm surprised. I had the impression she very much enjoyed herself this afternoon." He cleared his throat. "Although I can't say the same for the duke."

Melbourne frowned. "Did something happen?"

"No, it's actually his lack of gusto with whatever he and Her Majesty might be doing. It bothers me. Surely you have noticed?"

"Hmm." Melbourne leaned back in his seat. "King Leopold has made it clear that Albert should have a singular objective. To secure an engagement with the queen. Although, I second your concern having caught the duke looking at the queen in a less than auspicious manner a number of times. I'm not sure what he sees when he looks at her, but it certainly isn't marriage."

James glanced at the huge grandfather clock in the corner of the room. "I have to get to the duke's rooms, but I felt I must say something. What of Victoria? Is she as taken with Albert as she seems?"

"She is. In fact, I sense her growing bolder in her intentions toward him by the hour." Melbourne steepled his fingers under his chin, his gaze pensive. "She told me this morning that she is a good deal changed in her opinion of marriage, which can only mean she intends to propose."

"You do not look particularly happy about the prospect."

"Oh, I will be." Melbourne lowered his hands and blew out a breath. "I daresay I'll be ecstatic if their union means greater good for the country, yet I fear the reaction to a German prince on the throne will not be received as favorably as she'd like to think. Not by Parliament or the public."

"But you think theirs a positive alliance?"

"I do, both for Victoria, who needs someone steady like Albert beside her, and for the state. A firm marriage between a country's queen and a man willing to do all he can to support her is destined to be a great union. Having said that…" Melbourne rubbed his hand back and forth along his jaw. "She has confessed to becoming increasingly agitated by the duke's apathy."

"And what did you advise her?"

"What else? I told her in no uncertain terms that a woman cannot stand alone for long and that she should get on with the proposal."

James raised his eyebrows. "And how did she react to such…I beg your pardon, sir, unequivocal urging?"

Melbourne flashed a rare smile, his blue eyes amused. "There was no urging, Greene, I merely told her what she needed to hear. As I am prone to do on an annoyingly frequent basis."

"I should go." James walked to the door and stopped, his fingers on the handle. "Marriage is such a conflict to so many people, is it not? Lord knows I feel sick whenever my own marriage rears its head in discussion. There is no choice for so many of us. Just expectation."

"I assume your visit home involved such discussion?"

"It did, and it was bloody annoying." James scowled. "I will marry and return to my family estate in my own time and not before."

"And you told your father as much?"

"Yes."

"Then I wish you the best of luck."

James left the office and marched along the corridor; his hands curled into fists at his sides. Victoria was queen, so the urgency for her to produce an heir and secure the monarchy was somewhat understandable. She was head of state with responsibilities that stretched back hundreds of years. The pressure on her to do "the right thing" must be immense, a heavier burden than it would ever be for most.

Yet part of her continued to resist her fate in the same way as James whose anger simmered like the embers of a pyre, dangerous sparks dancing and flickering but not quite erupting. The more impatient his father grew, the more James resisted, his resentment increasing along with the wavering ability to retain his need to yell and scream, lash out and hurt.

Reaching Albert's apartments, James buried his irritation at the sound of unexpected laughter and entered the duke's bedchamber.

Albert stood in front of a tall mirror, Carr tying the laces at the back of the duke's waistcoat. Albert met James's eye in the mirror's reflection. "Ah, Mr Greene. I was beginning to wonder where you were. How is Lord Melbourne?"

James dipped his head in greeting, somewhat taken aback by the size of the duke's smile. "He is well, Your Supreme Highness. He sends his regards."

"I'm sure, I'm sure. And what of you? Have you managed to speak to anyone in Victoria's household about her preferences? I must admit I very much enjoyed her company on our jaunt around the castle's park this afternoon."

The lilt in Albert's German accent and his stiff decorum had most definitely softened, and James could not help but wonder if the change had been provoked that afternoon by the queen or the duke's supposed obsession with nature.

James cleared his throat. "I spoke to someone, sir, but I'm afraid she refused to reveal anything more about the queen or what happens in her chambers. My source has the utmost loyalty to Her Majesty."

"I see."

"And I very much doubt she will be swayed in her devotion. She is dedicated and committed to the queen's service."

"As I hope you will be to mine."

Something in the duke's tone stilled James, and he glanced at Carr who tipped him a wink. "*Will be*, sir? Am I not already—"

"If I should become more…how shall I say? Important to Victoria and the palace, I would rather like you to remain part of my household, Greene." He glanced at Charles. "Along with Carr, of course."

"It would be an honor, sir," James said, steadfastly ignoring the voice in his head telling him his return home would happen sooner than any royal wedding.

Albert held out his arms so Carr could slip on his jacket. "Good. I must say Victoria is proving an interesting, brave, and determined queen. A woman who knows what her role stands for and duty is profoundly important to her. I believe I could come to both admire and respect her on every level," the duke said, firmly. "Yes, our exchange of letters held substance, after all. If the queen wishes it, I would very much like to become her husband."

Chapter Twenty-Three

Violet carried her sketch pad and box of pencils through the Great Park, down a long slope that led to a pond with the most fantastical artificial waterfall. On such a rare afternoon off, she wanted nothing more than peace, quiet, and a tranquil view. She picked a spot beneath the shade of an oak tree, positioning herself on the blanket she had brought with her.

She had hardly stopped smiling since last night when the queen strode into her apartments and announced that she had asked the duke to marry her. The exclamations of congratulation and the pure joy of her ladies and Violet had been so raucous, Victoria had shushed them all into silence, not wanting word to reach her mother yet.

Just another sign of the fractured extent of their relationship, and how much the queen wanted to avoid the duchess's interference for as long as possible.

Holding a secret of such magnitude had Violet fit to burst with the humbling depth of the queen's trust in her. For knowing of the queen's engagement before others must surely prove her importance to Victoria. A bond Violet had forged through her own care, perseverance, and growth and established without any influence from her mother. A grateful validation that went some way to evaporating a little of her overbearing shadow.

Violet hovered her pencil over her partial sketch of

the waterfall, a landscape she hoped to find the courage to gift the queen once finished.

"I might have known you would choose to waste time at the first opportunity."

Violet jumped and looked up, her peace entirely shattered as loathing shrouded her. "Mama. What are you…?" She narrowed her eyes. "Did you follow me?"

"I was on my way to the queen's apartments and saw you leaving with that ridiculous book under your arm. I knew well enough where you were likely headed."

Violet shot her a glare before facing the pond. "I wish to be alone."

"And what makes you think I have any more want of your company than you have of mine?" Her mother walked to a bench close to where Violet sat and took a seat. "I am here because I've heard rumors that you are still spending time with Melbourne's lackey and are well on your way to ruin. So once again, I must step in and save you from your own stupidity."

"My own stup—"

"Stupidity, Violet."

Violet steadfastly stared ahead, anger burning hot in her chest. "I am not stupid, and I do not need saving, Mother. I have never felt so alive, so free…" Violet faced her. "So *seen*."

"And clearly Mr. Greene sees you. Sees every part of you, no doubt."

"I refuse to justify your words by responding to them. And for your information, James Greene is nobody's lackey and never will be. He is a good man. A proud, hardworking man."

"So it is as I thought."

"What is?"

"You have feelings for the cad. Why, your cheeks are red with your passion and defense of him."

"Don't be ridiculous."

Her mother's eyes sparkled with malice. "You are a fool if you think I will allow you to be associated with such a man. You are naïve and malleable, Violet. James Greene will eat you alive."

"As you so often try to do, Mama, yet I am still in one piece and breathing freely."

Her mother shot from the bench and gripped Violet's chin with such speed, she barely had time to blink, let alone react.

Her mother's nails dug deep into Violet's skin, her eyes dark with fury. "Now, you listen to me. The duchess believes the queen will propose to the duke this very evening. If you want to keep your position once Victoria is married, you must make yourself invaluable to her. Not behave like a harlot besotted by a man who has lain with more women than I can count." She pushed Violet's chin away and clenched and unclenched her fingers as though they pained her. "You have me to thank for every privilege you seem to be enjoying, but your life will only remain that way if I allow it. You are the duchess's spy and will remain so during the queen's marriage. If I think you are not up to the job, then I will see you dismissed and replaced with your sister."

Hating the tears that burned behind her eyes, Violet resisted the urge to touch her throbbing chin. "If the queen marries, she will not be under any obligation to have the duchess live with her. Her control will be over, Mama. As will yours."

"You will continue as I command until I tell you to stop. Whether or not the duchess and I are at court is of no matter. Wherever is chosen for the duchess to live, you will write or visit with news of the queen and what she has planned."

"Heavens above, can you hear yourself?" Violet trembled with frustration. "Am I never to make a single decision of my own?"

"What decisions would you like to make, my dear?" Her mother sneered. "How soon you can throw your virtue to the wind for Mr. Greene? Or when you can return home to your father so you can sit around and do nothing all day? You *are* nothing, Violet. A nobody. You have no right to think or dream, care, or want. What do you know of the world except for what I have allowed you to see? What do you know of people apart from those I've allowed you to meet?" Her eyes hardened. "You will stop this association with James Greene and do as I say."

Her mother abruptly turned and stalked away, not looking back once.

Violet watched through her tears until her mother had disappeared out of sight. Trembling and consumed with hatred, Violet stared at her half-completed sketch. Every part of her tempted to rip it from its binding and tear it into shreds. The landscape she had so lovingly worked on for the last two weeks felt like nothing but cruel, artistic torment.

The sense of freedom and beauty she had captured was now tainted with disdainful mockery. She would never live in the country as she sometimes dreamed, would never walk about her own gardens, her children at her heels and a husband waving to them from the house's doorway.

"Stupid, foolish..." Violet angrily swiped at the tear

that rolled down her cheek. "You know nothing, will always be nothing, *are* nothing."

She looked across the park, and her heart stumbled.

A distance away, James sat as still as a statue astride a huge piebald horse. He seemed to be looking directly at her. Violet could not move, barely dared to breathe. An overwhelming urge to stand and run to him swept through her, and she gripped her sketchpad as though it might anchor her to the ground where she sat.

But then he dismounted, his eyes never leaving hers.

Gripping the reins, he led his horse closer.

Violet could not take her gaze from him and willed him closer, the cross words they had exchanged evaporating with her need to speak to him…to be with him.

He tethered his horse to a low-hanging branch, before sitting on the ground beside her. "I saw your mother leave." He touched her chin, his gaze concerned as he checked her face, gently tipping her chin this way and that. "I saw her grab you."

Her cheeks warming, Violet moved from his grasp. "It was nothing novel." She forced a wry smile. "Nothing about my mother is ever novel."

"Then maybe it is you who needs to change, Violet," he said, softly. "Show her she can no longer control or treat you like this. That from now on your place is with the queen. Your mother is no longer in charge of your destiny."

"Unfortunately, it is her wish that I remain beside the queen, so she believes herself still in control of all that I do. The longer I remain at Victoria's side, the longer my mother can use me to the duchess's advantage. If I defy her and refuse to feed her fragments of what the queen has planned, my mother will ensure my place beside Victoria is taken by my sister."

"You have a sister?"

"Yes, she is in service in the same house I was trained. It is my mother's legacy that we both follow her to serve at court." Frustrated tears pricked her eyes as she thought of dear Elizabeth, her quiet, much more reserved sister being used in the same way. "The queen and I share the same history having grown up with controlling mothers and bear the same need to be free of them. Maybe I will have to marry to be rid of my mother just as the queen believes she will be able to exile the duchess once she weds Albert."

"You would like to marry one day?"

She smiled. "You sound surprised. Am I not worthy of becoming someone's wife?"

"Of course, you are." He gripped her hand, his dark eyes blazing with passion. "It would be a privilege for any man to call you his wife."

Heat crept into her cheeks, and Violet slid her hand from his as the urge to kiss him rose in her heart. "And what of you, James? You said that you had no wish to marry yet, but surely you would like to eventually?"

His gaze dropped to her lips before he stared at the waterfall, his jaw tight. "I daresay it is inevitable. The same as you have similarities with the queen, I do with Albert." He glanced at her. "When he arrived at court, he was not as happy as he is now at the thought of marrying Victoria. Their union was prearranged as far I can tell."

The secret engagement danced on her tongue, but if the duke had not told James, Violet would not betray Victoria's trust. "I see. But he would like to marry her now?"

"Yes, I think he would."

Hoping her growing, futile affection was somehow hidden from him, she forced a smile. "There, you see? There is no reason that you, too, won't feel the same way about someone one day."

"I fear *one day* may be far sooner than I'd like. My father is ill and grows impatient for me to take his place as head of the family, secure myself a wife and heir." He quietly laughed. "The romance of it stirs the heart, does it not?"

Violet stared at his turned cheek. He seemed so relaxed and carefree, it would be easy to believe he had risen in court from a lowly station, studying hard, his work acknowledged and rewarded. She really was proving herself stupid.

She looked at her drawing, feeling further away from him than before. "I forget who you are, James."

"What do you mean?"

Violet stared into his wonderful eyes. "I forget that you are to be a baron one day. That so much responsibility will be placed on your shoulders."

He looked into her eyes, and he took her hand. "When I'm with you, I'm not the heir to a baronetcy but a normal man, Violet. A normal, happy man."

He leaned closer and stole her breath with a gentle kiss on her lips.

"James…"

He dropped his forehead to hers. "There is every chance I will become as vile as my father once I marry and take over the estate. That is something I would never want you to see, Violet. Not ever."

"What do you mean? What is wrong with your father?"

He brushed his lips to hers a second time before abruptly standing. “I should go.”

Violet quickly pushed to her feet, her sketchbook falling to the ground. “Don’t go. Not yet.”

“I must or else I have no idea what I will say or do next.” His smile was wolfish, teasing, but it did not dilute the sadness in his eyes. He walked to the tree, untied his horse, and mounted. “I will see you soon.”

Violet lifted her hand to shield the sun from her eyes as he cantered across the great expanse of grass to the castle, her heart aching as she concluded James’s internal misery ran just as deep as hers.

Chapter Twenty-Four

On the 23rd of November, Victoria made her Declaration of Marriage before an assembly of Privy Councilors at Buckingham Palace. With that done, Violet and the rest of the queen's household was relieved from the burden of the engagement secret.

Happily humming to herself, Violet immersed herself in tidying the queen's bedchamber. As she stacked some books on a shelf by the window, her mind wandered to James. Her work and his meant they had seen very little of one another over the last two weeks, and Violet's feelings bounced from longing to spend time with him, to knowing the longer she stayed away from him, the more chance she had of preventing further damage to her heart. A heart she could no longer deny was fast becoming James's.

Their shared frustrations and uncertain futures had formed a tangible bond between them that would almost certainly lead to one, or maybe both, being hurt. His future, no matter how much he resisted it, had been set in stone by his ancestors. Whereas hers remained in her mother's hands until Violet found the courage to sever their relationship completely.

But how could she do that when the moment she gave up her position as her mother's minion, the vile role would immediately pass to her quieter, more malleable sister? Elizabeth was kind and reserved, enjoyed spending time with her father as Violet once had, and it sickened Violet to think of her sister as a replacement pawn who, at any moment, could be plucked from peace to suffer the cruel fate of being under her mother's watchful eye day and night, week after week, month after month.

Violet stared through the window at the gardens, her entrapment feeling entirely permanent now that she was aware their mother had Elizabeth waiting in the wings.

Lady Kingsley entered the room, carrying a huge vase of fresh flowers. "Good morning, Parker."

Violet turned and dropped into a curtsey. "My lady."

"How are things going along with you and dear James?" Lady Kingsley asked, placing the vase on the low windowsill. "I have barely seen him since the duke departed for Germany."

"Neither have I. I imagine Lord Melbourne is keeping him busy with whatever is involved in preparing a new consort. There must be a lot to arrange so the duke's transition takes place without provoking concern or upset at court or for the public."

Lady Kingsley raised her eyebrows. "Well, you appear to have given the matter much thought, Parker. If this knowledge didn't come from your conversations with James, who on earth have you been speaking to?"

"My mother, of course." Violet sighed, moving away to dust the surface of the queen's bureau and rearranging the ornaments on top. "She has only increased her reverence that I continue to act as a snitch on the duchess's behalf now that the queen's engagement has been announced."

"You have to find a way to free yourself of her." Lady Kingsley put her hands on her hips. "Her control over you is ridiculous when you enjoy such esteem with Victoria."

"Oh, believe me, my mother's dominance over me lessens every day," Violet said, her determination rising. "I have made it clear enough that I will not violate the queen's trust."

"So why does she persist?" Lady Kingsley stepped closer, her voice lowering as she glanced at the open doorway where voices gathered as the queen's ladies entered the adjacent room, returned from their morning walk. "The wedding is imminent and all too soon the queen will insist her mother is installed in a house of her own, far away from court. Once that happens, the Duchess of Kent's power over Victoria is finished, as your mother's will be over you."

Violet picked up a beautifully hand-painted jug and carefully ran the cloth over its surface. "Possibly, but there are consequences I must consider when it comes to my mother that go beyond me and my future."

"Oh?"

"I have a younger sister, and my mother has already threatened to bring Elizabeth to court as my replacement. I will not allow her to suffer the same fate as me. I love her too much." Violet replaced the jug on the bureau. "If my mother is forced to leave court, she is vindictive enough to ensure I go with her, but rather me than Elizabeth."

"Victoria will not let you go. Not now. Her love for you is proven in how often she summons you beyond your usual hours. How much she enjoys your company and the passionate protection she shows you. And what of James? He is well?"

"I believe so, but…"

"But?"

Violet turned away from Lady Kingsley's curious gaze. "It is for the best that we have not seen one another for a while."

"Has something happened between you?"

Keeping the vulnerability of her heart to herself, Violet shook her head. "No, but I am enforcing the distance as a safeguard to the future."

"What do you mean?"

"I suspect James will be appointed to Albert's service when he returns. And, if he is, James is all too likely to come into the duke's confidence."

"And that is a bad thing?"

"As far as my mother is concerned, yes. At first, she warned me to stay away from James, threatening my reputation and position with the queen as a consequence. Now Albert and the queen are to marry, the duchess has surmised that the duke could be instrumental in arranging her reconciliation with the queen. A far more powerful and influential figure than I could ever be."

"What does that have to do with James?" Lady Kingsley's frown vanished as understanding lit her eyes. "Your mother wants you to get as close to James as possible so he can conspire with you to ensure Albert plays a part in encouraging the queen's relationship with the duchess."

"Exactly. The duchess is under the impression that family is important to Albert, and he will urge a reconciliation. She even thinks they won't be long married before he'll want Victoria's agreement to start a family."

"Good Lord." Lady Kingsley sighed. "I had hoped he and Victoria might enjoy some semblance of a honeymoon before the whole court stands waiting for a child."

"It seems not. I'm also quite sure, when the time comes, my mother intends to choose my husband as though I, too, should consider duty over love."

"She really is the most…"

"I agree, but I will not allow her to use the only man I have ever had feelings for."

"Feelings?" Lady Kingsley placed her hand on Violet's arm. "Parker, have a care. James is the kindest, most wonderful man, but he is also a charmer and a flirt. As much as I like you, and I don't mean to be derogatory, but James will have to marry well one day. You know that. You will only end up heartbroken."

Violet stood firm against a wave of humiliation and forced a smile. "Don't worry about me, Your Grace. I will be just fine."

Lady Kingsley's gaze wandered over Violet's face before she smiled, her hand slipping away. "Good, because James is little more than a dalliance for a woman to enjoy. He is not the marrying type, but whether he likes it or not, his hand will be forced to some unfortunate woman one day. Mark my words."

Unable to resist the opportunity to probe a little deeper into Lady Kingsley and James's relationship, Violet turned to the bureau and wiped her cloth over another trinket. "And what of your feelings for James? Have you not at least fleetingly considered him as a husband?"

Soft footsteps sounded behind her as Lady Kingsley came to Violet's side. "No, and our flirtation came to an end once he began speaking to you. James and I had fun, Parker. Nothing more. If you think you can do the same and keep your heart under lock and key… Well, a woman has needs, does she not?"

Victoria walked into the room, her cheeks flushed and her smile wide. "Lady Kingsley, Parker, whatever are you doing huddled over there like that? Are you gossiping by chance?"

Violet dropped to a curtsey as Lady Kingsley walked closer to the queen. "Not at all, Your Majesty. I was just giving Mistress Parker some motherly advice about men preying on a woman's chastity."

Heat leapt into Violet's cheeks as she rose, hardly daring to look at the queen.

"Is that so?" Victoria laughed as she took a seat at the window. "Well, as long as Parker is under my care, she will have all the protection she needs. From men or otherwise."

Several other ladies entered the room and gathered around the queen, Lehzen requesting that tea be ordered, and Victoria's embroidery brought from the bureau. Grateful for the return of habitual commotion, Violet finished cleaning and hurried from the room, lest any more be said about her chastity.

Chapter Twenty-Five

James entered the queen's drawing room behind Melbourne and bowed.

"Your Majesty." The minister brushed past Lehzen where she stood in the center of the grand room and stopped in front of the queen. He kissed her outstretched hand. "You are looking decidedly happy this morning, ma'am."

"Well, I am now, Lord Melbourne. I am now." The queen walked to the sofa and sat, arranging the skirts of her navy-blue dress around her. "But I most certainly was not before I received a wonderfully reassuring letter from dear Albert in today's post."

"Oh?"

"Oh, indeed. If you consider the continuing debates surrounding the popularity of our union, the paltry income he has been allowed and how suspicion constantly encircles him, it would come as no surprise if he called the marriage off. Wouldn't you agree, *Lord* Melbourne?"

The minister glanced at James, his expression clearly conveying his disquiet at having his assistant stand witness to Melbourne's potential dressing down from the queen. "The duke is entirely in love with you, ma'am. He would never do such a thing," Melbourne said, facing the queen. "However, might I suggest that, if you wish to discuss private matters regarding the duke's feelings, we—"

"Of course, he would never do such a thing as call off the marriage! It is not I whom vexes him. It is you and your government." She pinned him with a glare. "All this opposition. It's not just dear Albert's income but a hundred other things, including doubt about his credentials as a Protestant. It is insufferable."

"The concerns of Parliament might be troublesome, ma'am, but they must be attended to. If the beginning of your marriage is to be free of grievance, it is best that these issues are resolved beforehand."

"That may well be, but it makes the stubbornness of certain ministers no less palatable."

James bit back a smile knowing full well how Melbourne's frustration with the queen grew the more beguiled she became with her future as Albert's wife. In fact, the minister's impatience seemed thinner with each passing day. It was becoming usual that Melbourne spoke of little else as he paced left, right, and center through his office, barking orders at James and anyone else brave enough to intrude on the prime minister's time. The situation was far from funny but still…

"Alas, it is testament to my future husband's wonderful personality," Victoria continued. "That Albert is willing to concede to Parliament's request that he only appoint English staff to his household rather than his own preferred German. A sacrifice I suspect will be accepted with blasé assumption by government."

"He has agreed?"

"Yes. He has also accepted Mr. George Anson as his appointed private secretary."

"Well, that is excellent news, ma'am. I will inform government—"

"But on one condition." Victoria turned to Lehzen, who stood at attention at the queen's elbow. "Kindly ask Parker to fetch the letter from atop of my bedside table, would you, Lehzen? The one sealed and for the attention of Mr. Greene."

James pulled back his shoulders, fought to hide his surprise. "A letter for me, Your Majesty?"

Melbourne glanced at him, his cheeks pink. "This is most irregular, ma'am."

The queen smiled at James, her blue eyes softening as she ignored Melbourne. "It seems you made a truly wonderful impression on my beloved Albert while he was here. So much so, *you* are the condition on which he has insisted if he is to employ Mr. Anson."

Melbourne cleared his throat. "Ma'am, I am not sure that I understand."

"It is quite simple," she said, slowly facing Melbourne as though he were an afterthought, and it was only James who concerned her. "Albert will agree to Mr. Anson as his private secretary on the condition that Mr. Greene becomes Anson's assistant."

James fought his smile as his gratification soared. So Albert had remembered his words about James being appointed to his service, after all.

"But, ma'am." Melbourne's jaw tightened. "Greene works for me. He is an integral and important part of ensuring my work proceeds smoothly."

"That may be so, but I will not refuse Albert's request," the queen said, firmly. "He deserves *something* he desires. Does he not?"

"Well, yes, but—"

"Then when the time comes you will release Mr. Greene to the duke's service. I am not asking you, Lord

Melbourne. I am commanding you."

James dipped his gaze to the floor lest Melbourne detect his delight.

As much as he enjoyed working for Melbourne, an appointment to the queen's consort was not only a huge rise, but a position of noted esteem. One his family would be unable to intercept. It seemed another delay to him permanently returning to the estate had miraculously fallen into place. Not that his father would see this turn of events as a miracle, rather as a royal pain in the backside.

"Ah, Parker," the queen said, her gaze moving to the bedchamber door. "Do you have the letter?"

"Yes, Your Majesty."

Violet entered the room ahead of Lehzen, and James's heart jolted. She did not as much as glance at him as she walked to the queen and handed her a sealed envelope before stepping away, her hands clutched respectfully in front of her.

The queen traced the duke's script on the envelope with her finger, an almost dreamy look in her eyes before she abruptly turned to James. "Now, Mr. Greene. It is my utmost wish that the duke's regard for you continues as it has clearly been established thus far."

James bowed. "Yes, ma'am."

"Alongside Mr. Anson, I am making you personally responsible for the ease of my future husband's return, prior to our wedding and thereafter. You will ensure he is content and made welcome wherever he goes. Do you understand?"

"I do, ma'am."

"You are to prepare the rooms next to mine for the duke and correspond accordingly with him in order to understand his requirements for décor." She held the envelope out to Violet. "Parker, if you would kindly give this to Mr. Greene. Now, Lord Melbourne…"

The queen's and Melbourne's conversation faded as Violet came closer. Their eyes locked as James took his time sliding the envelope from her fingers. "Mistress Parker."

She softly smiled, her beautiful blue eyes on his. "Mr. Greene."

James lowered his voice. "It seems you and I will once again be in each other's company from time to time."

"Indeed, it does."

"Parker!" Lehzen's voice cracked across the room. "Enough chitchat. Back to your duties."

Battling the urge to glare at the baroness, James gave Violet a discreet wink before she curtsied to the queen and hurried from the room. Forcing his attention back to Victoria, James stood tall as he waited for Melbourne to finish speaking.

"—then I assume I am free to employ Mr. Greene's replacement? Will I lose him immediately?"

"Greene can remain in your service for the required length of time needed for him to pass his knowledge to your new appointment," Victoria said. "But I would prefer that he start preparing for Albert's arrival as soon as possible."

"As you wish, ma'am."

"Very good." The queen turned to James, her eyebrows raised. "Do you have any questions?"

"Just one, ma'am. Might I ask how soon before the wedding the duke is expected?"

The queen gave a theatrical sigh as she rose from the

sofa and wandered to the window, her back to the room as she stared out across the gardens. "How I wish I could tell you my beloved Albert will be in the palace corridors tomorrow, Mr. Greene, but it is not to be. He has promised he will do his utmost to arrive at least a week before our special day, and I pray it is so."

"Which gives the palace ample time to ensure everything is to the duke's liking, ma'am," James said, doing his best to placate the queen even though his mind raced with the scale of what needed to be done.

It would soon be Christmas, and the palace would become a grotto of celebration and headaches. Once they began the new year, James would only have a few short weeks in his new appointment before Albert returned.

"I will write to the duke immediately," he said, feeling Melbourne's glare boring into his temple.

"Thank you, Mr. Greene." Victoria faced the stony-faced minister. "See, Lord Melbourne? Mr. Greene entirely understands his new position, so you can stop your blustering and congratulate your assistant on his elevation."

Melbourne turned, and James arched an eyebrow in a gesture of complete innocence.

The minister gave a pinched smile. "Congratulations, Greene."

"Thank you, sir."

"I hope you have considered your family's reaction to this new appointment." Melbourne's eyes glinted with undeniable triumph. "After all—"

"Surely, your family will be overjoyed?" the queen asked, her brow furrowed.

James slowly turned from Melbourne to face the queen. This new situation would not sit well with his father. Not at all. He coughed, Melbourne's undisguised and unexpected spite sticking in his throat. "I will need to inform my father of this promotion as soon as possible, ma'am. He is keen that I return to the family estate and may not welcome this news as much as I."

"Whatever do you mean? He should be immensely proud of your elevation at court."

"I fear that may not be case. My father does not always share my enthusiasm for my place here and feels I should be at home, preparing for the baronetcy."

Victoria studied him for a moment before she waved dismissively. "Nonsense. Your father is still a young man by most standards. Do not worry, Greene. I will write to the baron myself, and that should put an end to his concerns."

James struggled to hide his satisfaction and dipped his head. "Ma'am."

"And on that note," Melbourne said, his cheeks red. "Mr. Greene and I will take our leave. We have much to get on with."

"Indeed, you do." The queen smiled sweetly as she returned to the sofa and reached for her embroidery on the table next to her. "I will see you at dinner."

"Ma'am."

James bowed to the queen before he and Melbourne left the room. The moment the doors closed behind them, the minister turned on James, his eyes bulging. "This new appointment will mean extra work and longer hours before you even begin to think about new pastures. I cannot afford for there to be any mistakes in the transition from you to the person appointed to take your place."

"Of course, sir."

Melbourne pushed his hand into his hair. “I swear the queen takes infinite pleasure in dropping the unexpected on me. The closer she gets to marrying, the more she seems to enjoy rousing my temper.”

James pinched his lips tightly together.

He had no doubt Melbourne was more than a little nervous that the queen was already heavily influenced by Albert’s wants and wishes, despite the duke being thousands of miles away. What did that say about how strong Albert’s persuasion would be when he was at court? In her bed?

“Well, come on, then.” Melbourne strode forward. “We haven’t a moment to waste.”

Chapter Twenty-Six

"Ohh, how I hate my mother!" The queen fumed as she stormed into her bedroom.

Violet quickly stood from the floor where she had been petting Dash, the queen's beloved spaniel.

Victoria's cheeks were red, and her eyes blazed with fury as she plucked off her gloves. "Time and again, she insists that I am not preparing for Albert's arrival as I should be. That I have no idea of a gentleman's needs the way she does. The woman is a constant thorn in my side. How would anyone as cold-hearted as her know about true love?"

Violet stared at the floor, unsure whether to respond.

"Do you know," Victoria continued, not seeming to particularly address Violet, Lehzen, or the queen's dresser as they each stood at attention in different areas of the room. "She even suggested that I am letting my household run free and Lord Melbourne to act as my consort. How dare she!"

Violet lifted her gaze an inch or two as Victoria walked to her dressing table and sat, her dresser immediately attending to her. Violet glanced at the open doorway as conversation began between the queen and Lehzen. Should she make a hasty exit? It was highly likely if Victoria had been with the duchess, she had seen Violet's mother too, and the sight of her daughter would only amplify the queen's anger.

Even though Violet's role within the queen's apartments continued to expand with each passing week, the coercion she suffered from her mother and the duchess remained unchanged. Not that Violet hadn't altered in her compliance. Her confidence had increased so much that she became ever more certain she would find a way to ensure her sister's freedom as much as her own.

Yet standing up to her mother was one thing, quarrelling with the queen's mother quite another, and clearly the duchess had fathomed as much. For the last week, every message, every order or command of Violet had been written or delivered by the duchess rather than Violet's mother. Moreover, since she had learned of James's future intimate access to Albert, the pressure the duchess put on Violet to compel James to her purpose was relentless.

Not that Violet believed the duchess's wishes would ever be met.

Victoria's glee that her nuptials meant her mother would soon be gone from court was apparent in everyday conversation. So much so, it was assumed the Duchess of Kent would be evicted from court before the queen rose the morning after her wedding.

"Parker, you have my every sympathy." Victoria met Violet's gaze in the mirror. "Your mother is like a limpet attached to my mother's every word and action."

"I'm so sorry, ma'am."

"You are not to blame for your mother or mine. They are poison. Both of them." The queen shook her head. "On top of that, I'm afraid I have further bad news, Parker."

Tension inched along Violet's shoulders. "Ma'am?"

Victoria sighed, the anger in her eyes softening with sympathy. "It seems your father has taken ill, and I have no choice but to grant your mother's request that you leave court and return home so that you might nurse him."

"My father is ill?"

"Yes. And you look equally as surprised as I am that your mother would not request leave so that *she* might return to him." Victoria's jaw tightened. "But, of course, we know she and my mother are not entirely human."

Suspicion unfurled in Violet's mind. "I had no idea my father was unwell."

Her father had seemed robust enough when he last wrote to her. Had something happened? Or had her mother reached the end of her patience and found a way to deliver on her promise to remove Violet from the queen's service?

She looked at the queen. "I can't help but suspect a ruse, ma'am. My mother has been looking for a way for me to return home."

"It's possible, Parker, but your mother appeared genuinely disturbed, if not a little distraught. I am reluctant to doubt the word of someone who appears to be suffering, even if that someone is Mrs. Parker. You will leave at the week's end, and your sister will take your position in your absence." The queen smiled softly. "Do not look so downtrodden. You will soon be back."

So her mother *had* delivered on her threat. She had found a way for Elizabeth to take Violet's place. Furious, Violet clasped her hands tighter. "Might I write to my father in the first instance to discover what ails him, ma'am? I just cannot trust my mother's words."

"That maybe so, but I have given her my agreement.

I'm sorry, Parker, but it is sometimes advisable to choose your battles. Do as your mother asks, and you will soon return."

Sickness coated Violet's throat as Lehzen nudged her and nodded, encouraging her to accept the queen's advice with grace. Yet acquiescence stuck in Violet's throat despite Lehzen's support. As the weeks progressed, the baroness acted more and more benevolently toward Violet. Not overly so, but enough that Violet had begun to believe they worked together amiably. The improvement in their relationship was proof of the progress Violet had made alone.

Not that it mattered now. By orchestrating Violet's return home, her mother had cut out her daughter's heart and stolen her joy…just as she said she would.

Violet gave a semi-curtsey. "Yes, ma'am."

"Do you know I've just the thing to take your mind off leaving. At least for today." Victoria smiled, her eyes glittering with mischief. "How does a picnic sound?"

"A picnic?" Violet looked from the queen to Lehzen and back again. Bright, winter sunshine shone outside the window, but the temperature hardly gave outdoor eating any appeal. "I don't understand."

"I think it's time someone from my household explored the arrangements thus far for the duke's arrival. If I speak to Lord Melbourne, he'll only tell me what I want to hear. It would be good to have you find out the truth. What do you say?"

"I will, of course, do anything you ask of me," Violet said. "But I don't understand how I'm the right person to—"

"I understand from Lady Kingsley that you have quite the friendship with Mr. Greene."

Heat leapt into Violet's cheeks. "We are friends certainly, ma'am."

"Well, then." The queen's smile widened. "You will soon learn I am not one for discouraging a little romance and courtship for my ladies, yourself included. I might be separated from my beloved Albert, but that does not mean my heart is closed to my ladies' happiness. I want you to go to the apartments next door and invite Mr. Greene for a picnic this afternoon. Even at this time of year, there is something so irresistible about sharing food outside with someone of whom we are fond. I'm sure Mr. Greene will agree."

Violet smiled at the mischievous twinkle in Victoria's eyes.

"Tell him I have instructed it so he can inform you of his progress with the duke's apartments and that he is to come to you with continuing updates from this day forward." The queen grinned. "Nothing could be simpler. Now, off you go."

Violet left the queen's apartments and headed along the corridor to the duke's rooms. She slowed her steps as she neared the entrance. It would only be more painful to see James now that her time at court drew to an end. Her insolence with her mother had led to an inevitable reality Violet did not want to face.

With such all-consuming power over each of her children—her husband too, it seemed—her mother's control was eternal. Yet deep inside, Violet vowed to keep stoking the rebellious, independent fire that burned inside her. A volatile anger that had every possibility of exploding the next time she saw her mother.

As it was the queen's command that she leave court, Violet could not disobey, but once she was home, if she found her father well, she would make plans for her permanent return to court. Her mother's days of dictating her future were over. As much as she loved her father and would ensure his comfort, if he were truly ill, his wife should be at his side. A fair and loving man, her father only wanted his family happy, and Violet was confident he would support her wish to remain at court.

Striding forward, she knocked on the closed suite door.

When no one answered, she entered the anteroom.

"Be careful, man! Do you want to see me in the bloody tower?"

James's voice rang above the scuffle and clang of industry as Violet stood on the periphery of what looked to be some frighteningly assiduous furniture placement. On the other side of the hubbub, James stood jacketless, his shirtsleeves rolled up to reveal strong forearms, his necktie gone, buttons undone just enough to reveal a smattering of dark chest hair.

Desire pulled deep at her core as she unashamedly drank in the sight of him, free of constraint and royal standards. At that moment, she imagined him as an ordinary working man, coming in from a day's toil. He would take one look at her, rush forward, press her up against the wall, and kiss her passionately until…

"Violet?" James yelled above the din. "What are you doing here?"

She almost leapt out of her skin. "James, I…I've been sent by the queen."

"The queen?" Irritation etched his face, clearly unhappy about being interrupted. "Just a moment."

He gave instructions to the men moving the furniture while Violet walked farther into the room, looking around and trying to get her shocking carnal yearnings under control.

Solid footsteps sounded to the side of her, and then James cupped her elbow. "Let's go into the next room. I can hardly hear myself think."

He led her into the adjacent room and closed the door.

"Why has the queen sent you?" he asked brusquely, his usually dark eyes almost black with irritation. "Please tell me she hasn't changed her mind about the duke having these rooms."

Although distracted by the inches of his exposed chest, his unexpected anger made her nervous. She had not seen him like this before. "No, not at all. She has sent me here to talk to you. She would like you to update me on your arrangements thus far."

"Now?" He pushed his hand into the fallen hair at his brow, his fingers gripping the strands as he glanced at the door as though desperate to return to his work. "I'm right in the middle of things. Can I report back to you later?"

"She's…" Violet hesitated, feeling foolish carrying out the queen's instructions when he was quite clearly busy and not at all happy. "She suggested we take a picnic."

"A pic…" His eyes widened before his cheeks mottled. "It's December!"

"I can pack some hot soup and bread. It will be…fun."

"Fun? I can't take myself off for a picnic when there is so much to do. What on earth will the workers think of me?"

His mood made her decidedly uneasy, but she could

not defer on the queen's request. She lifted her chin. "I'm sorry, James, but if the queen commands it, we cannot refuse. Besides, it will be the last time you will see me for a while."

He dropped his hand from his hair, his dark eyes boring into hers. "What are you talking about?"

"I have to go home. My mother claims my father is ill. Not that I believe a word of it, of course. But still, I must go."

"Your mother is exerting her power again?"

"I have little doubt."

He exhaled heavily, his gaze softening. "Give me an hour, and I will come. Where shall we meet?"

"In the folly."

"Very well." His gaze dropped to her lips before he reached around her toward the door and opened it. "You should go."

He stood so close, Violet could see flecks of blue in his eyes, smell the subtle maleness of him. Her treacherous heart swelled with silly, dangerous love. She forced a smile and ducked under his arm and through the open doorway.

Chapter Twenty-Seven

As James neared the folly, he wondered why Violet had chosen such a secluded spot for them to meet. It was late afternoon, the time when most courtiers retired to their rooms for a nap or to relax before the evening's formalities began.

The time when Violet was often free from her duties until the queen needed her again in the evening.

Was it her intention that they be entirely alone?

He turned the corner and stopped.

She had laid out a thick blanket and two cushions on the stone floor of the folly, the hazy, winter sun streaming through the pillars of the stone structure, its soft light surrounding her. James's heart stumbled. She looked different somehow. Lovelier than ever if that were possible, but also more self-assured, a little more comfortable. Wrapped in a coat and hat, she sat back, her arms propped behind her and her eyes closed. With her face tilted toward the sky, a gentle smile on her lips as though she basked in the sun on a warm, summer's day.

Never in his life had he met someone who gave him such peace whenever he looked at them. Who so easily lifted him, steadied him. It was as though Violet possessed an invisible power to calm his temper and fears in equal measure.

James swallowed as understanding hit him square in the chest. *God help me, I'm falling in love with her...*

As though sensing him nearby, she opened her eyes and straightened, lifting one hand to shield her eyes from the sun. "There you are. I was afraid you wouldn't manage to get away."

He forced a smile despite being entirely shaken and walked forward. "I was glad to escape, if the truth be told."

James swallowed against the sudden dryness in his throat. Falling in love was the last thing he should have allowed to happen. He had always known his role and that he would eventually marry a gentlewoman, if not a woman of the aristocracy. How in God's name could he bury the treacherous euphoria that bubbled inside him now that he understood the truth of his feelings? Suddenly, he yearned to hold, kiss, and touch Violet, right here, right now and be damned whoever might see them.

He sat down beside her and looked at the food she had laid out, arched an eyebrow to lighten the madness in his heart. "This is quite the feast. Did you raid the kitchens?"

"I would have prepared something smaller had I not seen you so hard at work." She passed him a cup of tea. "I assume you're famished?"

"I am." He took the cup. "Thank you."

As she poured steaming soup from a jug into two bowls, James stared at her turned cheek, noticing how quickly her smile diminished and a crease furrowed her brow. He would have wagered a hundred pounds that she thought of her mother rather than the food she handled.

"Violet." He touched her wrist, urging her to put down the jug. "Leave the soup for now. Talk to me."

She met his gaze, and James's heart hitched to see

tears in her eyes. He put down his cup. “Oh, my love.”

“Don’t…don’t call me that,” she said quietly, wiping her fingers under her eyes and looking at the sky. “I’d prefer your earlier agitation to kindness.”

Guilt whispered through him as he battled the need to pull her into his arms. Whenever he became overly stressed, his family traits surfaced, and this time Violet had witnessed it. “I didn’t mean to be snappish. I have so much to arrange and can’t help worrying from time to time if I am up to the task.”

“Of course, you are. The duke chose you especially. Whatever Albert saw in you impressed him enough to ask that you be moved from Melbourne’s service to his. That is quite the request.”

“Maybe. But you’re maneuvering the subject.”

“Only because talk of my mother will sour what might be our last time alone for a while.” She looked at the greenery ahead of them. “It’s so beautiful here. There was a time I dreamed of living in the country. Of falling in love and marrying a man who would cherish me as I would him.” She gave a wistful smile. “We’d have three children, two boys and a girl. Three dogs.” She glanced at him, her eyes glittering with unshed tears. “A Labrador and two spaniels. And we’d live as tenants to landed gentry who treated us kindly and with respect. A good and happy life.”

James barely dared to breathe. The life she described sounded idyllic but so far removed from his future it was laughable. He shouldn’t be here. Not when her dreams suddenly felt far too much like his own. A simple existence with responsibility only to his loved ones, rather than a hundred or more families who would one day look to him to ensure they did not starve.

"It's silly, isn't it?" she asked, softly.

"What is?"

"Dreaming."

Unable to bear another moment without touching her, comforting her, James took her hand, gently kissed her gloved fingers. "You will have all you dream of one day. I know you will."

She dropped her gaze to their joined hands. "I'm not sure my mother will ever allow me to be happy. Nor my siblings. She has proven that time and again."

"Then go home, Violet. Escape court *and* your mother." He stared into her eyes, willing her to hear him for her sake and, now it seemed, his too. "Your mother's ambitions lie at court. It is here that she wishes to see you rise and one day inherit the power she thinks she has gained. Surely, if you are away from court, you are free from her."

"You want me to go and never come back?" Hurt flashed in her eyes before she drew her hand from his and stared ahead. "I see."

"That's the last thing I want." James touched her chin, turning her to face him. "But I do want you to be happy. Life at court, or anywhere else where protocol and restriction is rife, is clearly not what you want. Why shouldn't you be free to live with children and dogs and nature? Concentrate on your painting. That is who you are."

"My painting?"

"Yes. That is where your passion lies, does it not?"

She softly smiled. "Yes, it does." She looked out across the grass. "I am painting what I hope will be a wedding gift for the queen. It is almost finished."

James smiled. "Victoria will be thrilled by such a

personal gift, I'm sure."

She sighed. "How do you know me so well, James?"

He slipped his hand from her face. "You have no idea how I would like to get to know you even better, but what I feel and want is irrelevant."

"Of course, it's not. Why would you say such a thing?"

"Despite my resistance to return home, I cannot abide the thought of being the heir who brings an end to my family's legacy. An inheritance that stretches as far back as the English Civil War. My obligations might frustrate me, but they also make me immensely proud."

"And your passion only shows me more of who you are." She smiled softly. "And I like you very much, indeed."

Even though it was clear she tried to bolster him, James desperately needed her to understand all that he wanted for her was happiness. "But those obligations do not apply to you, Violet. Your esteem with the queen has shown what a good, loyal, and hardworking person you are. Go home. Work far away from the palace at a place where you can fight for your independence, so that you might live the life you want. So that you might paint and become the artist you long to be." He took her hand. "Please. For me."

She stared back at him, her gaze unreadable, and James fought the passion burning inside him. He loved her. It was too late to stop his heart from whispering her name or his body from yearning for her touch, but that did not mean he would selfishly try to keep her at court. Nearby, where he could see her often. She deserved to be free to fly as only Violet could.

"Violet—"

"Kiss me, James."

"What?"

"Please."

He stared at her, the soft pleading in her beautiful blue eyes impossible to ignore. He leaned closer, and she pressed against him, her tongue gently touching his…and in that moment, James wanted her nowhere else but in his arms. Preferably forever.

Chapter Twenty-Eight

Violet stood on the steps of her family home and lowered her bags to the ground.

She stared at its Georgian façade as fondness and love, dread and resentment, mixed in a maelstrom of emotion leaving her no idea if she was happy or angry to be here.

It had been three months since she enjoyed a carefree weekend at home with her father and sister, but it felt so much longer. And now she had returned, she would prepare for Christmas alone with her beloved papa. After all, her mother was as unlikely to leave the duchess's side during the season as Violet was of giving her mother a yuletide hug. Of course, as an additional punishment to Violet, her mother would also prohibit Elizabeth from coming home for a visit.

Inhaling a strengthening breath, Violet pulled her key from her pocket as worry edged into her heart that her father might be genuinely unwell, and her mother had not been telling tales about his health. If that were true, she would not leave his side until he recovered, or God forbid… No, she would not think of his passing.

She pushed the key in the lock and opened the door.

Picking up her bags, she stepped into the hallway, just as the family's housekeeper emerged from the dining room.

"Oh…Miss Violet!" Mrs. Kettling's chubby cheeks

expanded, squishing her eyes to slits as she pressed her hand to her breast. "Oh, my word, what a wonder it is to see you. Your father will be so happy you are home. Come in, come in."

"It's lovely to see you, too." Violet smiled as she put down her bags and began to unbutton her coat. "How is Papa?"

"He's…well enough." The housekeeper frowned. "Not that I would know the state of him if I didn't force myself into his study three times a day with food and water."

"So he's not seriously ill? Mama gave the distinct impression he was not very well at all. Hence why I have left court to be here."

Mrs. Kettling planted her hands on her hips, her gaze uncertain. "He's not been out and about much, but I'd say he is going along as well as expected considering his usual stubbornness."

Violet hung her coat and hat on the stand beside her. "Then it is as I suspected. Mama wanted me home for reasons of her own rather than to care for her husband." She glanced toward the stairs. "Would you mind putting my bags in my room? I'd like to see Papa straight away."

"Of course. Of course." Mrs. Kettling shooed Violet away with a wave. "I'll make some tea and bring it up. Go on now, the master will be over the moon to see you."

Violet climbed the stairs and walked along the second-floor landing and knocked on her father's study door. Her heart swelled. She loved him as deeply as she loathed her mother.

"No more tea for me just yet, Mrs. Kettling." Her father's voice came from behind the closed door. "I am perfectly content."

Smiling, Violet entered the room. “Well, you might be content, Papa, but I am far from it considering how long it’s been since I saw your handsome face.”

“Violet!” Her father whipped off his spectacles and slowly rose from his desk, abruptly abandoning one of the watches he was employed to fix and coming toward her with his arms outstretched. “What a wonderful surprise.”

Violet stepped into his embrace and breathed in the scent of pipe smoke and glue that was so entirely him. The familiarity enveloped her in the safety she had been lacking throughout her time at court. Maybe coming home for a while would not be such a bad circumstance, after all.

Her father leaned back and studied her, his blue eyes sharp. “So it seems your mother made good on her threat.” He shook his head, exhaustion showing in the lines around his eyes. “That woman can be so immovable at times.”

Violet stared at him in disbelief, anger at her mother rising once again. “You knew she wanted me home and away from the palace?”

“Indeed, I did,” he said, returning to his desk, wincing as he cautiously lowered into the seat as though his body grieved him. “She tried to pull me into her scheming, asking me to write to you telling you I was unwell. I flatly refused and hoped she’d leave you be.” He shook his head, his gaze angry. “I might have known she would continue in her will regardless.”

Violet sat in a wingback chair alongside him and fought to keep the rage from her voice. “So you are not unwell?”

He glanced at her before turning back to the watch.

"I am not entirely fit but certainly well enough that there was no need for you to leave court."

Violet looked at the disarray littering the room. Boxes and trays were scattered on every available surface; rags and cloths, tools and leather straps spilling from jars in a myriad of colors. The jumble made her regress to the little girl who used to come in and out of her father's study, pestering him with her need to help. So patient and loving, he would often give her the trunk of brushes and paints from the high shelf above his desk. The same paint set he had used as a child.

That was when and how her love of paint, art, and brushes had started.

She looked fondly at his bowed head. "Her scheming to get me home is just the beginning."

"Oh?"

Resentment coiled inside of her as Violet told him about her mother's determination that she orchestrate reconciliation between the queen and her mother, the Duchess of Kent. "Yet now Victoria is engaged to Albert, such a reunion is impossible. I have no doubt Her Majesty will remove the duchess from court within a day or two of the wedding."

"Hmm, and I am certain your mother will find a way to hold you responsible for such an outcome." He picked up the watch and studied its minute mechanisms over the edges of his half-spectacles. "I fear your mother has lost all of her principles since she became so close to the duchess."

"Quite possibly, but her plan to punish me by sending me home has backfired in the most spectacular way."

"It has?"

She smiled. “Yes, because now I am seated beside you, I am immensely pleased to be here.”

He lifted his gaze, soft with love. “I’m glad.” The silent connection between them bloomed before he winked and returned his attention to the watch. “So tell me about Victoria. You are pleased to be in her service?”

“Oh, yes. She has shown me so much favor, and I’m sure she will call me back to court soon enough. Mother might have placed me in the queen’s household to carry out her dirty work, but she did not expect Victoria to take to me so kindly. This attempt to separate me from the queen will be short term. Mark my words.”

“I’m glad to hear it.” Her father winced, his color paling as he shifted in his chair. “Court life obviously suits you.”

Immediately, Violet stood and laid her hand on his shoulder. “Clearly, you are not at death’s door, but something is most definitely wrong. What is it?”

“I have a touch of pain in my ribs. Nothing to worry about.”

“And how long has this pain been bothering you, Papa?”

“Not long. A week or two at the most.”

“Have you seen the physician?”

“No, and don’t talk about such things around Mrs. Kettling. The woman is like a horse with a bit between its teeth. ‘I’ll fetch the doctor, Mr. Parker,’ ” he said, mimicking the housekeeper’s voice. “ ‘I’ll ask the medicine woman across town to come and look at you, Mr. Parker.’ ” He rolled his eyes before returning to the watch pieces scattered atop his desk. “Fuss, fuss, and more fuss.”

Violet’s heart filled with love for the man who

claimed to still love his wife, despite her long absences away at court and her obsession with the Duchess of Kent. He was such a wonderfully kind and patient man. "Papa, it will do no harm to be make certain there is nothing wrong. I will remain here into the new year." She slipped her hand from his shoulder. "Why don't I send for the doctor? Just to be sure."

"No. Now, go on with you. I have much work to do."

Horrible trepidation that her father suffered far more than he admitted niggled at Violet as she slowly walked to the door. Maybe her mother hadn't entirely lied and suspected something was amiss. Could her determination that Violet return home possibly have been founded in care rather than spite?

Violet turned the doorknob. "I'll unpack and then bring you a nice cup of tea."

Her father merely grunted, so she left the room and walked upstairs to her bedchamber where Mrs. Kettling had left her bags by the bed. Sitting on the familiar eiderdown, Violet dropped backward onto the mattress and stared at the ceiling.

It was right that she was home where she could care for her father and spend Christmas with him. Moreover, it was fruitless to remain angry with her mother. Even though it was clear she was not prepared to nurse her husband herself, her mother knew Violet perfectly capable of doing so. Whereas Elizabeth did not possess the same nurturing intuition, so it made sense for her to be at court in Violet's stead.

"All right, Mama, you win," Violet murmured as she pushed herself upright and looked at her bags. "I will not leave Papa until I am certain he is well. Victoria or no Victoria...James or no James."

Chapter Twenty-Nine

"James, please. Sit down."

Having been home for the Christmas season for almost two weeks, James's irritation neared breaking point as he kept his gaze on his mother and slowly lowered into his seat at the family dining table. He scowled. "We are barely into the new year, and once again marriage is all we talk about."

"Just listen to your father. Please."

His father glared at him from across the table, a glass of brandy hovering at his lips.

Trying his level best to remain in control of his rising temper, James addressed him. "I am not shirking my responsibilities nor running away as you constantly infer. I chose to spend Christmas at home, did I not?"

His father smirked before taking a hefty gulp from his glass. "Yet it is clear to one and all how desperate you are to flee back to the palace."

"Is that any surprise? All you talk about is my marrying or the estate. Both subjects that I am aware of and have every intention of honoring. In time. You have my word, but please just trust me and give me this time to serve the duke, a man who will soon be king consort."

Silence fell in the dark wood-paneled room, the crystal glasses and chandeliers above the vast dining table only emphasizing his father's repeated insistence that every piece of furniture, every carpet and tapestry, every tenant and servant in Cassington Park would one day be under James's management and care.

The problem was that any pride James might have felt constantly conflicted with deep claustrophobia.

"To be appointed assistant to the private secretary of the future consort is hardly something to sniff at," he said. "Once upon a time, you would have been shouting my elevation from the rooftops. Yet since I turned twenty-eight, it seems nothing else matters in my life past this house."

"It has nothing to do with your age, you fool!"

"No? Then why—"

"It has everything to do with mine! I am not well." His father's face reddened, a vein bulging in the center of his forehead. "You must marry and bring home a wife who is prepared to stand by you as your mother has me. I am proud of your achievements at court, and I understand the obligation you have to the queen's future husband, but I want your assurance that it will not be to the detriment of your inheritance."

Afraid his father risked a burst blood vessel, James calmed his tone. "How could such an affluent position become disadvantageous to my inheritance? Surely it will only serve to bolster our name and reputation?"

Picking up his glass, his father drained it and then held it aloft, his gaze unwavering on James. The footman standing behind his father came forward and took the glass before walking to the bureau to replenish it. Tension stiffened James's shoulders as he glanced at his mother. Her jaw tight, her eyes never left her husband. It seemed she shared James's concern that another drink was the last thing his father needed.

Once the newly filled glass was placed in front of

him, James's father curled his fingers around it. "You need to be here to truly understand what is expected of you. Yes, I have taught you a lot, but not enough, and time is running out. Your forefathers deserve your full attention and care to the estate." His father's voice cracked with emotion. "Not to the goings on at Buckingham Palace or Windsor."

Something wasn't right. Although his father wanted him home, this exaggerated condemnation of the palaces was far from usual. A royalist to the very marrow of his bones, his father's service and his father's before him had been the foremost reason why James had started working for Melbourne upon leaving the army.

James glanced at his mother, her paleness only accentuating the gravity of what James sensed hovering over the table. A secret unsaid.

He turned back to his father. "Are you dying?"

Silence stretched until his father picked up his brandy and sipped. "We are all dying."

"That does not answer my question. There has to be something more than what you are telling me behind this constant pressure for me to marry and leave court—"

"Fine." His father slammed down his glass, two spots of color leaping into his cheeks. "If you are determined to serve the duke, the least you can do is promise me the next time we see you, it will be to tell us of your engagement to a woman of the highest and most capable breeding. You will not make a success of your inheritance if you are unmarried and without heirs waiting in the wings. You need a wife, and I suggest you start with those ladies closest to the queen. They will understand exactly what you are asking of them when you propose."

Those ladies closest to the queen…

James wasn't sure whether to laugh or cry as Violet's beautiful face appeared in his mind's eye. So be it…

"You have not answered my question. I have a right to know." He stared at his father, a strange sickness deep in his stomach. "Are you dying?"

His father held James's gaze before he lowered his glass, looked down into the amber liquid. "I am ill, James. That is all." He lifted his head. "But that does not mean I do not think of my mortality, because I do. All the time."

James inhaled a long breath, slowly released it, not entirely sure he believed his father's demise was not infinitely more serious than he implied. "I will do as you ask and put as much intention into finding a wife as I will serving Albert. In return, I expect your full trust that I will carry out what I have said in fair time and leave me to my own devices." He abruptly stood, sending the legs of his chair scraping across the floor. "For now though, I bid you both good night. I leave for London first thing in the morning."

James strode through the lobby, and when he reached the grand staircase, he stopped with his foot on the bottom step. He looked at the portrait beside him, the first of a line of ancestors that ascended to the upper landing. Dark eyes so very much like his own stared back at him, his grandfather's smile amused. His temper had been as notorious as his father's before him and his son's today, undoubtedly, James's too once he became immersed in the pressures of the estate.

Curling his hand tightly around the banister, bitterness coated James's mouth, the natural but suppressed impulse to rant and rave, spit and snarl lingering just beneath the surface of his self-control. Whenever he felt unjustly challenged or prohibited the freedom to do as he wished, horrible burning anger simmered inside him. Anger he had managed to control thus far, but deep down, James knew that would not always be the case.

"Excuse me, sir." Branson approached and held out a tray bearing an envelope. "This came for you while you were at dinner."

"Thank you. I'll take it upstairs. Is there fresh water in my room?"

"Indeed, sir."

With a final glance at his grandfather's portrait, James climbed the stairs and walked into his bedroom, firmly closing the door. He tossed the letter onto his bed and proceeded to undress. Once washed and in his nightclothes, he lay back on the pillows and opened the letter.

Dearest James,

I hope you are well. I have been at home caring for my poor papa for the last four weeks, and I am sorry for not writing sooner. My daily prayers for his recovery have been in vain, and it seems my pleas will go unanswered. My beloved papa is dying, James, and so I will not be returning to court until after the burial that is certain to break my heart.

I wish you well in your new, exalted role and look forward to whenever I might next see you. It is my sincerest hope—if my grief allows—that I will return for the queen's wedding.

Please take care of yourself and, if possible, assert my love and loyalty to Victoria.

Yours,
Violet

James's heart beat fast, his jaw clenched against the anguish he felt for Violet's pain. The letter was dated almost a week ago. He could not leave her to manage her father's suffering alone. She had made no mention of her mother or any other member of her family being with her. The mere thought of her nursing her father and her sorrow with no one for company was intolerable.

Leaping from the bed, James grabbed his robe from the wardrobe and left his bedchamber. Descending the stairs, he looked around the huge hallway and frantically peered into the empty rooms.

"Branson? Are you there, man?"

Frustration and impatience whirled through him as James searched one room after another, cursing the labyrinth of his family home.

Rapid footsteps sounded behind him, and James turned, barely managing to refrain from grabbing Branson's lapels. "There you are! Please ensure my bags are packed and everything is stowed on the carriage as soon as possible after breakfast tomorrow. And I will need someone to drive me to Essex."

"Essex, sir? I thought you were returning to the pal—"

"Essex, Branson. Essex."

"Of course, sir." The butler gave a curt nod. "I will ensure all is packed and ready. Might I summon your father, sir? You look—"

"Like I cannot wait to leave? Like someone else might need me more than my family? Well, you're right, they bloody well do!"

James stormed back to the stairs and took them two

at a time. God willing, he would be in Essex and with Violet by early evening tomorrow.

Chapter Thirty

Violet carefully laid her father's hands on his chest before gently squeezing his cold fingers. She closed her eyes, and tears slipped from beneath her lashes. "I love you, Papa."

The loss of a father, who had loved her so unconditionally, struck raw and painful in her heart, and Violet bowed her head, willing her father's soul to God where she hoped it might rest in eternal peace. It was early morning, and the drawn drapes offered welcome respite from an outside world that Violet lacked the strength to face. She had never felt so lonesome.

An hour before, she had entered her father's bedroom and immediately sensed his passing. Still, she had been woefully unprepared for the profound and instant grief that shrouded her. He had been such a source of comfort in a family steeped in distance or ambition. She, her father, and Elizabeth, the only three of six who thought of others more than themselves, of service to make other's lives better and, hopefully, happier. Her mother and brothers, in contrast, were each so intolerant and unforgivably critical in their views of people and their circumstances.

A quiet sniffle proceeded Mrs. Kettling as she entered the room.

Violet swiped her fingers beneath her eyes. "Will you see that the clocks are stopped and the mirrors turned to the walls? We must ensure things are done properly regardless of how helpless I feel."

"Of course." The housekeeper sniffed. "You leave that with me."

Violet released a shaky breath, her heart heavy and her mind reeling with what needed to be done. "Have you mourning clothes? If not, I will arrange for some to be made for you."

"I have a mourning dress. Don't fret over me, child." Mrs. Kettling gently curled a comforting hand around Violet's shoulder. "You should write to your mother. It will take her a couple of days to come from the palace."

Violet looked at her father's still body. "I wrote to her five days ago telling her of his declining health. I made it obvious it was time for her to come home. There's every possibility she could arrive today or tomorrow."

"All the same, I think it best you send word again seeing as the master has now—"

"You're right. I should also let my brothers know. Mama will bring Elizabeth from the palace with her, I'm sure."

"I'll find the masters' regiment addresses, miss. Don't you worry, we'll ensure the funeral Mr. Parker deserves. I will also pull out your mother's and sister's mourning attire and check it over. I'm sure it has not been taken from its coverings since your grandmother passed. Oh, it will be such a shame to see you and your mama called back to court dressed in black, but that is the way of it."

"I hope now my mother might consider staying home permanently. After all, she is the new head of the household until John comes home."

"Do you think your brother will move his family here?" Mrs. Kettling's brow furrowed. "Only I'm sure they will already have a housekeeper and—"

Violet lifted her chin and clutched Mrs Kettling's hand where it still lay on Violet's shoulder. "Don't you worry about losing your position here. I will make sure John understands that if he intends to move in and take over things, you are to remain. You have served our family…my father, with so much diligence and care I will not have that go unacknowledged."

"But if he has a housekeeper who he is used to—"

"If I am forced, then I will find you a position elsewhere, but it will not come to that." Violet smiled softly and raised her eyebrows. "Maybe I could arrange for you to work alongside me in Her Majesty's chambers. How will that be?"

Mrs. Kettling quietly giggled and swatted Violet's arm. "Oh, heavens above. Can you imagine me at court? It would be like a charwoman taking high tea at Brown's."

Mrs. Kettling left the room, and Violet's smile dissolved as she pulled her chair closer to her father's bed. Grateful for some solitary time to reflect on how much he meant to her and how his love had been the balm that had soothed a little of her mother's harshness over the years, Violet laid her forehead on his arm.

Despite the strict way her mother ran their household, once her position serving the duchess was secured, she'd had no qualms about leaving her family to the care of her husband and their household staff.

Of course, the whole house had been happier living and working alongside Violet's father. Laughter often mixing with jesting as they went about their work and play. Their contentment was never made so obvious whenever Violet's mother deigned to visit, and every room filled with palpable tension once more. Then her mother would return to court, and Violet and her sister would close the door behind her, breathing a collective sigh of relief.

Violet blinked back tears and rubbed her hand over her father's cheek. "And then she bid me to join her at the palace. Oh, Papa, I never wished to leave you. I'm so sorry I didn't make more effort to visit."

The front door knocker sounded downstairs, and Violet turned to the open bedroom doorway. Mrs. Kettling's stout footsteps thudded along the wooden floorboards as she hurried to answer the door, and Violet strained to hear the muffled conversation.

Not recognizing the voices, she stood and pressed a gentle kiss to her father's forehead before making her way downstairs.

Halfway down, shock brought her to a standstill.

"I am indeed sorry, ma'am, but if you could just tell Mistress Parker that I am here, then…" James pushed some fallen hair from his brow, his agitation palpable. "I am sure she will allow me to speak with her. Even for just a minute or two."

"Mr. Greene, you claim to be acquainted with Mistress Parker, but I had no idea you existed until a moment ago," Mrs. Kettling said with a firm shake of her head, a rare wobble in her voice as though she fought tears. "This is a house in mourning, and I believe Mistress Parker would prefer to be left in—"

"Mourning?" His eyes widened. "You mean—"

"It's all right, Mrs. Kettling." Violet descended the remainder of the stairs, her gaze on James and her heart lifted by his obvious concern. “Please, come in, James.”

Mrs. Kettling bristled. “I am not sure your father, God rest his soul, would be happy for an unknown gentleman to enter the house with no one else here to ensure our safety.”

Violet smiled through her tears with her gaze locked on James’s. “I am sure Papa would make an exception, Mrs. Kettling. Mr. Greene is from the palace. He is Lord Melbourne’s assistant.”

“Oh!” The housekeeper dipped a hasty curtsey. “I do beg your pardon, sir.”

“Not at all. I am pleased to see Mistress Parker is so well looked after.”

“Oh, she is, sir,” gushed Mrs. Kettling, her cheeks pink. “She is my own heart, believe me.”

Tears pricked Violet’s eyes as the combined sadness of losing her father and the unrelenting joy of having James arrive on her doorstep merged, bringing a lump to her throat. “Let’s go into the parlor. Would you like a drink? Tea? Something stronger? I’m sure I can find some of my father’s brandy—”

“Tea will be welcome. Thank you.”

Violet nodded. “If you’d be so kind, Mrs. Kettling?”

“Of course.”

As Violet stepped toward the stairs, she stumbled, her grief washing over her once more. James swiftly took her elbow, his other hand at the small of her back.

She briefly closed her eyes. “Thank you.”

“Are you all right?”

“I am now.” She managed a small smile. “Thank you.”

He stared at her, his concern clear when he did not return her smile. “Did your father pass this morning?”

"During the night judging from his coldness this morning," she said quietly as they ascended to the next floor. "I found him just over an hour past."

"I am so sorry."

They entered the parlor, and once they were seated, James cleared his throat. "I left Oxfordshire as soon as I received your letter. I regret that I arrived too late to help you with your father's care."

"You are here now, so you are indeed helping me." Violet inhaled a long breath. "I wrote to my mother a few days ago telling her I was fearful for my father's passing, so I am expecting her home soon. I will write to my brothers, and they will help with the funeral arrangements." Tears welled in her eyes. "He was a wonderful father. So very different than my mother."

"Your love for him is clear."

"He was a good man."

They lapsed into silence for a few moments before James spoke again. "I have taken lodgings nearby, so you must allow me to do all that I can to help."

"You are very kind, but you can't possibly stay. What of your position at court? Lord Melbourne will be expecting—"

"The minister is not expecting me for another few days at least."

Touched by his care but knowing readily accepting his presence was steeped in selfishness, Violet shook her head. "But still, you can't stay here just for me."

"I can and I will." His gaze was tender but determined. "Your grief is what concerns me above all else right now."

Protestations battled on Violet's tongue, but it was no use, her need to have him with her was too deep. "Thank you."

Chapter Thirty-One

Four days later, James walked from the boarding house, the letter he'd received from Melbourne that morning tormenting him from within the inside pocket of his jacket. The minister might well have demanded that he return to court forthwith, but James had little intention of complying until he was certain Violet did not need him to stay.

Although her brothers had written to confirm they would be home as soon as possible, they had not yet arrived from their barracks. Neither had Violet's mother or sister returned from the palace. Her family's absence added more weight to Violet's troubles, and because of that James found containing his temper steadily harder.

Melbourne's impatience for his return had not come as a complete surprise considering it was the second week in January and he had left court before Christmas. But it had been a surprise that the minister confirmed Duke Albert would be arriving in early February, a week before the royal wedding on the tenth.

In truth, the arrangements were immense, and James had no time to lose. Yet he refused to leave Violet. It would have been a possibility had her mother arrived, but she had not sent a single word regarding her delay or even a note of her grief. It was despicable.

Arriving at Violet's house, he knocked and stood back, smoothing the lapels of his coat with gloved fingers. How would he tell her of Melbourne's summons when the circles beneath her eyes grew darker and her body thinner?

The door opened, and Mrs. Kettling ushered him inside. "Come in, sir. It is so cold out today."

"Thank you." James removed his hat and brushed the sleet from its brim as he looked toward the stairs. "How is Mistress Parker this morning?"

"Oh, well enough, sir. Well, enough." She took his hat and coat, her gray eyes glinting with unshed tears. "She is a strong girl. No one, not even her mother, can take that away from her."

Soft footsteps sounded before Violet emerged from below stairs clutching a letter, her gaze distracted.

Mrs. Kettling coughed. "Mr. Greene is here, my dear."

Violet jumped, her expression startled. "James, good morning." Her immediate smile seemed suspiciously forced before she turned to Mrs. Kettling. "I have left Cook and Lizzie with a few errands to run. Could you make sure the food is on hand with the grocer?"

"Of course. Don't fret now. We will see your father to his resting place in the best manner possible." The housekeeper's cheeks reddened. "Even if it is just you, me, and Mr. Greene at his graveside."

The swipe at Violet's mother and siblings was clear, and James couldn't help but bite back a smile. He was glad Violet had Mrs. Kettling beside her.

Once the housekeeper disappeared below stairs, Violet faced him, irritation storming in her beautiful blue eyes. She held the correspondence in her hand aloft. "A letter from my mother."

The ferocity in her eyes sent unease whispering through him. "What does she say?"

"I am so angry. She and Elizabeth will not be returning for the funeral. My mother claims it unseemly for women to attend funerals and that I should not do so either. She *demands* that I return to court. She demands as though she is Victoria herself. How dare she?"

James shook his head, fury for Violet stirring in his chest. "God above, what is it about our parents that they cannot see past duty and propriety?"

"She is so cold. How could she turn her back on my father as though their marriage meant nothing to her? She is like a devil in her ambition. A selfish, blind Beelzebub. All she cares about is the duchess." She tilted her face upward, clearly fighting tears. "It may not be the norm for women to attend funerals, but this is my father, James." She dropped her chin, her furious gaze on his. "I *will* go."

"Of course, you will, and so will I."

She paced back and forth, her neck and cheeks flushed, a stray curl touching her cheek. "She tells me to leave all remaining arrangements to my brothers and Mrs. Kettling. Apparently, the queen was distraught to hear of *our* loss and that I must come back so that she might comfort me."

"Well, that's something."

Violet abruptly stopped. "The queen's sympathy is of no conciliation at a time like this, even if I dared to believe my mother speaks the truth. Can you not see? My mother has no care that her husband is dead. That her children have lost a loving father. All she cares about is hers and her daughters' service at court. All she cares about is getting me back in the queen's household so that

I might carry out any or all of her and the duchess's underhanded mischief. I can't help worrying that Elizabeth is buckling under the strain of it all."

James clasped his hands behind his back, surmising now would not be a good time to attempt touching her. "You may be right."

"I *am* right."

Knowing that he would have to return to court, no matter how much he might not want to, James took a deep breath. The sooner he told Violet the truth of Melbourne's summons, the sooner they could work out what to do. "There's something else."

"What?"

"Melbourne has urgently requested my return." James braced for her reaction. "The dukes will be arriving from Germany for the wedding in two, possibly three weeks. I imagine it is mania at court. Whatever anyone's position."

Her gaze flitted over his face, her mind clearly racing. "Then you must leave."

"I won't leave, yet. I will stay until after the funeral, at least."

She began pacing again as she pushed the same unruly curl behind her ear with trembling fingers. "How could I have forgotten how close it is to the queen's wedding? Now I feel that I must be with her. But if I go, my mother will think she has entire control over me once again." She faced him. "Yet despite the loss of my father, I cannot imagine missing a wedding that I know will make Victoria so very happy. She has been so good to me. I should be with her."

"And you can be. Once you are truly ready. It would be a mistake to go before." Risking her wrath, he gently took her elbow and looked into her worried eyes. "Once you have buried your father, you can decide when you wish to return to court. The queen will have a hundred things to think about, and although I'm sure she'd be delighted to see you again, I cannot imagine her commanding your return."

Her gaze dipped to his mouth for a moment before she met his eyes, her shoulders dropping. "No. She is not my mother after all."

"Precisely."

"The funeral is in three days, and my brothers have assured me they will be here." She placed her hand on his chest, her gaze on his. "Go back to court. I will not keep you here when you are needed there. I will be all right."

"Violet—"

"Please, James. Go now, I haven't the strength to fight you. It is for the best that I am alone."

"But that's the last thing I want."

"But it's what I want. I appreciate your care for me, but, for now, each of us is needed elsewhere." She slid her fingers from his chest to take his hand before leading him to the closed front door. "I will write to you with the date of my expected return to court in due course."

Indecision warred inside him. A huge part of him wanted to stay, but another part was filled with pride to see her so changed, so determined without her mother casting a shadow over her. This was the woman he loved, the woman who inspired him and bolstered him to stand up for what he believed in and wanted. He could not go against her wishes as so many others had to her and him alike.

"I will be thinking of you every minute of every day

until I hear from you again."

She smiled, a tear rolling over her cheek. "And I you."

James stepped closer and slowly, tentatively, brushed his lips over hers. Encouraged when she did not move back but leaned in, he pressed his hand to the small of her back and eased her closer, deepening the kiss.

They silently parted, and she softly smiled. "I will see you soon."

With a curt nod, James turned and opened the front door, lest he never leave.

Chapter Thirty-Two

Two weeks later, having received not one but two letters from the queen subtly suggesting Violet's return, she had waved goodbye to Mrs. Kettling, Cook, and the family's maid, Lizzie, promising to visit to check all was well with them as soon as possible after Victoria was married.

But for now, Violet was back at court and eager to play her part in making sure the wedding went along without a hitch.

Battling the constant lingering grief over the loss of her father, she smoothed the skirt of her black satin mourning dress and entered the queen's apartments for the first time in over a month. At least here she was guaranteed not to run into her mother.

The queen's laughter bounced from the walls along with the excited chatter and giggles of her ladies. For the first time in weeks, Violet genuinely smiled, her relief at being back at court surprising her when home was where she had been needed for weeks. Yet Windsor and Buckingham Palace felt like home too, her father's death having taken away all that had kept her heart in Essex.

"I am so excited to visit the chapel today," the queen exclaimed as Violet entered her bedchamber. "For I will see it through new eyes as the place I finally become Albert's wife!"

Smiles and applause prevailed as Victoria's ladies

and Lehzen gathered around her, adjusting the rich, burgundy material of the queen's dress, or putting finishing touches to the pearls and feathers in her hair. Violet stood a short distance away, breathing everything in, the atmosphere filling her like much-needed oxygen.

"Parker!" The Duchess of Sunderland smiled as she approached Violet, her arms outstretched in welcome. "You're back."

"Your Grace." Violet dipped a semi-curtsey, and the duchess took Violet's hands, her kindness causing tears to prick the backs of her eyes. "And very happy to be so."

"I am so sorry for your loss. Come." The duchess squeezed Violet's fingers and pulled her in front of the queen. "Your Majesty, look who I found creeping about the place."

The crowd around Victoria parted, and Violet's heart hammered with sudden trepidation. What if she had misinterpreted the queen's letters and it was impatience that caused her to write rather than the possibility she missed her? The letters had been short and matter of fact, after all.

Violet lowered into a deep curtsey. "Your Majesty."

"Oh, Parker, what a wonderful surprise." The queen beamed and walked closer, her skirts swishing across the rich oriental carpet. "How are you? I was so sorry about your poor papa."

"I am well, ma'am," Violet said, relief washing over her as she rose. "Your letters gave me much comfort."

"I am glad." The queen's gaze roamed over Violet's face, her eyes twinkling with happiness. "And so pleased you are back in time for today's grand event."

"Ma'am?"

"I'm sure you know my beloved Albert is due at the palace next week?"

Violet smiled at the flush in the queen's cheeks and the romantic light in her eyes. "I do."

"Then you must accompany us to a viewing of the chapel. I am soon to be married there, you know."

"But I couldn't possibly come with you. I am hardly a lady, and I am sure some courtiers would not look kindly on my—"

"Nonsense." Victoria laughed. "I refuse to leave you here all alone when you have just returned to me. We will all go. Lehzen, my ladies, you, and, of course, Lord Melbourne." The queen took a fan from Lehzen who stood beside her, carefully eyeing Violet. "You can travel in the carriage with the Duchess of Sunderland, Mr. Anson, and Mr. Greene, and I will travel with Lehzen and the prime minister."

Before Violet could protest, the queen swept past her to the door.

"Come along, everyone." She laughed. "I cannot delay another minute!"

Violet could barely look at Lehzen. Surely, she would have misgivings about Violet accompanying the queen—travelling in a carriage through the city, no less—when she was a mere housemaid? Perhaps this surprise privilege would be a step too far for the baroness and she would say as much to Violet's mother, igniting further trouble when Violet had only just returned.

No matter how much she strove to believe she had escaped her mother's long-reaching fingers, the dread that knotted Violet's stomach proved just how much influence her mother still had over her. Her father's death and the angry sadness it had evoked certainly sparked an increase in her confidence, but she could hardly deny her anxiety was still there, chafing like a slow-healing wound. Her daughter attending the queen as she was today would either excite or anger her mother, depending on the role she wished Violet to play going forward.

She pressed her hand to her stomach and followed the others, battling to find the courage and conviction that the loss of her father had somehow given her. But now that he was no longer at home—that his open arms offering comfort and safety were no more—it suddenly made all Violet endured from her mother so much harder to bear.

Wrapped in furs, hats, and coats, the queen's entourage walked into the courtyard and approached the row of resplendent black-and-gold carriages that awaited them.

The first people Violet saw waiting to see off the queen were her mother and sister. Dressed in black, they stood alongside the Duchess of Kent who clearly held little regard for her companion's loss and wore a dress of the deepest red. Each of their faces were thunderous as they stared directly at Violet. Even though she began to tremble, Violet pulled back her shoulders and defiantly met her mother's gaze.

Do you see me, Mama? Despite all you have done and continue to do, still I stand and still I rise.

"I believe you are traveling with me, Mistress Parker."

Violet's heart jolted as she met James's beautiful brown eyes. She grinned and took his proffered elbow. "Indeed, I am."

Her mother's glare bored into her back as Violet walked confidently to the waiting carriage, one of its benches already occupied by the Duchess of Sunderland and George Anson. They were immersed in quiet conversation, their expressions relaxed and both seemingly impervious to Violet and James joining them.

Violet settled back against the plush velvet seat as James laid a blanket across their knees. He winked at her, his impish smile causing Violet's toes to curl in her boots. The man was an incurable flirt, but it was so wonderful to see him that she immediately forgave his wickedness.

As they set off through the streets of Windsor toward London, crowds gathered along the roads waving and cheering beneath the hazy winter sun. Complete and utter astonishment that she was among the entourage delighted Violet, the breadth of her smile so wide her cheeks ached.

"You look happy." James smiled.

Violet laughed. "I feel as though I am in a dream."

"It makes my heart sing to see you this way. I have been so worried."

"When I received the summons to return to court, I wasn't sure I had the strength, but now I'm here…"

"You're glad to be?"

"Yes."

"And your father's funeral? Did it go along as well as can be expected?"

"Yes. My brothers were there and Papa's devoted staff, of course. Some of his customers, present and past, came, too. That would have made him especially happy."

"Good." James's gaze lingered on her mouth, before he lifted his eyes to hers. "I want to ask you something." He glanced at Mr. Anson and the Duchess of Sunderland before stealing his hand discreetly over Violet's. "Now you are back, will you allow me to court you, Violet? Officially, I mean."

"Court—" Her heart hammered as she slid her hand from his grasp, her cheeks warming. "Do not tease me, James."

"I'm not." His dark eyes grew somber. "The question is asked in earnest."

Humiliation burned inside her despite the chill air, sudden tears stinging the backs of her eyes. "You know as well as I do that there can be no future for us as a couple," she whispered, glancing at the duchess, relieved to see her focus was on the crowds. "Why ask me such a thing when you know me to be grieving?"

"But—"

"No, James. No."

She looked into the street, her heart beating fast. She had come to believe James genuinely cared for her, yet here he was playing with her heart. Her hope that he might one day hang up his boots as the court's Lothario had been ridiculously naïve. Men like him enjoyed playing with women's affections as much as they did their bodies. His tormenting might well have been meant to cheer her or raise her spirits, but the opposite was true. Worse, it showed just how little he really knew her.

"Violet, please look at me."

She swallowed past the lump in her throat. "No."

"When I went home, my father was reluctantly impressed by my appointment to Albert's household," James said, his voice lowered almost to a whisper. "But he was also adamant I use the opportunity to find a wife."

"So you thought you would have a little amusement with me?" She glanced at the other side of the carriage again. "I thought you cared about me."

"I do, and my asking to court you is not done as amusement. I hope that we might deepen our relationship. The only instruction my father gave me was to select one of the queen's ladies, so that is what I am doing."

"It is not funny, James."

"Are you not one of the queen's ladies? Are you not travelling in the queen's train to view the chapel where she is to marry? You *are* one of her ladies, Violet, whether you accept that or not."

She shot him a glare, and he met her gaze with a hardened stare. "I have never been more serious about anything. Please, just consider what I am asking of you."

He faced the crowds alongside them and confidently acknowledged their waves with an elegant nod of his head, proving all too clearly how his comfort in such grand surroundings differed to Violet's complete unfamiliarity.

Unable to believe James's feelings for her were real, Violet spent the rest of the journey turned away from him. James, *her* James, had thought to tease her in the harshest way possible. He, above all, knew how little love she had in her life, and now he claimed he wished to extend their friendship in a manner that she had not dared consider—no matter how much her heart had wanted to these past few months.

They arrived at the chapel, and Violet hurried inside behind the Duchess of Sunderland, praying James gave her some much-needed space. She had no wish to speak to him now or even on the return journey back to Windsor.

The chapel's interior was a breathtaking vista of stained windows, flickering candles, silver and gold, polished wood, and worn gray stone. Violet stared in awe as she slowly walked along one of the aisles, tentatively gliding her fingertips across the edges of the pews.

Yet James's words overshadowed this unprecedented and undoubtedly once-in-a-lifetime moment. She had the sudden urge to run home, back to Essex, back to the life to which she would only ever really belong. Her position at court was neither genuine nor steadfast, she merely playacted something she wasn't and never would be.

"Parker, why so glum? Do you think of your papa?"

Violet jumped at the queen's voice beside her before dropping into a hurried curtsey. Guilt that she had been thinking of James and not her father pressed down on her. "I am just entirely enthralled by the chapel's beauty, Your Majesty. It is the most wonderful building I have ever seen. Thank you so much for allowing me to come with you today."

"It is my pleasure." The queen slid her hand into the crook of Violet's elbow. "But I do not believe you were thinking of the chapel. Walk with me."

Violet glanced at the queen's ladies standing a polite distance away, their eyes flitting over her, curiosity showing in their raised eyebrows or frowns. When she met Lehzen's gaze, the baroness nodded slightly, her gaze laced with encouragement rather than anger. Could it be that the baroness was coming to like her? Maybe even respect her?

"I have missed you at court, Parker," the queen said, quietly. "But now you are back, and I am to be married. That makes it more important than ever that I know you are happy to continue in my service."

"Oh, I am, ma'am. Truly."

"I really wish I could believe that, but I look at your face, so etched with anxiety, and know that you continue to fret about your mother and mine. But they will soon be gone, as I promised they would be. You, though, will remain in my chambers if that is your genuine wish."

Touched by Victoria's vehemence and care, Violet could not have been more grateful. "It is, ma'am. More than anything."

"Good. Then your future at court is settled."

Violet studied the queen's turned cheek as she stared ahead, smiling and nodding at her courtiers. She was so young and beautiful yet carried such gargantuan responsibility. Violet could not imagine how it must feel to walk in Victoria's shoes. How on earth she managed to be so caring and observant, especially of people lowly in her household like Violet.

Violet swallowed. "Could I ask you something…personal, ma'am?"

A soft smile curved the queen's lips. "Ah, so it is as I suspected. Your melancholy is steeped in the complexities of romantic love as much as the love you bore your father. Am I right?"

Violet cheeks warmed. She would never admit her true yearning for a happy ever after to anyone. The queen included, and James most of all. Not when, in doing so, she risked her mother discovering her amorous dreams and then doing her utmost to viciously destroy them.

"No, ma'am," she said. "My question is not about romantic love, but about us as women in a man's world."

"I see. What is it you wish to ask me?"

Gathering her courage, Violet pulled back her shoulders. "When you became queen, you held an admirable passion to lead your life and country on your own terms. So much so that—"

"Indeed, I did. I still do."

"Yet…"

A flicker of annoyance flashed in the queen's gaze. "Yet what?"

Violet's heart raced. "Yet now you are to marry the duke. Surely then any decision you make will not be entirely yours. Will the duke not influence you? I need to know what changed for you to allow a man into your life with such trust? What makes you so certain that Albert is the right man to stand beside you? That he will not do all he can to take your power and make it his own?"

Victoria silently appraised her, her study roaming over Violet's face before she gently cupped her cheek. "Love, Parker. Love changes all. Everything about Albert, from his looks to his countenance, to his intelligence and wit speaks to my heart. I am confident he does not seek to control me but help me. Only when a woman feels so strongly for a man that her life would be entirely empty without him should she relinquish any measure of independence. And with Albert, for me at least, that time has come."

"But…" Violet hesitated, knowing she stood on unsteady ground by verbally doubting the queen's word, but her need for reassurance remained. "Are you absolutely certain those things are enough to ensure it will always be *you* making the decisions?"

The queen's eyes glittered with abject resolution. "Yes."

A sudden dread of falling in love stirred in Violet, her mind racing with the perils of making a foolishly emotional mistake. If James were serious about courting her and she agreed, would it one day lead to him controlling her in some way or even many ways? Would he demand she give up her role at court? Would she have to surrender the somewhat frail power she had gained through her time serving the queen? That instead of her mother, it would be James who pushed and pulled the boundaries of her life? The prospect sickened her.

"You have turned quite pale, Parker. Let's us walk closer to the entrance," the queen said. "If my words have frightened you, I urge you not to marry until you feel as I do now. The duke will never rule over me as far as England is concerned, but as for our home and private life, I am happy for Albert to take the lead."

"You are?"

"Of course, I intend to be a dutiful wife to him in every way, and to my mind, the man is always the head of the household." She smiled widely and slipped her hand from Violet's elbow. "Come now, no more of this talk. We have a wedding to think of. Ladies, come closer, would you?"

As Victoria was encircled by her ladies, Violet looked across the pews, and her breath caught.

James stood a distance away, still as a statue, watching her. Her heart stumbled. He had the potential to be everything to her that the duke was to Victoria, but no matter the queen's assertions, Violet could not risk giving James her heart.

Her mother had told her over and over again that she would be nothing without her. Yet she was now a valued member of Victoria's household and would remain so even with her mother gone from court and living elsewhere serving the duchess.

How could she succumb to James's advances now

and have him endanger all she had achieved? She had to remain strong and do what she must to maintain her importance to Victoria. Sacrifice and surrender all—her heart's desire too, if necessary—because it was beside the queen that Violet's true happiness lay.

Chapter Thirty-Three

James stood by the carriage waiting for Violet to emerge from the chapel. The queen had already boarded the royal carriage, and everyone else would soon be away, but he refused to leave without taking Violet's hand and having her look him in the eye.

Her shock and horror at his suggestion that they deepen their relationship, that she accused him of tormenting her, had rocked him to his core. He had never been so sincere with a woman, and the fact Violet doubted him hurt. Yes, he was somewhat guilty of teasing and tormenting the opposite sex from time to time—mostly for a desired result that ended in a certain physicality—but that had never been the case with Violet and never would be.

The moment he set eyes on her, he was attracted to her, but once they had spoken, he knew she was different than any of his past dalliances. What he had not expected was his initial interest in her to bloom into a burgeoning love that was testament to his instinct and her beauty, intelligence, and charm.

"Mr. Greene, shall we?"

Turning, he looked straight into Violet's eyes, barely resisting the urge to step back. Deep coolness had settled in her blue gaze that he had not seen before, her chin tilted and not a twitch of a smile in sight.

Unsettling confusion whispered through him as

James offered his hand, and her fingers curled around his before she stepped into the carriage.

She nodded politely to George Anson and the Duchess of Sunderland, confidently meeting their gazes before taking her seat. Unease lifted the hairs on James's nape. It was as though the Violet he knew had walked into the chapel, been touched by God, and miraculously metamorphosed into someone wholly different. A woman in command, more regal and, ironically, looking and acting every inch the matriarch of a grand family.

It was also clear that this new Violet wanted nothing to do with him.

He climbed aboard, and the carriage jolted away.

Rare insecurity wound through James as he stared at the people lining the streets. Had Violet spoken to someone inside the chapel, and that person had said or done something to entirely change her attitude and care toward him? Or was this the real Violet, a woman he had no idea existed? One to whom he was by no means equal. Her aloofness and poise made him leap from feeling insulted and angry to abjectly nervous and fascinated.

When he could not abide her silence any longer, he abruptly turned.

"Have I upset you?" he asked quietly, sliding a sideways glance at Anson and the duchess. "If I have, I can only apologize."

Violet jerked her shoulders nonchalantly as she continued to look away from him. "Not at all. In fact, after speaking to both you and the queen, I know exactly who I am now and who I wish to be in the future."

So it was the queen with whom Violet had spoken inside the chapel. He dared not contradict the queen or in any way insinuate Her Majesty was mistaken for risk of

Violet turning her back on him forever. Her immovable loyalty to Victoria was just another reason why he loved and respected Violet so completely. However, whatever the queen had advised her meant he was ousted from Violet's plans without being given an opportunity to plead his case and prove his love.

James swallowed his annoyance, unused to being on the receiving end of such torment. "And who are you now?"

"Well, Mr. Greene…" She lowered her voice, her eyes twinkling as she leaned closer, her manner almost conspiratorial. "I am a person who intends to rise. Become the first woman not of noble birth to be lady in waiting to the queen. From that…" She shrugged. "Who knows? Maybe, when I am ready, I'll go on to marry a great man."

Dangerous irritation stirred inside James as she flashed him a smug smile before facing the street once more. James clenched his hands in his lap as the infamously volatile Greene temper simmered in his gut. He fought back with all his might.

He was not his father. Not yet at least.

Having always assumed the possibility of his all-consuming narcissism emerging once he had children, maybe it had prematurely bloomed now that James found himself in love with a woman who did not love him back.

Well, over his dead body would he leave things like this between them.

"You have fallen awfully quiet, Mr. Greene," Violet murmured, still looking into the street. "One would almost think you have run out of interesting, titillating things to say to a woman…at long last."

He narrowed his eyes at her turned cheek.

She faced him, her brows raised, but the glee in her eyes soon vanished as their gazes locked. Her cheeks mottled, and the skin at her neck moved as she swallowed. “And now you’re angry.”

He glared, his battered self-esteem smarting. “Not angry. Affronted.”

“Why? Is it only you who can torment and tease?”

“Not at all.”

“Then why—”

“Because if marrying a great man is one of your aspirations, I do not see why you would entirely dismiss me as a contender. After all, I am a man set to inherit a grand estate,” he said quietly from between his teeth, conscious that Anson and the duchess had fallen suspiciously silent. “I will one day be a baron with wealth and property. Is that not enough evidence of the great man you seek?”

Her color deepened, and uncertainty warred in her gaze. “Those things do not matter to me. A great man does not necessarily equate money. Don’t turn my words into something they are not.”

“I am merely questioning your agenda. If you are seeking a man as I’ve described, allow me to court you. To prove myself worthy of you. After all, in doing so, you will get a head start on your ambitions, will you not?”

She glared, her cheeks darkening until she turned back to the crowd and inched away from him.

James could not stem his smile as he looked in the opposite direction, raised his hand to wave every now and then. Violet’s anger permeated the distance between them. Despite being unsure about the temperament or agenda of the woman who had walked from the chapel,

James suddenly suspected he might come to like this version of Violet even more than the original. He could almost picture the future sparring between them, the passionate words and challenges, the erotic reconciliations…

"Fine." She whipped around to face him. "There is a play at Windsor's theatre on my night off. You will take me."

Completely stunned by this turn of events, James glanced at Anson and the duchess. They stared back at him with identical expressions of amusement and expectation.

He drew back his shoulders and faced Violet as though she were the enemy rather than the sweet object of his desires. "That sounds most agreeable."

"Very well. If Mr. Anson can spare you that evening, we will go."

She turned away from him, and James risked another look across the carriage.

He could have sworn both Anson and the duchess blinked back tears of mirth…no doubt due to his actions and expression rather than Violet's.

Chapter Thirty-Four

Violet hurried through a maze of corridors as she headed for one of the many exits from Windsor Castle. Excitement fluttered in her stomach, and her heart beat fast as she emerged into the small courtyard at the back of palace, a short distance from where she and James had agreed to meet for their night out.

The trip to the chapel had only been two days before, but Violet still very much felt like a new woman, one entirely affected by Victoria's words.

"*Only when a woman feels so strongly for a man that her life would be entirely empty without him should she relinquish any measure of independence.*"

That singular sentence had struck Violet so deeply, it was as though a whole new purpose—a new mentality—had opened inside her and suddenly the course of her life felt clearer than ever before.

Yes, she wanted to marry, have children, live in the country, but all of that would not come from a place—or at a time—that she had not considered very precisely and very carefully. These were not times when women could think with a head full of romance and dreams of domestic bliss. Despite being raised under the strict rules devised by the duchess and Lord Conroy, Victoria had managed to break free. Not from the responsibilities of her office, of course, but she was at liberty to make decisions with regard to her personal life and what made her happy. She was consciously walking into marriage with Albert of her own free will, content in the knowledge she would retain control of certain aspects of her life and willingly relent on others.

That was something Violet could have, too.

The higher she rose in the queen's esteem, the more independence she could gain and the more distance she could insert between herself and her mother. The coldness she had shown by not returning for her husband's funeral had been the final swipe of the sword that severed her control. Violet narrowed her eyes as she stared ahead. She would walk through fire before she ever allowed it to return.

The knot of fury that had lain in the pit of her stomach for as long as she could remember had slowly began to loosen, and it felt wonderful. Violet stopped walking, closed her eyes, and pulled a long, fortifying breath deep into her lungs. She planned to enjoy this evening, and having such bitterness in her heart would only ruin what she hoped would be a time of fun and laughter. Of risk and rebellion. She had no doubt James would have come to his senses by now and accepted his family meant for him to court a real lady in waiting, not a housemaid with fantasies of becoming a lady of importance—and a painter—one day.

Their friendship was too important to compromise with such nonsensical talk. She wanted to keep James close, to guard and respect the trust and flirtation that had grown between them. She wanted him to be her place of safety where she could return, if and when she needed or wanted and have him depend on her the same way. What more could someone like her ask for than to have that special person with whom she could talk, trust, and care for?

Hurried footsteps sounded behind her. “Violet! Wait right there, I wish to speak to you.”

Opening her eyes, Violet turned, her anger instantly ignited. “I have no wish to speak to you, Mama.”

“Have you no sympathy that I came from your room at the other side of the palace looking for you?” her mother panted, a hand pressed to her breast. “You really are the most trying girl at times.”

“Trying? Well, that is better than other words you have used in the past to describe me.”

“I spoke to one of the maids, and I understand you are going out for the evening?”

“I am, yes.”

“And who are you accompanying?” Her mother leaned around Violet, looking into the courtyard. “Is it Lady Kingsley? The queen told the duchess that the two of you are getting along well. A friendship with Lady Kingsley would be wholeheartedly encouraged by both myself and the duchess. She believes Lady Kingsley has the queen’s ear more than some of her other ladies, which will be all to our benefit.”

“Would it really? Can you hear yourself, Mama? Do you think you’ll ever have anything to say to me that doesn’t concern the court and your underhanded scheming?”

Her mother’s gaze grew so icy-cold that it would have once shaken Violet to her core. Now, though, she stared straight back with newfound confidence that most certainly surprised her mother judging by the way she stepped back.

“How dare you snap at me,” her mother said, confusion in her eyes despite her obvious anger. “I am ensuring that you behave sensibly and not make a mistake by going out for the evening with the wrong sort of people."

"Well, considering you have never allowed me any friends, the only people I could possibly go out with are those I have met at court. Are you saying servants, like you and I, are not suitable company?"

"Don't be fastidious." Her mother glowered. "Tell me who you are meeting. Otherwise, I shall follow you to the castle gates."

Praying that James did not come looking for her and remained at their predetermined meeting place, Violet lifted her chin. "I owe you no explanation, a name or anything else. My obligation to you is over, Mama. When you decided to bring Elizabeth to court and then stay with the duchess rather than return for Papa's funeral, the remaining iota of loyalty I felt for you vanished. I will never, ever forgive you."

"You really do hold on to such nonsense, Violet. Your sister is now returned home, is she not? And as for your father's funeral, what I did or did not do has absolutely nothing to do with you. He was my husband, not yours."

Violet trembled with anger, tears burning her eyes. "But he was my father, Mama."

"Yes, he was, and you attended his funeral. Be happy with that." Her mother sniffed and looked away from her across the courtyard, a muscle twitching in her jaw before she faced Violet again, her eyes cold. "Do you really think you are in any position to decide when your obligation to me has passed, Violet? I birthed you. I own you."

"No, Mama, you do not."

"Heavens above, you silly girl! You look at me with such resentment, but it is unseemly for women to attend funerals. You should have heeded my advice and let your brothers take care of everything. That is what your father would have wanted."

"He would have wanted his whole family around him. You and Elizabeth, too."

"Don't presume to tell me what my husband would have wanted when you have yet to find one of your own!"

"*I've* yet to find one? Goodness, are you allowing me to choose my own husband? That really is a surprise."

Her mother's eyes glinted with spite. "You think yourself so clever, Violet, but you are not. I will choose who and when you shall marry."

"No, Mama, you will not. I have fully explained to the queen how you and the duchess still seek to control me despite me repeatedly telling you both that my loyalty will forever lie with Victoria. She is far from happy that your conduct continues in the same vein. I imagine her irritation will make itself clear to you and the duchess soon enough."

"What is that supposed to mean?" Her mother glared, the color in her cheeks rising. "Do you know something?"

Violet smiled. "If I did, I would not tell *you*."

"You spiteful cat!"

"The queen listens to me, Mama. I am on the rise in her apartments, maybe even at court."

"Don't be so ridic—"

"And not from anything you have said or told me to do, but because I decided to start being honest with everyone around me. Everyone that you wish me to use and manipulate, to spy on and listen to."

"Why, you..." Her mother raised her open palm and struck Violet hard across the cheek.

Violet stumbled back but quickly steadied herself, refusing to lift her hand to her stinging face. Lord only knew what James would think when he saw the mark.

Tears burned behind her eyes, but Violet defiantly held her mother's glare. "That is the very last time you strike me. Your work with me is done. I have decided to give up my personal happiness in preference of ambition. I will make life decisions with my head and not my heart from now on, just as you wanted and taught me to do. Congratulations, you have molded one daughter the way you wish. Now, you just have Elizabeth's kindness to ruin."

Her mother's eyes narrowed to slits. "Who are you going out with tonight?"

"A friend."

"What friend?"

"A male friend, and we will be entirely alone." Violet smiled, immensely satisfied by the horror in her mother's eyes. "I have no care for how that might affect your reputation or mine. He is a man of good standing, after all."

"It's Mr. Greene, isn't it? He will see you ruined, you silly girl. He has no doubt lain with a hundred innocents just as foolish as you. Do you think him in any way surprised that you are wantonly flaunting yourself at him? Don't be a fool, Violet."

"If I am a fool, it is you who has made me one." Violet adjusted her purse on her wrist, her heart pounding with anger and fear that her mother's words about James could well be true. She sighed, feigning boredom. "I suggest you be happy with that and find some other way to reconcile the queen with the duchess."

"And what do you suggest? Considering you are so favored with Her Majesty?"

"That is up to you to fathom, because so help me God, if you try to make me a part of your scheming again, I will take a path far worse than going to the theatre with Mr. Greene."

Turning away, Violet grasped her skirts and marched along the graveled courtyard.

"Violet! Come back here!"

Her mother's high-pitched hysteria echoed around her as Violet's smile grew. She strode purposefully forward until she spotted James push away from the wall where he had been waiting for her.

"My God, what happened?" His gaze flitted over her face. "Your cheek—"

"Met with my mother's palm." Violet eased her hand into his elbow and pulled him forward. "It does not matter. Let us go. I plan for us to have an entirely raucous evening."

He glanced behind them, his jaw tight. "She can't get away with hitting you, Violet."

"There will not be a next time, believe me." She forced a smile. "Come. I want to enjoy myself, and that will not happen if my mother is part of our conversation."

Chapter Thirty-Five

James led Violet along the row of theatre seats, and once he was sure she was comfortable, he sat down beside her.

The red velvet curtain rose, and the first act of the evening walked onto the stage. The duo flung themselves into their comedic act of jesting, jabbing, and squabbling. It was just the distraction he needed. A necessary diversion that might go some way to easing the tension that swarmed inside him from the moment he'd discovered Violet's mother's violence toward her.

He forced himself to relax his clenched fists as he glanced at her. She laughed as she stared wide-eyed at the stage. The mark on her cheek had slowly faded from scarlet red to pale pink. How could he ignore what her mother had done? Most likely, not just on this singular occasion either.

Violet turned, the delight in her eyes melting his heart. "Why the glum face? They are joyous, are they not?"

James dragged his gaze from hers to the stage as the bigger of the two men leapfrogged over the other. He couldn't help but smile. "Yes, I suppose they are."

"You suppose?" She placed her hand on his knee. "You clearly need to laugh as I do."

Before she had chance to lift her hand away, James gripped her fingers, holding her there. Her smile slowly dissolved as James struggled with what to say, how to contain his anger at her mother and tell Violet how much he wished to protect her and make her happy. The seconds ticked by as he fell deeper into the blue of her eyes.

"What is it?" she asked, softly. "Why do you look so fearful?"

Even now, when he was in love and sat close to the only woman who had ever stolen his heart, fear showed in his gaze. Not love. Not care. Not affection.

Unadulterated fear.

Because he was a coward. A coward with Violet and a coward with his father.

He lifted her hand from his knee and placed it in her lap. "I just wanted to look in your eyes and make sure you were all right after your mother struck you." He stared at the stage, despising his weakness and the hollow existence that lay ahead of him. "I can see that you are."

"Of course, I am." She scoffed. "I am a new woman, James. Just as I vowed to my mother, from now on, my decisions will be entirely my own. I will be brave and forthright. Live in the moment, take risks. Even if comes that I have to leave my place at Victoria's side one day, or end up alone and unmarried, then so be it. I refuse to live another day under my mother's command. Or anyone else's."

He gazed at her beautiful face, her newfound confidence making her light up like the gas lamps surrounding them. "You will continue to serve the queen for as long as you wish. I can't imagine you'll ever do anything that would make her unhappy."

She turned back to the antics being played out on

stage, a slight crease furrowing her brow. "I'll certainly do my best to never disappoint her, but I'm sure my mother won't ever stop threatening to take me away from court. It might come that I must leave of my own accord just to bring a halt to her harassment." She gave him a strained smile, her eyes sad. "Which will be incredibly hard considering the queen is the only person who has come to like me for being exactly who I am."

"Not the only one."

She smiled. "Fine, maybe the second person. She doesn't see me as an apt servant or as someone she can use as a stepping-stone to whatever she wants done or needs, but as a real person." Her eyes filled with passion. "Victoria has made me see the true way of things for women, for all mankind. Compromise and honesty. That is the secret to lasting happiness."

Her huge eyes searched his as though seeking a response, but James could not think past the sudden hammering of his heart, the overwhelming desire to hold her in his arms and make love to her. All he wanted was for her to be as animated, happy, and beautiful as she'd been when she grasped his hand and practically ran with him to the theatre.

"We must be strong, James. Believe in what we want and hold fast. Once you feel certain all will be well, in here…" She pressed her palm to her stomach. "Everything a person wants becomes possible. Everything."

Her smile grew so wide, so infectious, James could not help but smile back at her. Her eyes bright with happiness, she turned back to the stage. As he watched her, James's euphoria slowly dissipated. The passion that burned inside of him whenever he was with her had almost become too much for him to bear, to control or suppress. More and more, he yearned to take her in his arms, bruise her lips with his, leave his handprints on her skin like a brand so that she might always be his.

That was not love, but possession, and he needed to get as far away from her as possible. Why had he thought to court her when one day he might become filled with hatred and show violence toward their children should she choose their happiness over his? But was he really capable of such reprehensible conceit when he felt such deep, unconditional love every time he looked at her? When the thought of their unborn children brought him such joy? When a huge swell of pride rose inside him to witness her confidence and jubilation of a future free of her mother's tyranny?

No. He had to court her, love her, and, God willing, hope for the day that she might come to feel half the love for him that he felt for her.

She laughed at the chaos erupting on stage before turning to look him, her face alight. James's mouth trembled with the strain of his smile, but he managed to hold it until she turned away again.

Dread encircled his heart. It was useless. Violet exemplified goodness, honesty, duty, and care. He would not risk destroying the very things that made her the woman he loved.

He straightened in his seat, fighting to bury his burning wants and desires, but even by the end of the show, over an hour later, his heart was in no less turmoil.

Taking Violet's elbow, he led her out of the theatre onto Windsor's streets, his mind decided that he must let her go. Further pursuit of her was selfish and defunct.

"Can we walk awhile?" she asked wistfully, as she

stared at the bright, perfectly round moon above them. "It is such a beautiful night."

"Of course. Whatever you want."

"What I want, James Greene, is to enjoy this night as though it is my last." She faced him. "Do you know this is the first time I have ever stepped out with a friend after dark? Let alone a male friend. My mother, of course, is outraged that I am alone with you unchaperoned." A mischievous smile curved her lips. "Which makes tonight all the sweeter."

"I'm glad to be of service." He looked ahead, afraid to keep looking into her eyes lest he act on his desire to pull her to a stop and kiss her thoroughly and firmly regardless of the people walking back and forth around them. He needed to change the subject. "Are you looking forward to the wedding?"

"Oh, more than anything. I'm sure it will be the most romantic spectacle the world has ever seen." She tugged him close. "Maybe you will catch the eye of that suitable lady your father wishes you to find."

"There is little chance of that." *When the woman I want is standing right beside me, her hand tucked in my elbow…*

"Whenever I am away from court…" She sighed. "I want to use the brief freedom to take risks and enjoyment rather than care and caution. Don't you?"

James thought of all the responsibilities he held now and in the future. "Such a thing sounds almost fantastical in my world."

She stared at him before lifting onto her toes to press a long, lingering kiss on his lips. His heart hammered as she gently pulled back, her voice quiet in the darkness. "Let's go back to the castle."

Disappointment wound tight in his stomach. He was not yet ready for the night to end. "I thought you wanted to walk awhile."

"I did, but not anymore."

"Then maybe we could—"

"Take me to your room, James."

He stilled.

Her gaze bored into his, her intention clear even if her confidence felt laced with uncertainty. "I want to be with you." She stroked her hand over his jaw, her fingers moving lower to trace the curve of his neck. "Even if I am destined to never marry, even if there is no chance of us truly being a couple, I will not forsake this…this feeling between us. Please, James. Take me to your rooms…make love to me."

Indecision warred inside him. He wanted to lie with her so much, to feel her pleasure, hear his name on her lips as she came undone.

"Violet." He exhaled a shaky breath. "I don't want you to regret—"

"I won't."

He stared at the woman he loved, his body tight with desire, his every sense filled with her and only her. How could he not claim this moment? To make her fully his just once?

Gripping her fingers, he tugged her forward and kissed her with every ounce of his hunger for her.

Chapter Thirty-Six

Violet had never felt so free.

She clutched James's hand as they skulked, whispering and smiling, through the castle to his rooms. Her heart pounded as they dipped behind pillars and suits of armor, bureaus and dressers, stealing kisses and caresses as they drew ever closer to…what? Violet had no real idea, but the thought of James touching her neither scared nor shamed her.

Only made her feel incredibly wanton, excited, and entirely uninhibited.

They hurried through corridors and into antechambers, on and on until at last, hand in hand, they arrived at James's door. He dropped her fingers only to unlock it before grasping them again and pulling her inside.

He eased her back against the closed door, his gaze darting over her face, her hair, her neck. "Are you absolutely certain? If we do this, I'm not sure I'll be able to resist doing it over and over again."

Violet grinned and leaned into him, pressed a long, lingering kiss to his mouth. "There is no evidence to say I won't feel exactly the same."

Worry clouded his face. "But we must think of the risks."

"The risks? Do you mean my mother?" Violet cupped his jaw in her hand, looked deep into his eyes in the hope of reassuring him. "She will never know about this. You might think I have her continued attention, but her care for me does not stretch beyond what I can do for her."

"I'm not talking about your mother."

"Then what—"

"Children, Violet. We must be careful."

Violet slipped her hand from his face, a strange sensation gripping her stomach as though a babe had already started to grow inside her. "Oh. Yes, of course."

"I will be careful. There are ways…" He shook his head, brushed some fallen hair from his brow as his gaze shadowed with his concern for her. "But if you no longer want to, then I understand."

Violet's heart beat fast, filled to bursting with love and desire for him. But a baby? The risk was too great, yet…

She swallowed. "You know how to avoid such things?"

"Yes, but nothing is guaranteed."

She chewed her bottom lip, stared into his eyes as slowly, second by second, her courage returned. The woman she wanted to be, the woman who stood firm in her decisions and took life by the scruff of the neck and wrought every last drop of happiness from it rose inside her once more.

"I want to do this, James," she said firmly. "I want to make love with you and only you."

For a long moment, he did not move, his gaze moving from her eyes to her lips and back again. Then he blew out a breath, pulled her close, and nibbled her neck, making her whimper as sensation after new sensation surged through her core. With his mouth covering hers, he walked her backward to the bed. When the backs of her legs touched the mattress, they stopped, and James untied the laces of her dress as he gently nipped and kissed her exposed nape and shoulders, pulling and pushing her free of her dress, bustle, and petticoats. At last, she stood before him in only her chemise, her face and body so hot, she feared she might combust. Momentary doubt threatened when he stood back from her, leaving her vulnerable and exposed as he undressed.

With each item of clothing he discarded, Violet's body reacted, tipping from ardent desire to deep fear that she was not up to the task she had orchestrated. What if the admiration in James's eyes changed to disappointment? Would he find her naivety, her virginity entirely pathetic when he had been with women experienced in both the bedroom and the world?

Standing before her in nothing but his vest and drawers, Violet lifted her hand to her mouth to stifle a nervous giggle. She closed her eyes. "Sorry."

"Don't be." He eased her hand from her mouth and kissed her palm. "I imagine there's nothing funnier than a man dressed only in his underwear, so it's just as well neither of us will have to endure it much longer."

She smiled as he carefully eased her onto the bed and lay down beside her. His kisses grew more ardent, and Violet welcomed the new feelings that warmed every part of her. The delicious throbbing between her legs, the deep pull low in her abdomen…

Closing her eyes, she silently willed James to lift the hem of her chemise and touch her most private place. She embraced her lust and opened her legs wider. His lips paused on hers before he inched lower down her body.

She stiffened as he eased her chemise higher. Did he intend to put his mouth…? Was he…? His breath whispered over her naked thigh and then gently fluttered the hair between her legs, his finger softly stroking her back and forth.

Violet swallowed, her fingers clasping the top of his head. "James…"

"Trust me," he said softly, lifting his eyes to her, his gaze confident and teasing at the same time as his fingers continued their exploration. "You will enjoy it, and it will make you ready. If you want me to stop at any time, just say."

The moisture drained from her mouth even as wetness gathered at her core. Her cheeks heating with embarrassment and lust, Violet nodded.

He winked and then lowered his head.

Violet gasped and squeezed her eyes closed as his tongue moved back and forth, flicked and licked, his fingers doing something that should have shamed her. Instead, she lifted her hips, inviting his ministrations, silently begging him to carry them out with more haste and more pressure. She groaned as he licked her again before sliding his finger inside, withdrawing, sliding it inside again…over and over.

"Something is happening." Violet closed her eyes, her mouth dropping open as words failed her. "Mmm."

Heat burned inside her, a delicious clamping, writhing sensation that seemed to grow more and more potent until he gently withdrew his fingers. She cried out in protest and opened her eyes. He hovered above her, his hand low between them, his gaze on hers.

Her breath caught as he eased inside her, just the

tiniest amount and withdrew, inched inside again.

"Are you all right?" he whispered. "Shall I go on?"

"Yes."

He smiled and then dipped his head to kiss her as he thrust forward again, and Violet grimaced as a sharp sensation pierced her, and then her body surrendered to his, and she followed James's lead, matching his steady rhythm. Together they moved, and she dug her nails into his muscular arms as he brought his mouth to her breasts, her neck, her shoulders.

The stirring she felt when he'd caressed her began to build again, and Violet moaned, her eyes closing. "James, I…"

A rush of pleasure swarmed through her body, and she relished every part of it. She was filled with love. Filled with James…

****

Afterward, time passed slowly and with complete satiety as they lay in one another's arms. Violet was so happy, talking softly in the darkness that when the clock on James's mantel struck midnight, panic rushed through her, obliterating her temporary peace.

She leapt from the bed and swiped up her chemise. "I must go. I have to light the queen's fires in a few hours."

James groaned and rolled from the bed. "I could so easily fall asleep with you. You give me such peace, Violet."

She quickly looked away lest he see in her eyes how much he was beginning to mean to her. She could not be foolish. Their lovemaking was her way of exerting control and independence. Nothing more.

Haphazardly throwing on their clothes, James

insisted that he see her safely back to her room. With her hand clasped in his, they hurried through the castle, stealing a rushed kiss at her closed door before he left and Violet crept inside, smiling like a loon. Quickly, she undressed and collapsed into bed, grateful and relieved that no one had seen her, the maids in her chamber softly snoring.

A few hours later, she was woken by the noises of a new day dawning. Even as she rubbed her tired eyes, her body was alert and ready to embrace a new day. She had never felt so alive.

"Has something happened?" a fellow maid asked as she joined Violet walking along the corridor to the queen's chambers. "You look like you might burst with happiness at any moment."

Violet merely smiled as she smoothed the apron tied at her waist. "It is a beautiful day, and I am excited for the wedding. Nothing more."

The other girl turned a corner toward a different part of the upper floor as Violet continued to the queen's apartments. She quietly entered Victoria's bedchamber where Her Majesty slept soundly. Violet smiled at Dash as the little dog lifted his head from his mistress's leg before flopping his chin back down on the bed covers.

Kneeling in front of the fire, Violet scraped and poked at the charcoal until the embers began to glow. She pulled some wood and then a scoop of coal from the baskets on the hearth and carefully placed them in the grate, giving the coals another poke.

"Parker? Is that you?"

Violet's memories of the night before scattered as she quickly stood and dropped into a curtsey. "It is, Your Majesty. I'm sorry if I woke you. It is still early."

The queen smiled and sat up higher against the pillows. “I have barely slept all night thinking of Albert and the wedding.” She reached for Dash and gently lifted the dog onto her lap, her fingers smoothing his long, silky ears. “I dread to think how little I will sleep as the days and nights draw ever closer to the big day.”

The big day. It was almost here. Violet returned the queen’s smile. She could not wait to present Victoria with her finished painting. She prayed the queen liked it as it had been created with every ounce of Violet’s love and gratitude for all that Victoria had done for her.

“Parker? Have you nothing to say? The duke will be here tomorrow, and nothing seems at all ready.”

Violet blinked. “Tomorrow?”

“Yes, and I can barely stand the wait. Come.” Victoria patted the bed. “Sit awhile and tell me what has your eyes full of stars. I can’t imagine the vibrant color at your cheeks and the breadth of your smile are entirely caused by your queen and your early morning service to her.”

Was her lovemaking with James plain to see in her expression? “I am not sure I know what you mean, ma’am.”

“Nonsense.” Victoria patted the bed again leaving Violet no choice but to comply. She sidled onto the mattress, and the queen grinned. “Good. Now, it’s no use trying to conceal that you went out with Mr. Greene last night. There is very little Lehzen doesn’t know about what each of my household is up to, you included.”

Very little? Violet tried to contain the sudden panic that leapt through her veins. Did Lehzen have spies watching Violet’s every move? She swallowed. “Mr. Greene and I went to the music hall, ma’am.”

"And then?"

"Then?"

Victoria lifted her brows, her eyes shining with mischief. "Did he kiss you? Take you in his arms?"

Violet's cheeks grew hotter than ever. "He…well…"

"He did, didn't he?" Victoria cried and clapped her hands. "Tell me everything. You must omit nothing. Albert talks of such virtue and morality in his letters, yet he also speaks of passion and love in a manner that leads me to suspect that he longs to touch me as much as I long to touch him. Is it possible you feel the same way about Mr. Greene?"

Violet laughed at the excited delight in the queen's eyes and slumped her shoulders in defeat. "Yes, ma'am. I believe I do."

"Then we will learn all there is to know about lovemaking together. We are but two innocent maids with all the intricacies and delights of true romance lying ahead of us. What do you say?"

Violet smiled. "I'd say true romance would be simply wonderful, Your Majesty."

Chapter Thirty-Seven

Court had been a hubbub of excited anticipation ever since Albert's return three days before. Now, it was the day of the wedding, and that anticipation would soon reach its climax.

Standing alongside his parents in one of the front pews in the Chapel Royal, James smoothed the lapels of his jacket, stretching his neck in the hope of loosening his collar a little. The tense atmosphere as the entire congregation breathlessly awaited Victoria's arrival was taking its toll on his nerves.

The entire ceremony needed to go off without a hitch, or else James suspected he and Charles Carr would feel the full force of the wrath Albert had been struggling harder and harder to contain as this moment drew ever closer. The man was stretched as tight as a piano string, solemn and entirely without humor on this most auspicious day.

James studied Albert where he stood, straight-backed and stern at the alter and inwardly grimaced, willing the man to relax. Despite his valets' reassurances, Albert looked painfully uneasy, his face pale, his body stiffly upright in his bright-red British Field Marshall uniform, lavishly and beautiful decorated with the Order of the Garter.

Until Victoria arrived, the duke was the pinnacle of attention. Did he not comprehend that people would draw their own conclusions on how he felt based on his expression and mannerisms? The man looked as though he was about to be hung, drawn, and quartered rather than wed.

As James glanced at the doors at the back of the church, his eye was instinctively drawn to Violet where she sat alongside some of the lower born members of the queen's household. Lower born but still in a notable location inside the chapel. Her position would not be overlooked by anyone. Violet was on the rise.

He smiled to see her so happy, her cheeks flushed as she looked all around her, her beautiful eyes wide and bright with awe, maybe even a touch of romance.

James's smile faltered, regret twisting in his stomach. Since their lovemaking, he had hardly seen her, the mania of the wedding having taken over both their lives. The longer they were apart, the more James had to accept that precious night for what it had been in Violet's heart and mind. A night of liberty. Nothing more, nothing less.

He swallowed, tried and failed to turn away from her.

Victoria's high regard for Violet was obvious and with her elevation came the success and self-worth she so passionately sought. He could not imagine that she would ever forsake all that she had worked for, all that she had endured under her mother's tutelage to marry him and become the mistress of a country estate.

"For the love of God, boy." His father nudged James with his elbow. "Stop staring at that girl and face the front."

Shooting his father a glare, James straightened his shoulders. "She is a girl I am actually rather fond of."

"Don't be absurd."

"Why is the notion absurd?" James asked, somewhat enjoying his father's gruff disbelief. "She is one of the queen's ladies, after all."

His father's gaze lingered on James's before he looked across the aisle. "She is very pretty, I grant you, but far below the position of the women you should be pursuing." His jaw tightened. "I am tired of your insistent, senseless woman-watching. You should be courting one of the ladies carrying the queen's train not eyeing a woman sitting way behind us."

"You want me to find a wife, Father. That is what I am doing."

"Not any wife, James. The right wife and that girl over there is far from that. Your mother and I have been waiting weeks for news of your imminent betrothal, still the days continue to pass in silence."

"The wedding has kept me and the queen's household busy. There has hardly been time to sleep, let alone court anyone. Maybe when Victoria and Albert leave for their honeymoon, I will find some time." James drew in a long breath, glanced again at Violet. "Not that I foresee the honeymoon lasting longer than a few days. Melbourne told me the queen refused Albert's request that they indulge in some extended time from public view. It seems Victoria deems a few days ample time away."

"That's because she knows her duty. As you should. You need to marry, James. Enough is enough."

Before James could respond, his mother leaned in on his father's other side. "This is neither the time nor the place for this conversation. Please, save your discussions for—" She quickly looked behind her, a smile softening her face. "Oh, how wonderful. Judging by the commotion at the door, the queen has arrived."

Everyone rose to their feet, the scuffle quickly quietening as a hush descended over the gathered members of the royal family, dignitaries, and everyone else in between.

The choir boys began to sing as Victoria slowly walked along the aisle on the arm of the Duke of Sussex. She looked elegant, beautiful, and exquisitely innocent in a simple white dress, an orange blossom woven into a headband rather than the expected royal robes and glittering crown or tiara. Violet had told him Victoria was intentional in her choice of what to wear on this most public of days. Her wish being that the whole country understood she was marrying Albert, not as a queen, but as an ordinary woman.

The procession passed him, and a smile pulled at James's lips as Victoria's promenade was intermittently impeded by her bridesmaids' eagerness to assist her, which only resulted in them getting in one another's way in a rabble of knotted hands and trodden toes. James looked across at Violet, pleasure rippling through him to see her hand at her mouth, her eyes alight with laughter.

He was in no way surprised she was as amused by the spectacle as he. Their shared sense of humor was just another reason he desired Violet as his wife. Her ability to laugh, despite the stresses and strains of court life, made her more suited to the demands at Cassington Park than any plentiful dowry or title ever would. Something his father clearly did not understand.

James glanced at him, and his resentment wavered. His father's skin was gray, stretched tight across sharp cheekbones, his white hair growing ever thinner and his jacket appearing too big. His father's declining health could not be mistaken. If he was dangerously ill, his increasing wish that James return home with a wife would surely mean his father would come to accept James's choice of bride? Whoever she might be.

At last, Victoria stood beside Albert, their hands clasped as the wedding ceremony began.

Burying his trepidation about his own nuptials, James noted how much Albert had relaxed now that Victoria was at his side. Admittedly, he still looked as though the gallows were possible even if not entirely imminent. But there was a marked improvement, regardless. Whereas any resistance Victoria might have once had to marry was entirely gone. There was not an iota of compunction on her pretty face or in the stance of her petite frame. She looked like a woman in love…a queen who had found her king.

James rocked back on his heels, satisfaction washing through him. Despite his reputation, he was a staunch romantic, and a lump formed in his throat as he watched the scene before him. Victoria stared up at Albert, the orange blossom in her hair trembling. An assured testament to her nerves, despite the firmness of her responses.

Here was a couple, each just twenty years of age, embarking on a marriage that must succeed. Their union meant they were now the country's new parents who would be relied upon to see their people safely through future dangers that might threaten Britain's shores. Not to mention how soon Victoria's subjects would begin to demand a young prince as security of the crown.

Every marriage deserved the best start of mutual love and respect, and as James looked at Victoria and

Albert now, their vows exchanged and their wedding complete, he saw nothing but those two vital emotions as they looked into one another's eyes.

The royal couple slowly passed him, and James looked at Violet once again. She stared back at him, her gaze unreadable. Did she still think of marriage as she had once told him was her dream? Or did she now only think of freedom and independence?

Deep inside, James could not silence the belief Violet was meant to be his wife. That it was only her who could stop him embodying his father and grandfather before him. Her patience, care, and love were the balm that would heal the terrible paternal legacy that had riddled his family for generations.

Chapter Thirty-Eight

Satisfaction warmed Violet as she stood in front of her painting of the waterfall, which she had given Victoria as a wedding gift. It now hung in pride of place above a bureau in the queen's bedroom at Buckingham Palace. Victoria had been so thrilled with it she had ordered Violet to paint more landscapes so that she might send them to influential people who she believed would appreciate Violet's talent as much as she did.

Whether or not Victoria's predictions of forthcoming commissions came true was another matter entirely, but Violet loved the queen all the more for her belief and enthusiasm.

With Victoria and Albert enjoying their honeymoon at Windsor, Violet was stationed at Buckingham Palace along with several others from the queen's and duke's households, the royal couple only requesting the service of a select few while they were away.

Violet was glad of the extra time to herself, especially considering today was the day her mother—and Victoria's—departed the palace for their new home on Belgrave Square. A relocation that stuck in the throat of both women, and Violet had every intention of enjoying unfettered witness to their misery.

Although her mother had summoned her to visit her at the duchess's apartments that afternoon, Violet decided to first track down James so that she might spend a moment or two with him rejoicing in her mother's leaving. Her heart quickened with impatience to see him as she made her way through the palace to Melbourne's office.

Even though he refused to say it, James knew as well as she did that the stolen kisses they had occasionally indulged in since their single night of lovemaking would have to come to an end sooner or later. So despite Violet's feelings and care for him deepening daily, so did her determination to carve out a life of her own making.

One day, James had to marry and marry well. She was consciously protecting her heart and would not allow it to become any more his than it was already. Neither would she allow her mind to ponder whether she was any different than James's other lovers. Women who had kissed and no doubt lain with him and then gone on their way once both parties were done with his service…so to speak.

Yes, she had wanted James to show her the way of the bedroom, of how things were between a man and woman who cared for one another, but she did not use him as a toy as she suspected certain ladies in waiting had. She loved him, and there had been no other man before James. No other man she had so fervently wanted to touch and teach her. James was important to her, and she imagined he always would be.

As long as she was vigilant and kept things between them on a steady, mutually enjoyable keel, all would be well for her and him.

Reaching Melbourne's office, she firmly knocked on the door and stepped back, hoping her sources were right and Melbourne was currently away from the palace.

"Come in."

Relieved James's voice came from the other side of the door, Violet stepped into the room. "Good afternoon, Mr. Greene."

"Violet." He pushed his pen into the holder on his desk and rose, coming forward with his hands extended. "This is a most welcome surprise."

Her body immediately responded to him, and an insistent, impatience desire rose inside of her just as it did every time they were reunited after a spell apart. She slid her hands into his and glanced past his shoulder to the open doorway behind him. "Are you alone?"

"Completely," he said, pulling her firmly into his arms.

His warm mouth covered hers, and Violet melted against him, returning his kiss and relishing the way she reacted to him every time they were alone together. How she had ever lived without his kisses and caresses, she had no idea.

"I am on my way to see my mother. It's her final day at the palace," she said, as she stepped back, purposefully enforcing space between them. "Victoria and I will soon be finally free of our mothers. Hopefully forever. And, for me, I didn't even need to marry to make it happen."

His smile faltered, his gaze shadowing with something she couldn't decipher. "No," he said curtly, before returning to his desk. "You didn't."

Inexplicable tension descended, and Violet followed him, sat on the chair on the other side of his desk. "What is it?"

"Nothing. I just have much to do before Melbourne returns from his cabinet meeting. He's asked that I prepare as many papers as possible for the queen's signing when she returns in the next day or two."

Although unconvinced work distractions caused the upset that passed over his face, Violet was unwilling to press him when she might not like what he had to say or if the blame for his anguish lay with her.

"I see," she said. "But I thought you now worked solely for the duke?"

"Officially I do, but Melbourne has been good to me and with Albert away…" He shrugged. "I'm happy to help the minister while I can. Working here is preferable to returning home for a few days."

Violet settled back in her seat and stared at his bowed head as he looked at the papers in front of him. "You cannot avoid that your father is ill forever, you know. I saw him at the wedding. He does not look very well at all."

"You think I don't know that?" he snapped, and Violet's heart stumbled to see such anger in his dark eyes. "Have no fear, just like Albert, I too, will be put out to stud sooner rather than later."

Violet flinched at the crude remark.

He stood and walked to the window, gripped the frame so hard his knuckles turned white. "My life at court could be the most exciting and interesting it has ever been if the talk of the changes Albert intends to make are true, but no, all I can think about is the reality that I must return home. This time for good."

Violet frowned. "What changes?"

He turned, waved his hand dismissively. "It does not matter. What matters is that I do not have the luxury of enjoying the progression. I must go home and do what is expected of me."

"Does this mean you will not be working for the duke after all?"

"It looks unlikely."

Hating the sullen sadness in his voice as he resumed his seat behind his desk, Violet longed to touch him but dared not when his temper had been so completely roused. "When will you leave?"

"Once I have done what I can for Melbourne, I will make a final report to Anson and then return home. Who knows? Once my parents learn that I do not have news of an engagement, they may well send me straight back to court with a list of ladies in waiting to whom I must propose, one by one, until I receive a positive reply."

"Don't you…" Violet looked toward the window, hating how much it hurt to ask her next question. "Have a possible candidate in mind by now?"

Silence stretched, and she turned. His gaze burned into hers, clouding once more with something she couldn't decipher. Anger? Outrage? Hopelessness? So much stormed in their depths.

He abruptly stood and came around the desk.

Looking into her eyes, he took her hands and eased her to her feet, his jaw tight. "It's you, Violet. Do you not understand? Goddamn it, it's you I want to marry."

How she longed for him to ask her, and she say yes, but that was impossible when their lives were so irrevocably different. James did not need a humble woman like her beside him, but a lady who knew how to oversee an estate, knew how to direct staff, not one who had once been a servant herself. "James—"

"Whatever the future holds, I want you to know the truth of my heart." He lifted his finger to her brow and brushed back a curl. "I love you, Violet. I really do."

He kissed her deeply as tears leapt into her eyes, but she ardently kissed him back, hoping her mouth and tongue told him how much she loved him, too.

The moment they parted, Violet slowly walked backward to the door, her lips bruised from the intensity of their kiss. "I must go. Write to me when you can."

Hurt and confusion stormed in his gaze. "You're leaving? Now?"

"Yes, I must see my mother. Goodbye, James."

She fled along the corridor, lifting her skirts and dashing as fast as she could across the palace to the duchess's apartments. Once there, she leaned against the wall by the antechamber door and caught her breath, her mind reeling with James's confession and her heart aching to return to him.

But she could not. Would not. She must remain strong.

The door beside her abruptly opened, and Violet leapt away from the wall.

"What on earth are you doing?" her mother demanded, her blue eyes cold. "You look a complete mess."

"Good afternoon to you too, Mama."

Her mother glanced into the room behind her and pulled the door ajar before gripping Violet's elbow. "You cannot possibly see the duchess looking so unkempt."

Plucking a pin from her hair, Violet set about trying to tidy herself. "Are you almost ready to leave? I assume you asked me here to help you pack?" She could not stem the joy in her voice. "Which I am, of course, happy to do without question."

Her mother narrowed her eyes and roughly gripped the collar of Violet's dress and yanked it straight. "I'm sure you are, but your glee will be short-lived." Her mother smirked as she swatted her hand down the front of Violet's dress as though it were plastered with dust and dirt. "The duchess would like you to serve at the new house with me. I am sure the queen will be more than happy to comply. All she cares about now is Albert."

Violet's heart beat with undeniable panic. Would her position with the queen be forever tenuous? She swiped her mother's hand away from her. "Will you never give up, Mama? I will not leave Victoria's side for as long as she needs me or else I marry."

"Marry?" Her mother huffed a laugh. "Don't be a fool, Violet. You are living the most luxurious life you will ever manage. Why give that up for a man?"

Her mother was right, but James's face would not abate from Violet's mind. "You know love is real for some people."

"There is no such thing as real love."

A jolt struck Violet's heart as she thought of her poor papa hearing such a callous declaration from his wife, but she would not give her mother the satisfaction of mentioning him now or showing an iota of her grief. "I believe Victoria and Albert are in love."

"Then you are a fool indeed. They were preordained to wed, Violet. Their destinies decided many moons ago. It is fortunate that they seem to tolerate one another so well, but love? No such thing."

"You're wrong. I have witnessed how passionate they are toward one another, how in love they are already. A love I am sure will deepen with time. What if that is what I want one day? What if I change my mind and dedicating my life to the queen as you have yours to the duchess is not what I want?"

"You really do have stars in your eyes," her mother

sneered. "Is this nonsense provoked by your futile feelings for Mr. Greene? His family would never approve of you, my dear. Never. You are little more than a way to pass his time, trust me."

Ignoring her mother's callousness, Violet tilted her chin. "The queen believes in love, and if I told her I had found it, she would let me go with her blessing."

"Oh, she would, would she?"

"Yes."

"Then go now, you silly, naïve little girl. Get out of my sight and look for your so-called love. I have no need for such stupidity, and neither does the duchess. She will do well enough with just me and Elizabeth."

"Oh, I'll go, Mama. But trust me when I say that if you recall Elizabeth, she will not be with you for long. I will see to it that she is taken away from you as you wished me away from Victoria." Violet started along the corridor. "Goodbye for now. I hope you and the duchess are very happy together in your new home."

Chapter Thirty-Nine

Sitting across from his father in the drawing room at Cassington Park, James swirled his crystal cut glass and watched the brandy ripple and settle. "You are not accepting what I am telling you."

"Because all I hear is endless bellyaching. Endless chatter about the past rather than the damn future." His father puffed on his cigar, the end glowing and fading until he was wracked by a deep and prolonged cough. He pulled a piece of paper from his dressing gown pocket with trembling fingers and held it out. "Here. Your mother and I have drawn up a list of suitable women for you to consider. Both from court and in the county."

Torn between annoyance over his father's audaciousness, concern for his failing health, and the irony of his prediction coming true that he would come home to find a list of potential wives compiled and waiting for him, James drained his glass and stood. He walked to the drinks cabinet and unstoppered the brandy decanter. "There is no need for a list."

His father coughed again, swapping the piece of paper for a handkerchief and coughing into it. "I beg to differ."

"I am in love. I have already chosen the woman I wish to marry."

"What? Who?"

"Who she is does not matter," James said,

concluding now was not the time to tell his father the woman who held his heart was the very one they had spoken about at Victoria's wedding. "What matters is I have found her, and she is wonderful."

"I demand to know who she is!"

"No. You will not spoil this for me."

"Spoil—good God, boy. This is not some frivolous matter. The woman you marry needs to know what is expected of her."

"And she will." James poured a hefty measure and returned the decanter to the tray. Taking a long drink, he sat down opposite his father. "Debate who I will marry has never been the cause for me dragging my heels."

"Well, what the bloody hell is?"

"The fear that inheriting Cassington will eventually turn me into a mean and brutal tyrant. That has been the cause of my reluctance all these years. That is why I joined the army, and that is why I fled to court as soon as I returned. If I was not fearful of becoming like you, your father, and grandfather, then I'm sure I would embrace my future wholeheartedly. As such a prospect cannot be guaranteed, my reluctance continues."

"That's how you see me, is it? As a tyrant?"

"Both myself and George have the scars to prove your past brutality, and from what I've seen of the staff, their continued fear of you proves little has changed as you have grown older. Why would I want to marry? Have children? Why would I want to risk becoming the sort of man who beats them?"

A flicker of shame passed over his father's face before he lifted his chin, pride gleaming in his eyes once more. "You always were a fanciful sort of boy. The world is harsh. Fathers and landowners must be strong, in charge, and clear in their authority. Anything less invites revolt and discord. You will learn that soon enough."

"Which is why I am not yet willing to take up my position as your successor. First, I need for you to accept that when Cassington is mine, I will do things differently. Give me your blessing and acceptance that your way and your father's way of running the estate is not how things will remain in the future."

His father glowered, his cigar hovering at his mouth, and his eyes narrowed as he stared at James through a spiral of smoke.

"Once I take over," James continued, "I intend to instill progression and alteration to the current processes and procedures that have been set in stone for decades. The alterations might take a while to implement, but they will happen." James took a sip of his drink. "It is also likely that several merchants and gentry who have dealt with the estate in the past, possibly for generations, will not like these changes and choose to ostracize me. Buy their livestock and produce elsewhere. So be it. I want it to be known across the county that I am not you. That I will not become my forefathers purely to keep things as they are."

Silence stretched as his father's cheeks mottled.

After a few seconds, he leaned forward and stabbed out his cigar in the marble ashtray beside him. "This estate has been in the family since the early part of the last century. The land and building of the original house funded by your self-made ancestor. You cannot toss aside decades of our family's way of doing business because it does not suit you." His father shook his head. "I have been hard on you and your brother because that is what is needed when a father grooms his sons for their futures. Men of our position cannot be weak with their wives, their children, tenants, or staff. Not ever. Do you understand?"

"No, I do not. Neither do I consider fairness, compassion, and mutually beneficial negotiation as weakness." James tightened his fingers around his glass. "It is as though you are encouraging me to find a wife and start a family so that I might bring them into order, show off my prowess rather than create a happy, loving home where my loved ones will thrive."

"What a lot of nonsense!" His father stood, another cough wracking his chest as he leaned on the back of his wingback chair. "You are to be a baron, not a father from the bloody village. Grow up, James. This is our life, and it's time you became part of it."

The stoop in his father's shoulders grew more pronounced, his face turning more and more ashen, his gait hesitant.

Sickness coated James's throat as love and sympathy twisted inside of him. No matter what his father might have done in the past, he was dying, and that was not something to which James could close his heart. "How long do you have, Papa?"

His father held James's gaze before he shuffled across the room and lowered into a seat by the window. He stared out into the darkness. "The doctor foresees less than six months."

"Then we do not have the time to waste arguing." James stood and walked across the room, slowly lowered into a chair opposite his father. He studied his face, almost ghostly in the moonlight that filtered between the open drapes. "I would like you to listen to my suggestions and revised methods now, so that we might discuss them before you die. Whatever has occurred between us, whatever has happened in this house, it is still my hope that you pass peacefully knowing the estate is in good hands."

"And if I agree to listen to your ideas?"

"Then I promise to do all I can to persuade the woman I love to marry me by year's end."

"Year's end?" His father shook his head. "No. It needs to be sooner. I need to die knowing you are married and her with child."

"I will not promise that. She deserves to be courted and know she is adored for who she is, not for what will be expected of her. She deserves the time to fully understand what lies ahead if she agrees to become my wife. I will not marry her without her knowing everything about me and my family. That part of the deal is nonnegotiable."

"And if I die and you are still a single man? You could go back on everything you've said to me. No wife, no heir. Just sell the place out from under me without a care."

"I will not do that."

"Why should I believe you?"

"Because you have no choice but to trust me." James leaned forward. "I will take over the estate, but I will not become you. I will not hurt my wife, my children, or anyone else. I will be the next baron and build on the prosperity already in place, I promise you. But that is where your legacy ends, everything else will be very different." James was defiant as he offered his father his hand. "Do we have a deal that you will listen to me and let me do things my way?"

Their eyes locked.

Then, slowly, his father reached out and clasped James's hand. "We have a deal."

Chapter Forty

Violet carried an enormous basket of fruit into the queen's study and placed it on the vast table lining one side of the room. She stood back, admiring the wonderful hues and textures.

"Parker?" the queen snapped. "Why has that fruit put such a smile on your face?"

Victoria sat stiff-backed and scowling at her desk, an open ledger in front of her and the red state box at her elbow. Lehzen was in her customary wingback chair a few feet away, hunched over some embroidery. The queen's expression and tone were far from amiable…just as both had habitually been for the last two weeks.

Violet swallowed, still fearful of the precariousness of her position. "I was just thinking how I would like to paint this basket, Your Majesty. It is a gift for you from the prime minister."

"Do not speak to me of Lord Melbourne. The fruit is no doubt his delicate, understated way of telling me he suspects me to be with child. Odious man. Over and over for the last few evenings, he has dared to suggest such a thing by asking me how I feel. Whether I am looking forward to what the future will undoubtedly bring. Does he think me stupid enough to long for a child?"

Violet dipped her gaze but glanced at Lehzen from beneath lowered lashes. They had discussed the possibility the queen might be pregnant a few nights ago.

It had been several weeks since Violet had washed and laundered fresh napkins for the queen's monthlies. Maybe Melbourne wasn't being entirely presumptuous in his speculation.

"I have no desire to talk about babies. Babies can wait." Victoria pushed her papers to the side. "Tell me something to cheer me up. I am tired of state matters. Not to mention how bored I am of Albert walking about the palace, complaining he has no place at court. What on earth he thought our life would be like together, I have no idea."

Violet scrambled to think of something entertaining to share, but her life consisted only of serving the queen or stolen moments with James since he had returned to court two weeks ago. A return where he had again declared his love for her and asked if he might court her. Even though she had tentatively accepted his sincerity, she was still too afraid to surrender to her feelings.

He had such responsibilities ahead of him, and if she agreed to their courtship and they married, those responsibilities would also become hers. She would lose her place beside the queen, and leaping from her mother's control to James's was not an option.

"I know," the queen exclaimed, her mood veering once more to joviality as she rose from her desk and joined Lehzen in front of the fire. "You can tell me how things are going along with you and Mr. Greene, Parker."

"Mr. Greene, ma'am?" Violet forced a smile and tried to keep her voice calm. "Our friendship continues to grow. He is very kind to me and—"

"Oh, come now. You have already confessed to caring for him, and now I've learned that he would like to court you." Victoria smiled. "Lady Kingsley told me just yesterday how things have moved on between you and how Mr. Greene is adamant that he loves you despite his father's reservations."

"Lady Kingsley said that?" Warmth leapt into Violet's cheeks as realization dawned that James continued to share everything and anything with her grace. He had barely mentioned Lady Kingsley for weeks. Did he continue to occasionally bed her, too?

Sickness coated her throat. "He has confessed his deepening feelings for me."

"And do you welcome his attention?"

Violet glanced at Lehzen who clearly struggled to tolerate what she undoubtedly considered innately banal conversation, judging by the way she stabbed her needle into her work.

"Well?" pressed the queen. "Will you agree to Mr. Greene's courtship, Parker? It is the most appealing elevation on your part, is it not? You do know Greene will one day be a baron?"

"Yes, ma'am, I do. But..." Violet walked closer. Maybe the queen could advise her. After all, no matter how many times Violet told James their courtship would end in heartbreak, that his family would never accept her as his wife, he refused to listen. "Considering his future, I can't help but worry that Mr. Greene's attentions to me hold no prospect. Certainly not a happy one. I am a maid, ma'am. He needs a lady beside him. More than that, wouldn't it be foolish to hope that he and I might marry and live a good life when, in doing so, I risk giving up all that makes me so very happy here?"

Lehzen gave an inelegant sniff. "That is very true, Parker. An intelligent observation indeed."

The queen sat back in her chair and regarded Violet

through narrowed eyes. "I must confess, I was probably too caught up in the romance of you and Mr. Greene to consider the realities of you courting. Lady Kingsley is so excited that you and he seem to be falling in love that I became as hopeful for your romantic success as she." Victoria pursed her lips before speaking again. "I think it best that you relay your fears openly and honestly to Mr. Greene."

"I've tried to make him see sense, but he refuses to listen to what I am certain will eventually happen."

"That you will be replaced by a lady once the roses clear from his eyes?" The queen gave a curt nod. "I completely understand. I am sure Albert now looks at me through a far clearer lens than he did before we wed."

Lehzen laid her embroidery in her lap. "The duke adores you, ma'am. That will never change. As for you and Mr. Greene, Parker, do not deem yourself important enough to bother the queen with these matters, or in any way assume Mr. Greene's reputation is no longer relevant now that he has set his sights on you. I fear you will be wholly disappointed."

"Now, now, Lehzen," the queen said, sternly. "I won't have you tarnishing Mr. Greene without just cause. The gossip about him and his ways has lessened over the last few months, and I have every confidence that is because of Parker. Now…" Victoria smiled at Violet. "I have a message I would like delivered to Albert. Why don't you take it to his apartments? Hopefully, while you are there, you will come across Mr. Greene and maybe have the chance to talk."

Violet swallowed. "Yes, ma'am."

Why was it she could kiss James, make love to him, but the thought of having a serious conversation with him still filled her with apprehension? Maybe that said more about her than him. With her liberty from her mother, maybe she had become a harlot who wanted fun without commitment.

"You must air your grievances even if they cause trouble," the queen said, firmly. "Why, the duke and I have had our spats already, and we have barely been wed more than a few weeks." Victoria laughed, but her eyes disclosed her anxiety. "Disagreements are people's way of getting to know each other. Now, the letter is on my desk."

Violet walked to the desk and picked up the envelope addressed to Albert.

"Off you go, Parker. We will speak again later."

Once she stood outside the door to Albert's apartments, Violet took a fortifying breath and purposefully knocked.

The door opened, and Charles Carr greeted her with a bow. "Mistress Parker. You have a message from Her Majesty?"

Before Violet could fathom an excuse why she needed to speak to James in particular, the problem was solved when the door opened wider, and he appeared, his beautiful dark eyes on hers.

She smiled despite her unease. "Mr. Greene."

With his gaze still on hers, James addressed Mr. Carr. "Charles, could you take the queen's message from Mistress Parker and give it to His Royal Highness? I'll be along shortly."

A heartbeat passed before Charles cleared his throat, his amusement obvious. "Of course."

Once they were alone, Violet released a breath. "If Mr. Carr wasn't gossiping about us before, he certainly will be now."

"And what if he does?" James gripped her fingers and eased her forward. "I want the whole court to know how I feel about you, you know that."

Violet stared into his eyes and saw nothing but sincerity. What more did she want him to say? To prove? Was she being unfair to him *and* herself by incessantly questioning what was in her heart?

"James, I know it's unusual I am afraid to be courted when most women want the security of a husband, but…"

"You are not most women, Violet. I knew that from the very beginning." He exhaled. "But I am pleading with you to trust me. When my father dies—"

"You will be a baron, James. Your position is a prominent one. I am a maid. I thought what was happening between us…" She shook her head. "Everything is becoming so serious when I thought we were merely—"

"Having fun?" His eyes darkened with undisguised resentment. "My days of having fun are rapidly coming to an end, I'm afraid."

"As our mine."

"Why?"

Violet darted her gaze along the corridor. "I believe Victoria will soon need me more than ever and our stolen time together will become ever more seldom."

"What do you mean?"

Violet lowered her voice. "I suspect the queen is with child."

"Well, that's splendid news." James smiled. "Albert will be overjoyed."

"Maybe he will, but I fear the queen will not. The

life she enjoys with Albert now could well be over once the pregnancy is announced and the baby born. I do not blame the queen for fretting. Every woman knows that once she bears children, her life is never the same again. Whatever her station."

Disappointment showed in his gaze. "You do not wish to have children?"

Violet smiled, the thought of motherhood warming her. "Oh, yes, one day maybe."

"Your mother has not deterred you from becoming a mother yourself?"

"Just because our parents did not raise us in the best way does not mean we will be the same. At least, I hope not."

Hope sparked in his expression, and Violet immediately wished she had softened her conviction. "Although, that does not mean—"

"I know. I'm just glad you wish to have children."

Violet stared into his eyes. When he was happy, she was happy. When he was worried, she worried. How could such a connection, such want of someone, be wrong? Yet there was still so much about their being together she was reluctant to trust.

"Why not ask Lady Kingsley to marry you?" she asked quietly.

"Abigail?"

"Yes."

He frowned. "Because she and I were never anything more than lovers. Confidantes. Friends who trust one another with their secrets. Nothing more."

"Nothing more?" An indiscernible jealousy seared Violet's heart. "Haven't you just described the perfect marriage?"

"No, it's different with Abigail." He reached for her hand, but whatever he saw in her eyes made him push his fingers into his hair instead. "She isn't you, Violet."

He looked so disappointed. So lost. He loved her. No man could have a look of such despair on his face and not mean what he said. Violet's heart pounded. How she loved him too…

She took a deep breath. What was the use in fighting her heart when he already so firmly held it? She had to take a risk. Run toward a chance of true happiness. "All right."

Optimism sparked in his eyes. "All right? You will allow me to court you?"

"Yes." Violet had little hope of stemming her smile. "But I want us to take things one day at a time. I will not forsake the freedom I finally have from my mother just to become trapped within the confines of your position as a future baron. I have to be sure a life with you will not quash the liberty I am desperate to keep."

"Of course, anything you want. You will lead the way. You are sure? You will allow me to court you?"

She laughed. "Yes, James, I'm sure."

Violet turned and left him standing in the doorway. She hurried back to the queen's apartments feeling a little lighter, a little more certain. That, despite all her mother had put her through, she still wanted children had opened her eyes. That tiny nugget of longing had been the deciding factor that had pushed her to trust James.

To trust their love.

To trust herself.

Chapter Forty-One

"No one understands how much having this baby will change things!" The queen fumed.

Violet grimaced and gripped the linens she carried as she ground to a halt outside Victoria's bedchamber. Her screech was promptly followed by the crash of an unfortunate porcelain object being thrown against the flocked wallpaper.

"Madam!" Lehzen admonished. "You must calm yourself. Think of the baby."

"The baby? Everything is about the baby, Lehzen. Everything!"

The queen's pregnancy had been confirmed three weeks before, and ever since tension had risen in Victoria's household and, more worryingly, between the queen and Albert. The thought of impending motherhood was not as joyous a notion to Victoria as it was to the rest of the palace and parliament.

Entering the room, Violet walked to one of the bureaus to put away the linens. The queen was sitting up in bed, a deep scowl on her face and a discarded, barely touched breakfast tray beside her. Her fingers fussed with the laces of her nightgown; her gaze permanently fixed on her abdomen as though the baby she carried might burst forth at any moment.

Violet opened the bureau doors and thought how she might offer some small comfort to the queen, to help soothe her frayed nerves. With each day that passed, Victoria became increasingly harder to calm, increasingly volatile and irrational. None of her ladies, Lehzen, or Violet escaped her notice these days. Everything and everyone annoyed her.

Linens safely stowed away, Violet moved to the bedside table to clear the water glass and handkerchief the queen had used through the night.

"What are you doing skulking around, Parker?"

"I was just about to clear—"

"Well, don't! Have I asked for anything to be cleared? Anything to be taken from me ever?"

"I'm sorr—"

The loud stomp of boots from the adjacent room eclipsed Violet's response, followed by a rush of feminine gasps and hastily muttered, "Your Majesty," before Prince Albert burst into the bedchamber, his face puce with anger.

The queen sat up straighter, clutching the bedsheet to her breasts. "Albert, what on earth—"

"I will not tolerate it any longer, Victoria!" he shouted, his voice stern with a strident German lilt. "I am your husband, not Dash, your bloody lapdog. You have no right to keep me on a leash."

Victoria glared. "What in heaven's name are you talking about?"

"This." He shook a letter in the air. "Demanding that I keep my days and nights free of anything that might take more than an hour or two of my time. That I must be here should you need me. That I might make myself available to you at the drop of a hat. You are pregnant, woman, not ill."

Violet glanced at James who had hurried in behind

Albert and practically skidded to a halt when His Majesty abruptly stopped at Victoria's bedside. Judging by James's exasperated expression, he had tried and failed to deter Albert from his current outburst.

James looked at her and briefly squeezed his eyes shut as the queen and her consort embarked on a shouting match of accusations and demands as though no one else were in the room.

"Your Majesties!" Lehzen's voice cut through the quarrelling like a cracked whip. "If you will please allow me to clear the room so that you might have some privacy."

Albert stood taller, his glare honed on Lehzen. "Yes, I think that best."

"Oh, do you?" Victoria snapped. "Well, I do not, and as this is my bedchamber and my household, it will be me who commands it. You will stay, Lehzen, as will you, Parker."

Violet inwardly grimaced as the queen tossed her husband such a look of utter triumph, Albert's cheeks—and no doubt his temper—grew impossibly darker.

James moved closer to Albert, seemingly in accord with Violet that something must be said to stop such a public disagreement between the monarch and her consort. "Sir, I really think it best…"

The duke faced James, his eyes blazing with fury. "You will stay out of this if you know what's good for you, Greene."

Violet's mind raced with what to say and how to say it so the quarrel might be diffused or at least calmed enough that their majesties resolved it quietly behind closed doors.

Her heart hammering, she cleared her throat.

"Ma'am, might I speak?"

Every eye in the room turned to her, and Violet forced her shoulders back, her knees trembling, but her gaze firmly on Victoria.

"Yes, what is it, Parker? Spit it out."

Violet stepped to the foot of the bed. "You have given me such wisdom, encouragement, and love since I came into your service. You are strong and vibrant, ma'am. The most revered queen in the whole of Europe."

The queen stared for a long moment before her gaze softened, her shoulders lowering. "Well, thank you, Parker, but your kind words do nothing to solve the predicaments between my husband and I, and they do nothing to solve the issue of my pregnancy."

"Forgive me, ma'am, but I think if you remember how much you have helped me and so many others, I am certain it will help you." Violet gripped the intricately carved, wooden bedframe, her heart thundering as the duke's and Lehzen's glares bored into her. "It is more vital than ever that you remain strong, ma'am. For every day of your service, you have had men of court and parliament question your authority and reasoning. Yet you have not faltered as their sovereign for a moment and, instead, pushed those gentlemen forward, commanded them to serve their country with authenticity, honesty, and honor."

Victoria smiled and lifted her chin, regalness that had been missing for weeks shrouding her as she pointedly looked at her husband. "You are right, Parker. And I will continue to do so for as long as I have breath in my body."

"Then…" Violet swallowed. "If I might so bold, ma'am?"

Lehzen stepped forward. "Parker…"

Victoria raised her hand, her gaze on Violet. "Go on."

Violet gripped the bedframe tighter, terrified that her next words might just be a step too far and the queen would slap her as Violet's mother would have.

"You are preparing to become a mother, ma'am," Violet said quietly and with care. "The most demanding role any woman can possibly have. I beg you, Your Majesty, accept this gift with open arms, courage, and commitment as I and all your subjects know you capable of. Do not allow anyone…" Violet glanced at Albert who stared back at her with interest rather than anger. "Your beloved husband included, allow you to falter. We are here to serve and assist you, ma'am, and always will be. No matter how many royal children might follow during your reign, you will be surrounded by people who love and care for you and your happiness."

The ensuing silence was so dense, so entirely still, Violet felt as though the world had stopped moving, everything grounded in time, frozen by her insolence. But she was not placating the queen, she meant every word and believed in Victoria completely.

Yet her words were also borne out of fear that if Victoria faltered in pregnancy without her mother beside her, there was every possibility Violet would without hers when her time came. What if, after everything she and Victoria had achieved, it was proven that they needed their narcissistic mothers? That they were nothing without them…

"Thank you, Parker." Victoria nodded. "All you have conveyed has touched me deeply."

Violet curtsied and stepped back from the bed, her

pulse racing as the queen turned to Albert. Smiling softly, he approached the bed, his eyes entirely on his wife as he cupped her cheek.

"Everyone please leave," Victoria said, her gaze locked with Albert's. "And close the door."

Somehow, Violet managed to sedately walk behind Lehzen and James as they left the bedchamber, quietly closing the door behind them.

Lehzen turned, a deep line between her brows, her gaze flitting from the closed door to Violet. "I suggest you make yourself scarce for a while, Parker. Go along now. I will speak to you later."

Violet dipped her head. "Yes, Baroness."

James stood back and held out his arm, encouraging Violet ahead of him into the corridor.

They walked a few feet along the gallery before laughter bubbled in Violet's throat. She looked at James, his lips pursed tightly together, his eyes shining. "Don't you dare laugh."

He grinned. "How can I not?"

She swatted his arm. "I'm serious."

"Did you see Lehzen's face? What a picture."

They walked a little farther before James tugged her into a small alcove. "What happened to you back there?" he asked, his eyes filled with amusement. "Are you all right?"

"I really don't know." Violet laughed, caught somewhere between hysteria and disbelief. "Everything I said fell out of my mouth without thought or censure. I am sure once the queen has had time to ponder my outburst she will not be as happy as she was just now."

"I think you are entirely wrong. Victoria appreciates your directness as I do."

"Thank you."

He tightened his grip on her fingers, his expression turning solemn. "What you did in there, how you spoke to Victoria, is exactly why I want you, no one else. You are strong, brave, and everything you described in Victoria. You, Violet Parker, are the woman I have been looking for all my life."

Violet looked into his dark eyes, her heart filling with love for this wonderful man who continued to show more and more of who he was, the more time they spent together. He was kind, hard-working, cared for his family despite their unrelenting pressure on him.

"I love you, James," she said, fear knotting her stomach. "I just hope it never comes to light that I am nothing without my mother because I fear you might be stuck with me anyway."

"That fear will never be consummated, my love. The love the queen bears you has nothing to do with your mother. Nothing at all. Can you not see that?"

Without waiting for her answer, he dipped his lips to hers, and Violet pulled him closer, deepening their kiss and sending up a prayer that she never came to regret showing her heart to the man who, despite all her worrying to the contrary, was responsible for giving her genuine freedom.

James's faith in her, his kindness, the way he looked at her…everything he did, lifted her day by day, week by week, until now she could stand tall and imagine a life of her own making.

Chapter Forty-Two

It was a beautifully warm day, and James paused reading to look across Windsor's lawns at Victoria and Albert. They sat on the grass near the pond, their heads almost touching as they spoke to one another intimately, as though they were alone rather than surrounded by courtiers. Having treated their households to a day outside so that their attendants might enjoy the early May sunshine, their majesties had instructed everyone to do as they pleased and indulge in a day free of duty.

The mood was buoyant.

Smiles abounded, music played courtesy of the trio set up beneath a huge oak tree, and people sat or larked about on the grass.

As a man passionate about the arts, pursuits, and technology, Albert was becoming a consort who actively encouraged people's opinions and desires and urged them in their innovation, whatever their rank. He seemed to genuinely care for all, and his conduct with royalty and staff alike had begun to yield a small, yet heartening, amount of influence on Victoria. She was more relaxed, more willing to allow Albert to share her burdens and fears. Something Melbourne wasn't particularly happy about but something Anson, Albert's private secretary, applauded.

"James? Is everything all right?"

"Everything's perfect," he said, lifting his hand to

his brow to shield his eyes from the sun.

Violet smiled down at him from where she sat in front of her easel, her brush hovering over the canvas. "What were you thinking about? I always wonder what you are up to when you smile that way."

"I was thinking how happy Victoria and Albert are these days. Much has changed over the last few weeks. In no small part due to you, I would say."

"Oh, nonsense. They just needed time to get to know one another." She looked across the grass where Lehzen sat alone with her embroidery, her beady eyes constantly straying between the royal couple and the linen on her lap. "Although, I fear the baroness is beginning to begrudge their closeness, rather than enjoy it."

James followed her gaze. "Doesn't she begrudge everyone in one way or another? She is not happy that our romance is now known throughout court either."

"No, but you must not condemn her too much. Victoria is her life and has been for many years. I think she is genuinely afraid of losing her to Albert."

"Losing her? Victoria was never hers in the first place, was she?"

"No, but…" Violet turned back to her canvas, her brow furrowed. "I think Lehzen still sees their relationship as governess and child, rather than queen and servant." She dipped her brush into the paint on her palette before touching the bristles to the canvas. "It is not a particularly healthy relationship for Lehzen or the queen. Albert certainly does not hold Lehzen in the same regard as Victoria. In fact, he often accuses the baroness of being overly attentive."

"Can anyone ever be overattentive to a monarch?"

"Well, I have certainly heard Albert say to Victoria

that Lehzen is stepping over the line. Projecting her thoughts and feelings a little too easily and too often for his liking."

James put down his book and reached for his discarded jacket. "Then it will be interesting to see how things play out. Albert and Victoria grow closer with each passing day." He delved into the inside pocket and pulled out an envelope. He slid his thumb under the seal, already aware that the letter was from his mother, having recognized her writing. "Melbourne's influence over her is certainly waning, I wouldn't be surprised if Lehzen's weakens next."

He turned his attention to the letter.

Dearest James,

I hope this letter finds you well, my darling.

I hate to be the bearer of bad news, especially after receipt of your last letter. Learning the name of the lady you are courting and how happy Mistress Parker makes you gave me untold pleasure. However, I'm afraid I must ask that you return home once again.

Your father suffered the most awful fit yesterday evening and is in a truly woeful condition, my darling. His entire left side has been disabled, his cheek and mouth hanging from his bones as though—

James's hand trembled around the paper, his heart beating fast. "My God…"

"James? What is it?"

"My father." James pushed to his feet. "He has suffered a fit."

"Oh, my goodness." Violet put down her brush and palette before snatching a rag to wipe her hands. "Is he all right?"

"No. No, he's not. I must go to him. Right away."

She stood from her easel. “We will pack up here, and I will come back with you to your room. I can help you—”

“No, stay here.” James looked across at the lawns. “I will speak to Albert and leave immediately.”

She gripped his wrist. “Your pulse is racing.”

“He asked me to return home so many times, urged me to find a wife. What if I am too late and my father dies without everything he wanted in place?”

“You cannot think like that. You have told them we are courting, and they have shown none of the disapproval my mother has. He must be content that you are taking his wishes seriously. Do not worry.”

He looked around the people gathered in groups across the lawn and along the terrace at the back of the castle. “Sometimes I long to take you away from here. I am beginning to see that court is little more than a menagerie of heirs and spares from noble families looking to make suitable marriages. Would you not like to be far away from court sometimes? Somewhere you only have to see your mother if you wish rather than being forced to see her whenever the duchess visits with the queen?”

She gave him an encouraging smile, squeezed his hand. “Just go home and care for your father. All will be well.”

He stared into her beautiful blue eyes, guilt pressing down on him. The truth was, he had avoided telling his parents Violet’s station and instead only listed her attributes, details of her beauty and closeness to the queen, steadfastly avoiding answering his father’s questions about Violet’s family, status, or wealth. Now, James wondered if he had been holding out for his father's passing so that he might never have to answer those questions.

"I love you, Violet," he said, hating his cowardice but knowing in order to protect her, his omissions were necessary.

"I love you, too." She lifted onto her toes and kissed him. "Write to me as soon as you can."

Lest he not leave at all, James abruptly turned and strode across the great expanse of grass. Victoria and Albert laughed as they fed one another pieces of fruit from an enormous silver bowl on the blanket in front of them.

When James's shadow fell over them, Albert lifted his gaze and blinked at James as though he had forgotten he and his wife were not alone. "Mr. Greene. What can we do for you?"

James bowed to both Albert and the queen, his hands clenched behind his back. "Your Majesties, I am sorry for intruding. I have received some bad news and must return home immediately. I'm afraid my father has suffered a fit of some description, and as I am unsure of the situation at present, I must request an indeterminate amount of leave. I will, of course, write with an update as soon as possible."

Albert's eyes darkened with concern. "I see."

"Well, of course, you must go," Victoria said, as she looked at Albert. "You can spare Mr. Greene for a few days, can you not, my love?"

Albert nodded. "I can indeed." He lifted Victoria's hand to his lips and kissed her knuckles. "I will be gone just a few moments." He lowered her hand and stood, pulling at the hem of his waistcoat to straighten it before addressing James. "Let us take a short walk."

James stepped in beside Albert as he started to walk. Uneasy, when all he had expected was an acceptance or refusal of leave, James waited for the duke to speak.

"You have my permission to leave court, of course, Greene, but I ask that you speak with Anson first to ensure your absence will not inconvenience him too much. I believe he lasted just an hour outside today before returning to his work." Albert flashed a brief smile. "He feels he has too much to be getting on with to lie around in the sun. His words, not mine."

"I will, sir. Of course."

Albert stared at him for a moment, hesitation clear in his eyes before he spoke again. "This may appear a strange question, but how interested are you in slavery? Or rather its abolition?"

"Well, greatly, sir. It is one of the most important aspects of debate and government at the moment."

"Has Anson told you anything of what my first speech is about or when it is to happen?" He shook his head, his smile wide. "No, I doubt very much he has considering I told him and Melbourne to keep things as quiet as possible for the time being. I'm not sure if Victoria will approve of my involvement."

"Involvement, sir?"

"Indeed. I will be addressing the Society for the Abolition of Slavery on the first of next month. Victoria abhors slavery, of course, but must consider her position as constitutional monarch and keeps her silence on such controversial matters."

"Do you need my help with the speech, sir? I can always find the time to work on it while I am away—"

"Absolutely not. This speech will be mine and mine alone," Albert said, his gaze firm. "No, I am telling you this because it will be my first public speech, and I wish for every single person in my household to bear witness to it. Therefore, if things progress positively with your father, I ask that you return no later than the eve before."

"I will do my very best, sir."

"Good, then I will see you on the thirty-first of May at the very latest."

With a curt nod, Albert returned to the queen.

James stared after him. The next time he returned to Windsor or Buckingham Palace, there was every possibility he would be a baron.

But still, he did not want the title. Still did not want to risk becoming the person he most dreaded…his father.

He had three weeks until Albert wanted him back at court, and James would put them to good use on the estate and aiding his father's rehabilitation. He turned to where he had left Violet. She was just a dot in the distance, yet her love for him drifted across the grass and into his heart. Was he doing the right thing by her?

A horrible culpability rose that he might come to hurt her. Come to lie and conceal, rant and rave, regardless of how well he had managed to control his temper thus far. He had to be strong. He had to deliver on the good life he promised her.

Chapter Forty-Three

In her bedroom at Buckingham Palace, Violet pushed a final pin into her maid's cap to secure it and then made for the door. She had been rushing around all morning and had lain down for a quick nap before her evening duties, only to oversleep.

Her nerves jumbled, she reached for the door and yanked it open. "Oh!"

Another maid stood just outside, her fist raised as if to rap on the door. The poor girl leapt back. "You scared me half to death, Violet." She laughed. "Whatever is the cause of such haste?"

"I will be late for my duties if I don't leave this minute." Violet stepped into the corridor, closing the door behind her. "That's not why you are here, is it? The queen hasn't sent a message for me?"

"Oh, no. This came for you with the afternoon post. It has a grand seal on it." She held out an envelope. "So I hastened to catch you before you started work."

Violet only had to glance at the handwriting to know it was from James. Her heart lifted, she had not heard from him in over a week. "Thank you."

The maid smiled and hurried on her way, a pile of mail in her hand.

Pressing the envelope to her breast, unexpected tears filled Violet's eyes. How she worried he had forsaken her and his time away had made him reconsider their courtship. Conversely, their time apart had only strengthened her love for him, but with his father so very ill and James's responsibilities growing, he might come to accept that she had been right all along, and she was far from being a suitable wife for him.

What if in this letter he told her their courtship had reached its end?

Violet prayed with all her might that it wouldn't be the case before stuffing the envelope into her apron pocket. She hurried through the palace to the queen's apartments, half of her panicked for her potential tardiness, the other half desperate to find a quiet corner where she might read James's news. At first, his letters had arrived almost daily, but as he entered the third week of being away, his letters had suddenly stopped which Violet feared could only mean something had happened to entirely consume his attention.

A lump rose in her throat. Mostly like his father dying.

Reaching the queen's apartments, Violet entered the drawing room and curtsied to the queen where she sat with the Duchess of Sunderland and Lady Kingsley looking through some papers and letters in front of the huge stone fireplace.

"Good evening, Parker." The queen sighed before she returned her attention to the letter in her hand, her gaze sad. "We are just looking through some of Albert's letters to me before we were married. Life was so much lighter and freer of problems then."

"It's always nice to reminisce, ma'am."

"I suppose."

The queen's melancholy only grew worse as her pregnancy progressed, her need to be with Albert twenty-four hours a day never waning and the friction between him and Lehzen escalating. It was as though pressure built within the palace walls from every direction.

When it was clear Victoria had no further conversation for her, Violet entered the bedchamber to start her evening duties. The room was empty, and James's letter crackled in her pocket as she walked, demanding her attention. Unable to resist, Violet softly closed the door.

She walked to the bureau and slid open the top tray, extracting the creams and potions Victoria liked applied to her face, hands, and décolletage every evening, as well as her best-loved scent. Once Violet was sure she would have sufficient reason to be standing at the bureau should the queen or anyone else enter, she quickly took James's letter from her pocket and opened it.

Dearest Violet,

I am writing just as I finish readying for my return to court. By the time you receive this letter, I hope to be no more than a day away from the palace. My father is much improved. He is beginning to regain movement in his arm and leg, and his speech recovers a little each day. Thus, why I can return.

Your letters in the weeks I have been away have been a great comfort to me, and I thank you deeply for your care and support. Life will certainly change for us both from now on, but I will speak of that more when we are together again. Too much has been left unsaid or omitted in the time we have been courting and now there is a need for complete honesty...

Violet looked up, staring blindly ahead. What did he mean "too much has been left unsaid or omitted"? She thought their relationship had been honest and open. Had he been lying to her? Keeping secrets?

...Prince Albert has written to me often, and between his writing, Anson's, and my input, I believe his first speech will be one of immense importance and propel him upward in the view of the government and public alike. I am proud to serve a man I think will prove himself worthy of his place beside our great queen.

But, for now, I must go. I hope to see you very soon.

James

Violet slowly closed the letter, her heart heavy. There were no words of love or endearments. No promise of their romance continuing once he returned. A tear rolled over her cheek just as the door opened and the queen and her ladies entered, Lehzen behind them.

Violet quickly swiped her fingers over her cheek and hid the letter behind her back, sinking into a curtsey.

"Whatever is the matter, Parker?" The queen frowned. "You look like I've walked in and caught you stealing." Suspicion shadowed the queen's eyes. "I haven't, have I?"

"No, ma'am. Of course not." Violet's heart hammered, her fingers crushing James's letter. "I would never—"

"Then what do you have hidden behind you?"

Heat crept up Violet's neck as she looked from Victoria to her ladies to the baroness. They all stared back at her expectantly, some clearly more amused by her discomfort than others.

Facing the queen, Violet pulled the letter from behind her back. "It's a letter from Mr. Greene, ma'am. I know I shouldn't be reading personal correspondence when I am supposed to be working, but he has been away so long and—"

Lehzen stepped forward, two spots of color darkening her cheeks. "You are absolutely right, Parker, you should not be wasting your time on personal matters." She shot out her hand. "Give that to me. It will be returned to you once you have finished for the evening."

Violet briefly closed her eyes before holding out the letter.

"Wait." The queen swept closer and put her hand on Lehzen's arm, pinning her with a stare. "Confiscating Parker's letter will not be necessary, Lehzen. You may go." She looked behind her at the gathered circle of ladies. "All of you. I wish to speak with Parker alone."

Violet's heart pulsed in her ears. The queen might have shown tolerance, but she looked far from happy, the strain she suffered showing around her eyes and lining her mouth. Her pregnancy was taking its toll on her petite body, her exuberance curtailed when she still had several months until the birth. Violet swallowed. Victoria's patience and gaiety were rare these days, her vitality waning. Who knew how she would punish Violet for her impertinence?

The women trailed from the room, Lehzen the last to leave and throwing a glare at Violet over her shoulder before she closed the door.

Victoria walked to the sofas in front of the fire. "Come. Sit with me."

Violet followed and sat, clutching James's letter in her lap.

"It pleases me that you and Mr. Greene are now officially courting, Parker. Not only does it demonstrate the depth of feeling Mr. Greene must have for you to defy society, but also that I believe true love should cross every divide. Class included." She paused, her sympathetic gaze steady on Violet's until she inhaled a sharp breath, her bosom rising. "Alas, such unions, such romances are rarely successful. You do know that?"

"Yes, ma'am. I do. I think Mr. Greene and I both know that our…romance cannot continue as lightly as it has been with his father so seriously ailing. His poor state of health was why I was desperate to read Mr. Greene's letter. I have not heard from him for a week and feared the worst."

"I see. And there was nothing else worrying you about his letter?"

"Well, I did wonder—"

"If Mr. Greene might be writing to say he wishes to end your relationship?" Victoria raised her eyebrows. "And has he?"

Violet looked down at the letter. "No, but neither is he in any way affectionate."

"And what of his father?"

"He is very much improving."

"Well, that is something at least."

Violet nodded, her selfishness shaming. "Yes, ma'am."

"We must rally, Parker! We are both young and in the prime of our energy and beauty. You should not waste yours on any man who cannot give you the best chance of having real joy in your life. Don't you think that you and I deserve happiness with a mate after the way we were raised by our mothers?"

Pleased to see the zeal returning to Victoria's eyes, Violet sat straighter and a gave a firm nod. "Yes, ma'am. We do."

"Even if sacrifices must be made, it is important that when we find love, we do what we must to maintain its joy. Do you know what has been bothering me, Parker?" She looked to the closed door, her cheeks reddening. "What has me in such a terrible mood these past few days?"

"No, ma'am."

Victoria clasped and unclasped her hands in her lap. "As time passes, the more likely it is that I will have to dismiss Lehzen or else risk losing Albert's love."

Violet stared. So what she had suspected was true. But still, the notion that Victoria might dismiss Lehzen was unimaginable. "She has been your most trusted servant your entire life, ma'am. I know she and the duke sometimes do not see eye to—"

"Sometimes? More apt never." Sadness seemed to weigh heavily on the queen's shoulders as they drooped. "With Lehzen gone and my estrangement from my mother, how will I cope with the trauma of childbirth and then an infant?"

The queen's voiced cracked, and Violet inched closer on the sofa. "You will have me and all your ladies to help you, Your Majesty," she said, firmly. "You are surrounded by so much love, and our new prince or princess will be, too. You will both be cared for."

"And I very much appreciate you all, Parker, but it is our life partners with whom we must concentrate on building a true bond." The queen's tone changed from glum to staunch, her gaze boring into Violet's. "It is vital that we build a strong and lasting connection with our love match. Yes, we might need others from time to time, but it is our husband or wife with whom we must aim to build a beautiful life. Even over our children. Do you understand?"

Violet nodded, although she did not really understand the queen's meaning at all and worried that her fear of giving birth was making her a touch hysterical. She and Violet had not received true love from their mothers, but Violet still believed children should matter to a mother above anyone else. Their spouse included.

"When Mr. Greene returns," the queen continued, "you must spend as much time together as possible, but please, hold back your heart and virtue for the time being. Do not let him take either without a marriage proposal. If you do not heed this advice, Parker, and he should later reject you, I fear your full recovery will be impossible."

Violet nodded, her heart hammering that Victoria did not know that both Violet's heart and virtue had been James's for months. "I understand."

"I have heard on very good authority that Mr. Greene has high hopes for you both, but a woman must look after herself until her love makes a true commitment."

"High hopes, ma'am?"

A smile lifted the corner of Victoria's mouth, her blue eyes lit with teasing. "Well, if he can tell my beloved Albert that he one day wishes to marry you, I do not think Mr. Greene has any intention of rejecting you, do you? But it does pay for a woman to be prepared. That way, if the worst should occur, she can still hold her head high and walk away, her cheeks dry and her pride intact."

Relief swept through Violet, tears pricking her eyes. "He told the duke he wishes to marry me?"

"Yes." The queen smiled. "He did. If you love Mr.

Greene how I love Albert, you must do all you can to make your dreams come true. Just don't forget the lessons we have learned under our mothers' hands. Love often comes with conditions. It can cause pain as much as it can make the heart soar." Victoria leaned forward, his gaze soft as she squeezed Violet's fingers. "I just want to protect you, Parker. I want you to be happy."

Violet blinked, and a tear rolled over her cheek. She was so entirely moved by Victoria's sincerity that she pushed protocol to the side and covered the queen's hand with her own and squeezed tight as if she and Victoria were friends, rather than monarch and servant.

"And I want the same for you, Your Majesty. Always."

Chapter Forty-Four

Movement in the distance caught James's eye, and he pushed to his feet on the steps of the stone folly nestled deep within the foliage of the palace grounds. Shielding his eyes against the late afternoon sun, he squinted across the yards of grass ahead of him as Violet emerged from behind a mass of shrubbery.

She carried her beloved sketchpad and box of pencils, no doubt brought as a decoy should anyone follow or come across her. There was no need for her to worry, James had seen neither person nor animal since he arrived half an hour before.

They were very much alone just as he planned.

Having returned to Buckingham Palace that morning, he had only managed to get a message to Violet a couple of hours before asking that she meet him prior to her evening duties. When no return message had been forthcoming, James left Albert's chambers and ventured through the gardens alone, praying Violet appeared.

Unable to bear seeing her and not being able to touch her, James met her on the grass. He stared at her beautiful face, looked into the eyes he had missed so very much. "Hello."

She smiled, a faint blush darkening her cheeks. "Hello."

The delight he'd hoped to see in her gaze was troublingly faint. Instead, caution dominated. Unease whispered through him. Something had changed. He wasn't fool enough to think he could go away, deal with own problems and worries, and have Violet unchanged and waiting for him. She was too strong a woman for that, but he had hoped for some pleasure in her eyes. A wide, heart-lifting smile. She greeted him with neither.

He forced a smile. "You look wonderful."

"Thank you. You…look well."

Her distance was so entirely unexpected it cut deep. She knew his father had been seriously ill, was he missing something? Or was his arrogance that she might jump for joy at the sight of him yet another sign of his familial conceit?

He tentatively reached for her hand, and when she allowed him to take it, James tucked it into his elbow. "I thought we could sit in the folly."

"Away from prying eyes?"

She smiled, but he wasn't convinced she was jesting.

Just because he had found their separation painful, his days depressingly gray rather than filled with light and possibility, there was every chance Violet found their time apart freeing. She was young and beautiful, intelligent and creative. Who was to say his absence hadn't altered her mind about their romance?

They stepped inside the folly and were shrouded in shadow as they sat on one of the curved stone benches lining its circumference.

"The doctors have told my mother and I that it would be best if we put our affairs in order. Father is stable, but they are reluctant to alter the prognosis that he is likely to die within the next few months."

"I'm so sorry."

Her eyes filled with sympathy, and he blew out a relieved breath. At least she still cared. "I came back because Albert wants me here for his speech, but I will need to return home immediately afterward. The last thing I want is for you to think I don't care for you, Violet, because I do. Deeply."

Her blue gaze wandered over his face as though looking for something. After a moment, she nodded and lifted his hand into her lap. She stared at their intertwined fingers. "I think Albert will let you return home without too much of a fight. He and the queen seem to be closing ranks."

"What do you mean?"

"They are relying on each other rather than those around them. I think Lehzen's days beside the queen are numbered, and I could easily be next."

"You suspected as much of Lehzen for a while, but you? That will never happen. The queen adores you. Anyway, whatever is happening for the queen to be relying on Albert, she will still need her ladies."

"You seem very certain."

"I am, considering the letters Albert has written to me. He grows ever keener to learn more about science and industry, about the real people of London, as he calls them. He wants to see the slums, the workhouses, everything. He talks of little else but societal change, and his desire to implement it. In order to do that, he will have to spend time away from the palace whether Victoria likes it or not. It is then she will need her ladies."

"Albert's interests are admirable, but the queen will most definitely hate his absence."

"I have the distinct feeling there is very little His Majesty will not wish to explore and learn about. It is a shame I will not be there beside him to see his ambitions unfold."

"So as Albert's life expands and grows more exciting, Victoria falls deeper and deeper into melancholy. Surely that is a recipe for disaster?"

"They love one another. They will work things out so both she and he are happy, I'm sure."

"Maybe." She sighed, looked again at their hands. "I just hope she regains her confidence once the baby is born. Maybe then she will have some years alone with Albert and their little one before the world starts expecting a baby brother or sister."

"Years might be a little generous as far as the government is concerned. They will want an heir and a spare in quick succession."

"And I very much doubt Albert will argue with that." Her jaw tightened. "Whatever he feels about his working life, Victoria insists he is the assured head of the family. She is adamant that she will always love and obey him in their personal life."

She paused, and then a glittering challenge sparked in her eyes. At first, James had no idea what she thought, and then comprehension dawned. Violet still suspected he meant to curtail her liberty, that he would expect the same deference from her if they married.

He breathed deep, knowing he must tread carefully. If she were to ever consent to being with him, the first thing he must prove is that he would never seek to entrap her.

"And you think she is wrong to do that?"

"Victoria is too great a woman to obey anyone. Her consort included."

"I agree. She should not obey anyone. She is the

queen."

"And a woman, James. Victoria is a woman."

"Of course."

Her eyes searched his. "Maybe I am wrong about them depleting the entire household."

"Why do you say that?"

She swallowed, her cheeks reddening. "Well, I cannot believe Albert will find you superfluous…especially considering the bond that has formed between you."

There was something about the tone of her voice. She said the final part of her sentence like an accusation. He studied her as she turned away from him, her chin high and clearly avoiding having to look at him.

"What is it?" He touched his finger to her chin, turning her head. Her blue eyes were filled with confusion and irritation but also a quiet pleading. "Violet?"

She exhaled a shaky breath and blurted, "Victoria told me something that I have difficulty believing."

He dropped his finger from her chin and frowned. "What?"

"She said you told Albert that you wish to marry me."

"She…" James snapped his mouth closed before looking away from her unwavering, forthright gaze.

He, Anson, and Albert had been in the duke's chambers one night before his last visit home, drinking into the early hours and regaling each other with stories of their past mistakes and desires for their futures. Never in a hundred years had James thought Albert would take any notice of his claim that he would ask Violet to marry him no matter the obstacle. And James certainly did not think Albert would tell his wife!

"I was drunk." He swiped his hand over his face. "Very drunk."

Her sharp intake of breath echoed around the small space. "Well, I thank you for your honesty." She stood. "I am glad you are back, James, but I'm afraid I must return to the queen. I give you all my best wishes for your father and family."

He leapt to his feet and gripped her wrist as she turned away from him.

She tipped her head back and glared, her eyes burning with hurt. "Let go of me."

"I haven't finished."

"You've said enough, and I've *had* enough. It is quite clear we are on different paths. It's time to end things between us, James. I will not keep going back and forth wondering if there is a future—"

He hadn't meant to crush his lips so roughly to hers, but he couldn't think or talk when she was looking at him with such undisguised hurt. She slapped her hands to his chest and pushed him away. "Stop that. Right now." Her cheeks were red, her blonde curls tumbling from their pins and falling to her temples. "You can't kiss me that way…not anymore."

She had never looked more beautiful. "Do you not know how much I've missed you?" he asked, his heart racing that this could be the end for them. "How much I've needed you?"

She planted her hands on her hips, her breaths harried. "All I know is you are clearly a man who takes what he wants when he wants it. All I know is you are a man who begged me to allow you to court me then—"

"Had far too much to drink one night and told

England's king consort that I will move heaven and earth to make you my wife because I cannot imagine a life without seeing your wonderful face and hearing your beautiful voice every day." James clenched his jaw against the overbearing passion that threatened to consume him, burn him alive if she refused him one more time. "I love you, Violet. I really damn well love you. Why in God's name can't you believe that?"

Her breasts rose and fell, her breathing rapid as her gaze swept back and forth over his face. Finally, she strode forward and gripped his lapels. Another search of his face and eyes, and then she yanked him down for a harder, more urgent kiss than the last.

Their lips bruised, their tongues teased and tangled, their fingers scoring into one another's hair. James pulled her closer, her breasts crushed to his chest, his erection straining…

She eased back and placed her hands on his chest, her cheeks flushed. "You really wish to marry me?"

"So much so I have told my parents everything."

"Everything?" Worry immediately clouded her gaze. "What do you mean?"

"I told them who you are, that you are a maid to the queen, and just how much you mean to me. I told them I love you and want to marry you. I made it clear there will never be anyone else and if they so keenly want to see me married and my wife, God willing, with child, then they will gladly welcome you." He inhaled a long breath. "But all my assertions to them mean nothing if marrying me is not what you want, too."

Her cheeks reddened, and then slowly, shyly—beautifully—the concern left her eyes and was replaced with palpable happiness.

Her tentative smile slowly grew to the most breath-stealing grin. "I want to marry you, James. I want to bear your children. I want *you*."

James whipped her into his arms, and she yelped as he lifted her off her feet.

He stared up at her, her hands braced on his shoulders, the sunlight dancing in her hair. "I want you to come home with me and spend a few days with my parents. See the estate, the horses, the dogs, meet the servants. I don't want you to agree to marry me until you have seen my home and are certain a life there is what you want."

She leaned down and kissed him. "It will be."

Yet nightmares of the man he might become unfurled in James's stomach as he slowly lowered her to the ground. "I want to make you happy, Violet. I have no idea who I will become once all the responsibility of Cassington Park lies on my shoulders."

"And I have no idea who I will be without my mother, without Victoria." She cupped her hands to his jaw. "We will just have to find out who we are together, won't we?"

Chapter Forty-Five

The carriage rumbled along the avenue leading to James's family estate, and Violet's breath caught as she saw Cassington Park for the very first time.

"Oh, my." She leaned a little further out the window. "It's the most beautiful house I've ever seen."

"Despite having lived in palaces?" James laughed.

She sat back in her seat. "Yes. Just look at it."

James's smile faltered. "I just hope you still find it beautiful once you've met my mother and father."

"Stop worrying. Everything will be fine."

"God bless your optimism, but you do not know my parents."

Despite her smile, nerves had not stopped leaping in Violet's stomach since she and James had left London two days before. The joy she felt having accepted his marriage proposal and knowing they would be man and wife as soon as possible meant they had travelled to Oxfordshire masquerading as a newly wedded couple. Eating meals together, talking for hours, and making love until the first light of dawn crept beneath the drapes of the room they had taken at a coaching inn.

"My love for you is too strong for anyone to break it," she said. "Your parents included. I have every intention of proving to them just how good a daughter I will be."

"Oh?"

"I will be my most charming, caring, and witty the entire time I am here. And…"

He lifted an eyebrow. "There's more?"

"They will come to understand why I am so close to the queen despite being a servant rather than a lady."

"You do not need to prove anything to them." James frowned. "You are perfect to me, and that's all that matters."

"Maybe, but…" Violet's smile dissolved, her bravado wavering. "I am not the titled lady they wanted for you, and you know how important it is to me that I prove my worth now that I am estranged from my mother. This is my first opportunity to do that away from the protection at court."

"You will be perfectly safe here. I won't let anything happen to you."

"That's not what I mean. I want to show my love for you by caring for your father and your mother. I might not come from a grand family or have a dowry, but I do have a maid's strength and a carer's touch. Maybe they will come to see the importance of that as Victoria has."

The carriage pulled up alongside the house's huge double oak doors, and apprehension took flight in Violet's stomach again. She exhaled a shaky breath. "Aren't we a little early?"

"Yes. I always do my best to surprise my parents with the hope they have less time to formulate a list of my inadequacies since they last saw me."

"A parental skill I know well, I'm sorry to say. Clearly, I will be perfectly at home."

But as Violet slid her hand into James's and alighted from the carriage, a horrible feeling of gloom shrouded her. Staring at the house's enormous façade, the magnitude of what she would be adopting as James's wife stretched her nerves close to breaking.

He touched her elbow. "Are you all right? You've suddenly gone awfully pale."

"I'm fine." Violet forced a smile. "Let's go inside. The sooner I meet your parents, the sooner I will learn what I am facing. The not knowing is far worse than the reality, I'm sure."

With James's hand at her elbow, they left the driver to retrieve their luggage and walked up the steps. With a final exchanged look of encouragement, James opened the door and held it wide for Violet to enter ahead of him.

Before she had time to gasp at the beautiful chandelier above her or the cream marble floor beneath her feet, a woman in her late fifties half-walked, half-stumbled into the foyer, a lace handkerchief pressed to her mouth as she let out a strangled sob.

Violet froze, knowing without a doubt that this elegant yet obviously distraught woman was James's mother. Her hair was the exact shade as her son's, albeit threaded with silver, and she had the same strikingly dark eyes that, in that moment, shone with tears.

"Mother?" James's hand slipped from Violet's elbow as he strode forward. "What is it?"

The click of his mother's heels abruptly silenced, her sharp intake of breath echoing around the cavernous space as her head snapped up and she quickly dabbed at her face. "James, we were not expecting you until this evening," she said, turning her gaze on Violet. "You really must cease this habit of arriving early."

"What's happened? Is it Father?"

His mother continued to stare at Violet as she struggled not to fidget under the older woman's solemn scrutiny. "Aren't you going to introduce us, James?"

Violet stood immobile as James took his mother's hand and brought her closer. "Mama, this is Violet, Violet Parker. The woman I love and who, I am proud to announce, is now my fiancée. I hope you will come to love her as I do."

"You are engaged?"

"Yes."

Violet dipped a curtsy. "Lady Greene, it's a pleasure to finally meet you."

Annoyance leapt into the other woman's eyes momentarily banishing the deep sadness that had been there a few moments before. "There is no need to curtsey, my dear. I am not the queen." She offered her hand, and Violet could not help but notice how it ever so slightly trembled. "I'm afraid, under the circumstances, you will have to forgive me for not offering my congratulations. I have far more upsetting concerns than my son's impromptu engagement."

"Of course." Violet swallowed against the dryness in her throat and stepped back. "Is there anything I can do to help? You are obviously distraught and—"

"There is nothing you can possibly do." Lady Greene's eyes filled with tears. "Unless you can bring my husband back from the dead."

James visibly flinched. "Father is dead? When?"

"Less than an hour ago. The doctor left just before you arrived." James's mother faced Violet who stood stock-still. "Considering my son's hopes that we might get along, please, call me Millicent. With my husband gone, I am forced to accept that titles and ranks have no real meaning, after all." She turned away as a black-suited butler approached. "Branson, I'm sure my son and his guest have luggage outside. Would you kindly take it to their rooms?"

"Of course, my lady."

Violet offered the butler—who also looked somewhat upset—a small smile, not sure she would ever get used to the others waiting on her as James assured her she would. She looked at him now as he moved away from his mother to pace back and forth, his fingers pushed into his hair. Every part of her longed to go to him, to comfort him, but Violet refrained when she had no idea how his mother might react to a display of open affection.

But the least Violet could do was speak to him. "James? What can I do?"

He stopped pacing, his eyes boring into hers before he faced his mother. "Is he abed?"

She nodded. "You can see him whenever you are ready. Branson and I have made him presentable in every way possible, the windows and mirrors in the bedroom are covered, at least. I will see to the others forthwith." She closed her eyes and pressed her handkerchief to her nose and mouth, inhaled deeply. After a moment, she opened her eyes and lowered her hand. "You are now a baron, my darling, and the master of the estate. I know he was hard on you, but your father always loved you."

Violet dropped her gaze to the floor, tears pricking the backs of her eyes knowing just how much James had loved his father, even though she doubted he would admit as much or how little love he received in return.

"Will you come with me, Violet? To see my father?" His jaw tight, James's eyes were dry if not heart-wrenchingly sad. "I would like you with me."

"Of course." Violet walked forward and stood in

front of his mother. "Please, Lady… Millicent, I ask that you lean on me while I am here. I recently lost my own beloved father and know how painful a time this is. It is my heartfelt wish to help in any way I can."

The older woman stared at her before she softly nodded. "Thank you."

James cupped his hand around Violet's elbow. "We will go up now, Mama. Why don't you ask Ava to arrange tea in the drawing room? We will join you shortly."

With another sad nod, Lady Greene walked away, and James led Violet in the opposite direction through the foyer into a darkened corridor. She stared at the polished wood, the shining marble, glinting glass and porcelain, trying not to consider how all of this extravagance and luxury now belonged to James. The grandeur somehow did not match the man she had fallen in love with, but it was his all the same.

They climbed a flight of stairs and walked along a carpeted landing before stopping in front of a closed door.

She glanced at him. "Are you all right?"

"Yes. I knew this day was coming." He exhaled heavily, his gaze on the door. "I am sure my brother, George, will be on his way here soon, if he isn't already."

"I wish I was meeting him under happier circumstances."

"We will do what we can to help Mama and then leave her in George's care when we return to court. Not for a week or so, of course, but—"

"There is no rush for you to go back. I can easily return alone and inform—"

"No, we go together," he said firmly, brushing a curl

from her cheek before dipping his head to kiss her. "I must present myself to Victoria as the new baron, and we will tell her of our engagement. The sooner we can make wedding plans, the better." He glanced again at the closed door. "It is what my father wanted, and now, at last, I am ready to comply."

Violet placed her hand on his chest. "Know he is proud of you, James."

He nodded, took her hand, and led her into the darkened bedroom.

Chapter Forty-Six

James stood in front of Albert's desk at Windsor, his hands clasped behind his back. "So once Mistress Parker and I have spoken to the queen, we will begin wedding arrangements."

"And how is your mother? I understand she took your father's death quite badly."

"She has found things difficult but is as well as can be expected," James said, following Albert as he stood from his desk and left the study to walk into his sitting room. "She will remain at the house after Mistress Parker and I are married." James softly smiled, once again in awe of Violet's kindness toward his mother when she had been less than welcoming. "My fiancée insisted upon it."

"As she should," Albert said with approval. "Family is important, Greene. The most important thing, in fact. I have every intention of doing my utmost to institute a union between Victoria and her mother. Before the baby is born, if possible."

James stilled. "Does the queen know?"

"No, but she will in time." Albert sat in a wingback chair and pinned James with a stare. "Why do you ask? You think it's a bad idea?"

"I would prefer not to offer an opinion with regard to the queen and her mother, sir, but I am certainly concerned that the duchess's maid, Mrs. Parker, does not further upset my fiancée."

"Ah, yes, of course. I remember the queen telling me something of their turbulent relationship. I will speak to my wife and—"

Charles Carr appeared at the door and nodded at James before bowing to Albert. "The queen, sir."

James straightened as Victoria entered followed by Violet and Lehzen. He briefly met Violet's gaze and winked before bowing before the queen, choosing to pretend he hadn't seen Lehzen's disapproving gaze. "Your Majesty."

"Ah, Mr. Greene or should I say baron?" The queen smiled warmly and offered her hand to James.

He pressed his lips to her lace-covered knuckles. "I have taken my father's title as he wanted, ma'am. I appreciate Your Majesties meeting with myself and Mistress Parker this afternoon. We have much we would like to share, and hopefully, you will give your blessings to our plans."

The queen grinned and snuck a look at Violet before she walked to her husband. Albert leaned down and kissed her cheek before taking Victoria's hand and leading her to the sofa. Once they were seated side by side, Lehzen took a chair by the door and removed her sewing from her ever-present bag.

James held out his hand inviting Violet to take a seat on the second sofa opposite their majesties. As he sat beside her, James felt more full of pride and strength than he had in his entire life. Being here in front of the queen and Albert with Violet by his side, his life suddenly had genuine meaning and purpose. He saw his future with complete and utter clarity, confident that in time everything he had resisted at home would be easier to bear with Violet there to help him.

"Are you with us, Greene?"

James blinked and faced Albert with a laugh. "Sorry, sir, I was miles away."

"And why wouldn't you daydream, Mr. Greene?" Victoria's eyes were soft with fondness as she stared at Violet. "Look at your fiancée. She is quite beautiful in her happiness."

Violet blushed as she grinned at the queen. "I am happy, ma'am. Truly."

"Then tell us your plans." The queen looked between James and Violet. "Have no fear, my beloved husband and I have discussed what your leaving us will mean, and as much as we shall be lost without you, we wish you every good will. Have you set a date for the wedding? Will it be at your parish, Mr. Greene?"

"It will, ma'am."

Victoria nodded and looked at Violet. "Do you have a date in mind, Parker?"

"Not as yet, but…" Violet covered James's hand with hers where it lay on the sofa between them. "I do not want to leave before the prince or princess is born, so maybe we will have the wedding at Christmas time."

"Oh, Parker, you are so sweet to think of me and the baby!" Victoria exclaimed. "I want you here as much as any of my special ladies. Thank you. Moreover, I think a Christmas wedding is always so romantic. You will look radiant in white with a bouquet of red roses."

James smiled. Violet's eyes were bright with happiness as she stared at the queen, a sovereign he had no doubt Violet would remain as devoted to as she would their own family.

"So," Albert said. "We should arrange something

for Greene and Mistress Parker as a way of demonstrating our blessing, Victoria. What do you suggest?"

"A wonderful idea, my love. How about dinner tonight in my private rooms?" She looked at James and then Violet. "What do you say?"

James nodded, thinking how pleased his father would be to see his son dining privately with the queen and her consort. For all his desperation to have James home, his father had been an elitist of the highest order. "That would be wonderful, ma'am. Thank you."

She smiled. "Parker?"

"I am honored, ma'am." Violet hesitated and threw a worried look at James. "But I couldn't possibly. I am your maid and—"

"And just weeks away from marrying a baron," the queen said, firmly. "No, tonight, you and Mr. Greene shall be our personal guests. Just the four of us. It will be wonderful." She looked across the room. "Lehzen? Please go to the kitchens and ask chef to prepare a celebratory four courses with the best wines, for myself, Albert, and our guests."

James looked at Lehzen as her disbelief was directed at Violet, then him, her cheeks red. "Yes, ma'am," she said, before purposefully pushing her sewing into her bag and standing. "I will see to that right away."

"Actually, just wait there a moment," Victoria said. "I think it is time we all took our leave."

She stood, and Albert immediately pushed to his feet to cup her elbow, James and Violet rising, too.

Gazing up at her husband, the queen touched Albert's cheek. "I will leave you to your work, my love. Might you spend some time in my apartments before our meal this evening?"

He kissed her cheek. "I will."

She smiled and then turned to James. "If I could take your arm, Mr. Greene?"

Nodding at the duke, James led the queen from the chambers, Violet and Lehzen following.

Once they reached the queen's apartments, Victoria slipped her hand from James's arm. "Thank you, Mr. Greene, Lehzen will escort me from here. You spend a few minutes saying your farewells to Parker before you see her again this evening." She smiled and leaned in conspiratorially. "I know how hard it is to be parted when one is so in love."

He laughed. "Thank you, ma'am."

James waited until Victoria and Lehzen had disappeared behind the closed door of the queen's apartments and then took Violet's hands. "Happy?"

"Very. I feel so privileged to dine with the queen and Albert. Privileged and a little like an imposter. This whole journey we are embarking on will take time for me to get used to."

"Believe me, it will take a while for me to get used to walking in my father's shoes. There is still so much I have to learn, and now understand why he wanted me home so often. I should have listened to him, confronted my fears, and got on with it."

"Our fears are real and sometime incapacitating, James. No one has the right to tell us differently. Not our parents or anyone else. You are worried about becoming as intolerable as your father because it has happened to every heir in your family for generations, but I have every confidence you will break the chain."

Thinking himself the luckiest man on earth to have

her for his own, James's conversation with Albert came into his mind. "And what about your fears regarding your mother?"

She looked along the corridor as though her mother might suddenly appear before turning to look at him again. "I rarely see her now that she lives away from the palace with the duchess, and I am happy with that. I will invite her to the wedding. After that, who knows?"

James inhaled a long breath. "Albert told me he intends to orchestrate a reconciliation between Victoria and the duchess."

She briefly closed her eyes. "My mother predicted as much. Albert is known for his belief in strong family bonds. I should have guessed this would happen. I imagine it will only be a matter of time until I see more of my mother along with the duchess, after all."

"But now you are stronger, more independent. More beautiful, engaged to a baron. Oh, and apt to dine privately with the queen and her consort." He winked. "I think dealing with your mother and the duchess will no longer be a problem."

She laughed. "Yes, I think you might be right."

He glanced in each direction along the corridor, and once he was sure they were alone, James pulled his fiancée into his arms and kissed her.

Epilogue

Over a year later... November 1841

Violet sat at her easel in front of the window in the sunlit room she had commandeered as her studio at Cassington Park…her beloved home.

Since her and James's wedding almost a year before, her love of the estate had grown exponentially, as had her care for her mother-in-law, the staff, and tenants. Contentment enveloped her as she laid down her brush and looked into the cradle just an arm's length away.

Nothing could have prepared her for the overwhelming love she felt for her and James's first born—the next heir to Cassington, Matthew, the future Baron Greene. Now four months old, Matthew had become the heart of the estate, not just for his parents and grandmother but for everyone else who lived and worked there, too.

As though the baby sensed her watching him, he began to snuffle and squirm as he awakened. Violet walked to the bureau and washed her hands with the water and soap she kept there before drying them and walking back to the crib.

"Well, hello there, young man. How are you this sunny afternoon?"

Her son blinked and smiled, his tiny fists rubbing his eyes as Violet lifted him into her arms. Softly humming, she walked to the window and watched James as he spoke to their head gardener, waving his arm back and forth as he encompassed the acres of green surrounding them.

"For someone who didn't want any part in running this estate once upon a time, your papa is very much at home now, isn't he, little one?"

There was a discreet cough at the open doorway behind her, and Violet turned as Branson entered the room and dipped his head. "Ma'am."

"Branson." Violet smiled. "What can I do for you?"

He came closer, carrying a silver tray. "A letter for you, ma'am. From the palace."

"The palace?" Violet adjusted Matthew on her shoulder before sliding the envelope from the tray. She stared at the seal, a small knot of excitement forming in her stomach. It had been two or three weeks since she had heard from Victoria which meant this letter held news of only one thing. "Would you mind taking Matthew to Nanny, Branson? I'd like to read this straight away."

The butler quickly put his tray on the closest side table and eagerly scooped Matthew from her arms. "Not at all, ma'am. Not at all."

Violet took the letter opener from the tray and broke the seal.

Dear Lady Greene,

I am writing on behalf of Her Majesty, the queen, to inform you that she is safely delivered of her second child. England's heir, a healthy baby boy, was born yesterday morning. The queen is feeling as well as can be expected and...

Violet lowered the letter and laughed. A boy…a

baby boy! Oh, the joy Victoria and Albert must be feeling. Now, little Vicky had a baby brother. A brother who was also the future King of England.

She rushed to the side of the room and flung open the French doors and hurried outside. The cold November breeze snatched her breath, but she didn't stop or go back for her shawl. A baby boy! Victoria and Albert would be so thrilled. Lifting her skirts, she hurried down the stone steps at the back of the house and onto the gravel pathway.

"James!" she called, waving the royal letter above her head. "James!"

He turned from the gardener and hurried toward her. "What's the matter? Is it Matthew?" He tightly grasped her hand. "Darling, what is it?"

Violet panted a laugh, pressing her hand to her stomach. "Nothing is the matter. I have the most wonderful news."

"Then why on earth are you running out here like that?" He frowned. "I thought—"

"James, it's the queen. She has given birth to a boy. A perfect and healthy baby boy. England finally has their next Prince of Wales. The line is secure, and all is well. We have our future king."

"Our future king. Well, well. Do we know what he is to be named?"

Violet scanned the letter and then grinned. "Edward. The future King Edward the Seventh." She stared into James's eyes, wishing she could fly to the queen instead of having to endure the two days it would take her to travel to Victoria's side. "We must leave for the palace immediately, my love. The queen will need me, and I must meet the little boy who is certain to grow up to be as great a monarch as his mother."

"Of course. Come, let us pack."

Violet slipped her hand into James's and pulled him close, resting her head on his shoulder. Finally, both she and Victoria had found the happiness they yearned for their entire lives. They each had husbands they adored and who adored them, and now she and Victoria had each given birth to that all-important male heir, securing their individual dynasties for the next generation.

Violet lifted her head and looked up at James, hope burning inside of her. "Her son is going to make her so proud. Just mark my words."

James smiled. "God willing, you are right."

A word about the author…

Rachel Brimble lives in the UK with her husband and beloved Labrador. They have two grown-up daughters, one living at home and the other living in beautiful Devon, England.

A member of the Romantic Novelists Association and the Historical Novel Society, when Rachel isn't writing, she is reading, walking, or knitting while watching an endless reel of period dramas...

Visit her at:

www.rachelbrimble.com
www.rachelbrimble.blogspot.com

Thank you for purchasing
this publication of The Wild Rose Press, Inc.

For questions or more information
contact us at
info@thewildrosepress.com.

The Wild Rose Press, Inc.

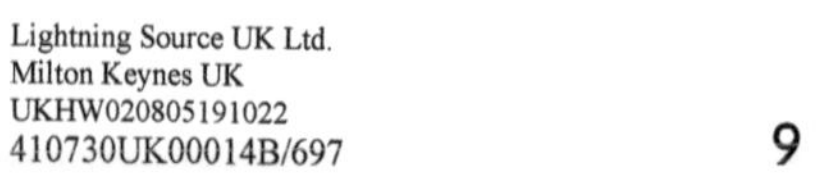

Lightning Source UK Ltd.
Milton Keynes UK
UKHW020805191022
410730UK00014B/697